The Falcon Princess

Jill Turner Claybrook

maple avenue

publishing

For Madie

Chapter One

MEG'S forest was still. As if nothing—tree nor creature—dared to stir. And yet she could feel it. Life surrounding her.

The sensation moved like fingers through her feathers and gently gripped the heart in her chest. Beat for beat. Inhaling, exhaling. She was the keeper here.

She looked down at the wild forest floor with her head cocked. She should stay low. Hidden from view. Her head bobbed several times, debating a move, then flicked up toward the great blue overhead. It beckoned to her. The ache for the rush deepened.

Just this once.

With a solid push, Meg's scaly feet left the pine-top perch. Her great wings stretched out and pushed against the air, swiftly taking her toward the clouds.

Hurry.

Higher and higher, she forced her way into the sky until a new sensation overcame her. Calm and free. Meg leveled her flight and lingered, reacquainting herself with the thin, crisp breeze that seemed to move through her. She rocked from side to side and glanced toward the land south of her forest. The white covering the ground was gone now, unlike the mountains to the north, and she could just make out the structures built by humans. Three castles, larger than her own, rose out of the ground, one far to the east, one straight south, and one just to the west. As it had before, the last held her gaze. A silent seeker, beckoning her to forbidden ground.

The pounding in her chest reclaimed her focus. The time to linger had passed. It was time for what she had come for.

After one steadying flap, her wings tucked back and her descent began. As her sleek, falcon form split the clear air, Meg grasped at the rush pulsing through her veins, hoping it would be enough to satisfy her for a time. Faster and faster, the earth seemed to hurtle toward her, until at last she was forced to spread her wings—a soft *fwap* as air caught underneath—and coast just above the tips of her trees.

Just that once, Meg told herself. *Until tomorrow.*

She ducked into the first gap she came across and landed gracefully on a fallen tree. Home was not far now. Mother would want her soon. Meg swooped a massive wing overhead and threw her body into a sideways, aerial twist.

When her bare feet touched the dark soil, the talons and scaled yellow were gone, toes and delicate skin in their stead. After adjusting her rough, brown tunic and black leggings, Meg tamed her chin-length black hair with her fingers and tucked one side behind her gently pointed ear, pierced twice through with a deep green crystal that gleamed in the fading light.

"What is for supper?" she mused, looking about with quick, jerky head movements. Not all bird ways left immediately with the change.

The sound of a well-known stream found its way to her ears, and she bounded through the tangled weave of green to get to it. An expert scan of the swift water revealed a silver streak beneath the surface.

"Hello, supper."

Slowly, Meg placed one foot on a submerged rock and leaned over the water's surface. With one swish of its tail, the fish darted forward. Meg's slender fingers followed. Her foot ached in the cold mountain water, but she knew to be patient. Inching forward a few more times, the fish relaxed into the current.

Quick as a fox, Meg's hands dived in and seized the creature in an unrelenting hold. The furious fish writhed wildly but with the tap of a rock, stilled to be carried home.

After a meandering walk, Meg left the wild growth behind and passed through an opening in the wall that surrounded her home, the black iron gate long held prisoner against the stone by the bracken and vines of her forest. Mickelby was inspecting one of their fruit trees and straightened when he saw her. She nodded and winked, and the old man returned the same nod and wink. It was their own greeting.

Mickelby was a human, not Raparean elf like her and Mother. How he had come to live with them, Meg did not know. Mother had forbidden such histories. And Mickelby never disobeyed Mother. But however he had come, the girl was glad he had. Like the gate and the towers and the orchard, he was part of her home.

She bounced up the short steps to the door of their slender castle—a two-story keep with four round towers on each side of the square. Just through the door was a hall that spanned the entire keep. Four tall columns supporting the roof broke up the space, and in one corner stood a grand fireplace made of smooth river rock. Meg knew every stone in the room and had talked to every figure carved into the columns.

Her quick steps silently crossed the space, taking her to the kitchen at the base of the far tower. Mother's chair at the table was empty. She wasn't out of bed yet. Meg exhaled a sigh of relief and set to work cleaning and preparing the fish. It was a good size and would feed the three of them well. One half of a fillet was placed on a tin plate raw for Mother. Meg sprinkled the rest with garden herbs and flavorful leaves from her forest for Mickelby and herself. Just as she laid the deep orange strips in the kitchen fire pan, the bedchamber door in Mother's tower scraped open.

"Hello, Mother," Meg said. "I have returned."

Moments later, a tall woman with short dark hair peppered with white and gold limped into the room. "Did you find it?"

"No." Meg lifted the plate and forced a smile. "But I found your supper."

Mother grunted and squinted one of her golden eyes before taking her seat. Mickelby entered the kitchen through the service door, a small basket tucked under one arm. Meg took the vessel and sliced and divided the plums and scrubbed carrots onto two plates. Then she crowned each pile with a steaming fillet.

"Mother," she said as she set a plate on the table. "Oh, and here." She broke off a bushy, green leaf from a discarded carrot stem and garnished the fillet as Mickelby had taught her. The bright green looked pretty against the silvery fish scales.

Mother sniffed and flicked the green aside.

Mickelby and Meg each took a plate and sat down at the table.

"And humans in the forest?"

Meg hated that question almost more than the other. "None, Mother." Answers were always the same.

Mother's eyes glowed. "Very good, my eyas. Continue your duty."

"Yes, Mother."

Aside from the crackle of embers and the crunch of carrots, the little kitchen fell silent. To entertain herself, Meg revisited the sky in her mind. The clear open air, the insignificant world below. Her forest of pine giants was large and covered so much, but from above, the mountains—in unobstructed view—became her giants. If she were ever allowed, she would explore those mountains and discover what made them white.

And what of the castles? The castles she could just barely glimpse. The one set against the west mountains was the nearest and appeared to be the largest. The other two castles seemed to match one another in size. The structures appeared empty from such a distance, but Meg knew they were not. Not yet.

Mother said the time of the humans was closing. Their deserved destruction near. Meg looked at Mickelby. His stringy, white hair barely brushed his shoulders and didn't touch anywhere on top of his head. His watery blue eyes added to the stark contrast of his coloring to her own dark hair and eyes. He was always good, always patient, and he almost made her believe other humans could be, too. As near as she had ever seen, Mickelby could not do anything the least bit wicked. She had never seen him change into a wolf or a mountain bear. The idea made her laugh outright.

Mother looked up sharply. Meg forced the smile from her face and looked down at her plate until she felt Mother's scowl leave her. She glanced at Mickelby again. No, he was always good, always patient. Never wicked. Mother said all humans were wicked. Murderous. Thieves. But what if—?

Meg took a bite of plum.

Her curiosity was getting dangerous again.

When the plates were empty, Meg helped Mother to her chair by the great fire in the hall, then cleared the dining table and rinsed the plates and cook pan in the basin. Mickelby remained in the kitchen with her, tapping his foot on the floor, just like he did after every supper. With the mess cleaned up, Meg pulled a winter squash from the storeroom, raised it overhead, and threw it to the floor, cracking it into three yellow chunks and sending seeds fleeing. She dropped the pieces into a heavy pot, placed the lid, and set the vessel on the smoldering kitchen fire.

Not yet ready to sit at Mother's knee, Meg sat down at the table next to Mickelby. He smiled at her, and she placed her hand over his.

"Mickelby, will you walk?"

The old man nodded and withdrew his hand to offer his arm. Linked together, the two ducked out the service door and into the night. The evening was cool and damp, a misty breath from the forest already circling the property. Meg guided her companion to the stone wall that surrounded the castle, where the grass was worn from many Meg and Mickelby walks.

Even the brisk air did nothing to clear the thoughts that fluttered in her mind. It was risky, but she went ahead.

"I went high above my forest, again," she whispered, carefully watching Mickelby's face. As predicted, he glanced at the castle. Meg squeezed his arm. "Look how far away we are. She cannot hear me when I talk small like this." Almost unconsciously, she looked at the castle, too.

"I have been thinking," she continued after a moment, "about the other castles and—" Before she could say more, Mickelby put his fingers to her lips, vigorously shaking his head.

But what if it is there. All her life they had been searching for the Imperald. Searching and wandering the forest. Never a trace. Never a whisper. She could tell Mickelby knew her thoughts. But he would not let her speak them. Mother would not have her even think them.

Mickelby gave her a firm look, then removed his hand and resumed their walk. He sighed and looked up at the sky. Meg followed his gaze. The stars were beginning to wake above the wisps of cloud and a sliver of moon smiled down at them.

It was a strange feeling, to want to be part of two worlds. When her feet were on the ground and she looked up, she felt a longing to be there. And when she soared in the sky—often higher than she was allowed—she looked down and felt as though there was someplace below she should be. She never felt filled inside her chest and yet felt happy to talk to old Mickelby and walk in circles around a tower.

In silence they finished their walk and went in. As she shut the door behind them, a call came from the main hall.

"Megnolia. I want you with me."

Meg bid Mickelby good night and went in to Mother. She took her place on the floor at Mother's knee and looked into the fire.

"Did you listen for it?"

"Yes, I listened." Meg tried not to sound impatient, but Mother had never been clear what she was listening for. 'I have told you,' she had said long ago. 'You will know when you are near enough. The Imperald searches for you just as you search for it.' Recently, Meg had begun to fear the Imperald had spoken to her and she just hadn't recognized it. Maybe it would tire of calling to her and stop.

"How much did you cover?" Mother asked, pulling Meg from her thoughts.

"Much. I have finished searching where you instructed me." Meg fiddled with the hem of her tunic, pulling at the frayed edge. *Stay, don't ask again,* she told herself. *No, never mind.* "Perhaps if you let me search outside our forest—"

"You will search where I tell you, Megnolia."

"But if it is out there, then—"

"No!" Mother winced and placed a hand over her chest. Her voice quieted. "I have said no. Do not ask me again."

Meg bowed her head to hide her face. She hadn't meant to make Mother angry. "Yes, Mother."

A disturbed stillness settled over the room as the fire greedily continued its meal of pine, the wood popping like breaking bone.

Mother settled back into her chair. "Everything depends on it being found. You must not fail. Say it."

Meg inhaled a calming breath and glanced above the fire at the mounted scepter, the empty cage of twisted silver in the center a reminder of what was lost. "The Imperald is my heart."

"It will not be long now." Mother said. "The end is coming. The pestilence. Thieves!"

The rest of the evening and into the hours of the night, Meg sat at Mother's knee. Mother used to fill this time with legends of their kind. Stories of her ancestors, great Raparean leaders—kings and queens of times past. How they carried the duty of keepers, protecting the mountains and the forests.

But Meg had not heard any stories for a long time. Most had faded from memory with each day turned to dusk. When the great fire burned low, Mother excused Meg to bed, and they parted, each to her own tower.

Chapter Two

WHEN the sky outside her window blushed at the rising sun, Meg's eyes opened. She stretched on her worn mattress and smiled at the friendly golden light. Soon she would have to go searching, but there was no need to rush. Mother was in bed again and would remain so for a few days. She didn't used to sleep so long, but even before Meg matched her in height, it had become necessary.

Though it came with a heavy bushel of guilt, Meg was always relieved when Mother went back to bed.

"Three days," Meg said to herself. "I have three days."

A bird chirped its morning tune somewhere outside. Meg whistled a return call and smiled when a little figure appeared on her window ledge. After one final stretch, she bounced off her bed and folded her wool blanket. Keeping to routine, she wriggled out of her linen shift and pulled on her day clothes.

While tying her belt, she paused a moment before her looking glass. Her black hair was already smooth from a few shakes of her head, and her round, dark eyes shone with a playful spark. She turned her head to examine the Imperald in her left ear, the only piece of the precious Raparean crystal they had—about the length of her little finger.

"What are you going to do today, Meg?" she asked herself, tracing a slow finger over the crystal. "Search your forest? Or will you…?"

The words wouldn't come, but the idea was still firmly rooted in her mind, knotted but irresistible. She clenched her fists and lifted her chin, a smile teasing her lips. "What a good thought, Meg. You should do that."

With a growl in her stomach, she bounded down her tower stairs, through the main hall, and into the kitchen.

Mickelby was already up and seated at the table with his hands folded. She winked and bid him good morning. He winked back and offered her a weak smile.

She stopped mid-step. "Mickelby, you do not look pleased."

He gave a little shake of his head and looked down at his hands. Meg frowned at him for a moment, then set to work. She lifted the lid off the pot she had put over the fire after supper. The coals had lasted long enough to make the pieces of squash soft. She dished up two plates and sprinkled each with some leaves Mickelby had dried.

She set one plate before Mickelby and sat down with the other. The roughly made table between them, each began to eat. It was their way, to eat quietly in the mornings. Just the two of them.

While she ate, Meg kept an eye on Mickelby. He fidgeted with his shirt buttons and sighed. He poked his squash and tapped his fingers. When her plate was empty, Mickelby took it and his own nearly untouched plate to the basin. Then he wiped out the heavy pot. Breakfast was his duty to clean up.

"Should we look at the trees?" Meg asked. "I feel like an apple."

With her arm in his, they walked out to the orchard. Although she was taller and could easily reach, he stretched up onto his toes and picked a golden apple for her. She rubbed it on her tunic until it shined and bit into the crisp, juicy treat.

"Mickelby, I keep feeling something. I feel like running. Like I can't be still. But however I move, it does not go away. Have you ever felt it?"

He nodded.

She lowered her voice. "Mother is sleeping again. What do you suppose would happen if I went to one of the other castles?"

He grabbed her arm and shook his head fearfully.

"She would never know. I would return before she awakened. You could come with me."

His grip tightened on her arm, and the apple almost slipped from her fingers.

"No, you are right." She patted his hand and felt it relax. "I would not really go. I just like to think about it."

She smiled to reassure him. But inside, her mind hummed with rebellion. She had hoped he would be willing to join her. Now, she was certain he would never disobey Mother and let her go, let alone guide her. But if he didn't know she left the forest...

"I think I will go searching now. Mother will want a good report when she wakes."

Mickelby slowly let go of her arm. He looked as if he was about to tell her something, but his hands dropped still at his sides. She took one last bite of her apple and tossed the core over the wall, then took a hold of his limp hand and gave it a squeeze.

"I will return in time to fix your supper."

He nodded with the shadow of a smile.

Meg left him in the orchard picking hard, green pears to ripen and went back to her tower. She looked around her room. What would she need? It felt strange to walk out of safety with empty hands. Humans came into her forest with their sharp sticks and long knives.

Trying to kill her. Nasty creatures, Mother called them. Meg reached under her mattress and retrieved a small, sheathed knife. A gift from Mickelby. She had never used it before. In her forest, she defended herself with talons. But perhaps it would be useful outside the forest.

Meg tied the knife to her ankle and, feeling better prepared, climbed out onto the window's ledge. Expertly placing her fingers and toes in the crevices between the stones, she climbed to the coned roof of her tower.

Three stories up was a good height, but it still did not allow her to see over the trees of her forest. She smiled looking at the giants around her, strong to their pointed tips and a green that made her draw in a deep breath. Like so many times before, she stood on her perch and let the climbing sun's rays soak into her skin. Then she took three quick steps and jumped.

As soon as her foot left the shingles, she swooped an arm overhead, drove her tucked legs up, and threw her head back, flipping her body in a sideways twist. Though she lost no size in height, she felt her bones lighten with the shift.

When her arms stretched out and legs untucked, the air caught beneath her feathers and she pulled up—above the tower and over the trees. Flying close to the tips, Meg headed in the direction of the west castle. She couldn't see it yet but knew where she would find it.

With each flap of her wings, Meg felt the heaviness push out from her chest. Perhaps today was the day. It had been a long time since she had felt so much hope. Mother's rules still nested in her mind, but she knew all would be forgiven if she returned with the Imperald in hand.

When The Edge drew near, Meg ducked toward the ground, angling her wings forward with the feather tips pointing down to slow herself, then wrapped her taloned feet around several lower branches of a tree. She considered finding a snack before she shifted back, but her stomach burned with anticipation. No food for now.

She swooped a wing overhead and pushed away from the tree, then flipped and landed on the soft earth, her elfin toes lightly digging into the damp soil. Keeping her same direction, she padded toward The Edge.

Soon the thick curtain of trees thinned, and she was able to see open space beyond her giants. Meg stopped. Then took two more steps. This was the closest she had ever come to The Edge. Mother would not be pleased if she knew. Meg took two more steps. Now *this* was the closest she had ever come. She was so close she could smell smoke from somewhere just beyond. Her heart quickened and began to feel afraid. Not of Mother. Not of open space. Not of humans.

She felt afraid she would turn back.

With each rising sun her curiosity had grown stronger. Soon it would be more than she could stand. And she was already here.

"Mickelby is human. And Mickelby is good," she said aloud. Something inside willed her to go further.

She took two more steps. The Edge was near. She made out the lines of a structure across the clearing. Not a castle, much too small. But it was so close. She drew in a deep breath, focused on the little hut, and broke into a run. She leaped over a fallen tree, branches and bracken scraping her skin, reaching at her feet as if to hold her back. Before she could think about stopping, she was out.

Out of the giants. Out of protection. Out of Mother's rule.

The clearing was open, and a breeze swished the bright, thick blades of grass and tickled her face. She scrunched her nose. "The air is moving. But I am not."

Perplexed, she hesitated. She closed her eyes and felt the air brush her skin again and move her hair. It was different than feeling it blow through feathers when she flew. She opened her eyes to the little structure across the meadow. Trees surrounded the clearing, but giants only lined where her forest began. The trees beyond were the same color and triangular shape but much smaller.

She adjusted her tunic and moved quickly toward the house, the wide-bladed grass foreign under her feet. She didn't have time to study every new thing. The sun was not yet mid-sky, but how long it would take to walk to the castle was uncertain.

She reached the little place and glanced around. No humans to be seen. A fenced pen on the other side caught her eye. Peculiar looking birds with small heads and round bodies poked around in the dirt.

She stepped over to the pen. "What are you? Birds, I know, but you do not look like the little birds in my forest." She squatted low and whispered, "Are you Raparean, too?"

The birds clucked and stared, baffled by her words.

"No. I thought you were too small anyway." She looked at the plump little things. "I cannot help but think you would be good to eat." One of the birds clucked a protest. "Be angry, but it is true, look at yourself. Just one of you would feed—"

"No one'll be touching my chickens," said a stern voice from behind.

Meg whirled around on her toes and pulled her knife from its sheath in one swift motion. A stout woman with rough skin and thick, crossed arms eyed her suspiciously. Meg stood. The woman looked up at her, and Meg thought she saw a flicker of fear in the woman's face. But she held on to her sturdy demeanor.

"Away with your little barb, sis, unless you want to meet mine."

She flashed the cook's knife hidden under her arm. "Put it away, I said."

Slowly, Meg sheathed her knife and drew some courage. "I only wanted to look. I am going to the big castle. Where should I go?"

"The 'big castle.' *Hmph*. You're a bit off your course if you ended up here. Go back on the path you came, girl, and don't bother this way again."

Meg cleared her throat. "I did not come on a path."

"Well, beat my hog, no wonder you're lost. What kind of—" The woman pointed toward a lightly worn trail. "Take that one there." She recrossed her arms, making sure the knife was in full sight this time. "And don't go wandering in the trees again, flip of a girl."

"Why?"

The woman leaned forward. " 'Cause you'll end up in The Death Woods if you do. And you enter them, bumbling like you are, you'll never come out." The woman narrowed her eyes and looked Meg up and down. "Where is it you come from that you don't know not to go wandering in the trees?"

"I am from…" Meg almost said the truth but caught herself. No humans came from there. "From the middle castle."

"The what?" The woman's hands moved to her round hips and her head cocked to the side, eyes full of suspicion and warning.

The look from the woman reminded Meg of a badger standing over her burrow, daring her to come closer. Feeling certain more of her answers would make the human's claws come out, Meg took several steps back before she turned and strode toward the path. When the woman called out for her to stop, Meg skipped into a run.

She sprinted down the path, ducking under branches and jumping unruly roots. She couldn't hear the woman anymore, but she didn't stop. She wanted to shift into falcon but told herself over and over to keep control.

"Stay, stay, stay," she chanted as she ran. She could not let anyone see her be falcon.

The path soon widened into a road. Meg raced past several turnoffs and ignored them all. The biggest path would lead to the big castle, she reasoned. When her lungs burned and her throat felt tight, she slowed to a jog, then to a walk. She hadn't realized there were so many trees outside her forest. She couldn't see anything but trees.

"I need to be higher." She thought about being falcon again and shook her head. "Think, Megnolia." The trees had tighter branches, not spread out for good climbing. She felt the air blow across her face again. It smelled like food. More humans were near.

"Further," she told herself.

Presently, the trees opened into a cluster of structures. Humans moved about, all different sizes of them. All doing different things. Getting water from a well, pushing heaping wheeled things. Small humans ran about, dirty faced but laughing.

One of them looked at her and stopped. Instinctively, Meg took a step back, hand ready to grab her knife. 'All humans are wicked,' Mother's words flitted in her head. She looked at the little one's face. Its cheeks were thin and the eyes large. The rest of it was scraggly. All of them looked scraggly. Unconsciously, Meg's lips curved into a smile. The little creature flashed a gappy grin and ran off.

"Someone needs to find that little human a fat bird to eat," Meg muttered to herself.

Beyond the trees on the other side of the structures, Meg could see the craggy section of the mountains, still a good distance away. The big castle was near there. She looked up at the sun approaching the middle of the sky. She needed to move faster.

"Are you in need of something, miss?"

Meg jumped. She turned to see a woman looking up at her.

"You aren't from—I've never seen you before. But you look…" Her words trailed off. She didn't smile, but her eyes looked anxious to help.

Meg liked the long braid that rested on her shoulder. *Mickelby is human. Mickelby is good.*

"How far is it to get there?" Meg asked.

The woman followed her pointing finger and looked back at her quickly.

"There? Not above a two hour walk. But what is it you're after?"

"I just want to see the castle."

The woman looked at her strangely and nodded. "There is a road just on the other side there. The one marked by a horse. It will take you to Davare's Heart." She looked Meg up and down. "But if you'll take my words, go back where you came from. You won't find much good there."

Meg narrowed her eyes. Why would she want to take the woman's words? She had her own. With deliberate steps, she made her way past the people and structures to the side of the village the woman had indicated and found two paths. One marked by a carved wolf, the other by an animal she assumed was a horse.

"Not above a two hour walk," Meg said to herself. "That does not sound far."

A two-hour walk was all that laid between her and the big castle.

Chapter Three

THE dwarf trees whispered to Meg and kept her in uneasy company as she moved down the path. These trees were not happy like her giants—she could feel the despair in their cores. They had no keeper.

The ground she trod was hard and tiring, unlike the soft earth of her forest floor, and when humans passed pulling hand-drawn carts of wood, nearly rotten apples, or wormy cabbages, she was forced to step aside into thick mud that trapped her feet. One of the humans stared back at her as he passed, but the others hardly gave her a glance. This land seemed neither dangerous nor pleasant.

The trees thinned, opening her view ahead, and she watched the castle grow taller and taller as she neared. Soon she stood on the outskirts of a confused mass of buildings, and a tickly feeling that had sprung up in her stomach turned into another bout of uncomfortable burning. There were many more structures here than in the first group she had come across. Many, many more.

The homes and buildings spread out in a labyrinth before her. Made up of small brick and wood, each building seemed to sag under the weight of its darkly thatched roof. Windows were covered with filmy glass or rough shutters, some were covered with planks of wood nailed in place.

And the humans. Meg ducked into a thicket of bushes, her back to the city. She rubbed her damp hands over her leggings as she listened to their shouting and laughter.

"Mickelby is human," she whispered. "And Mickelby is good."

With a deep breath of courage, Meg turned and stood just enough to peek over her blind. The humans shoved and bustled about. From where she stood, she sensed no danger. Saw no pointed sticks. Perhaps these humans would let her pass just as those on the path had. Meg stepped out of hiding and walked cautiously into the crowd.

Never had she seen so many faces. There were faces that appeared just washed and faces that hadn't seen water in days. Noses of all shapes and sizes—round, pointed, upturned, slender, and wide. The eyes that glanced at her were sometimes dark and familiar like her own and sometimes startlingly light and all shades in between.

And the hair! Some heads were white like Mickelby's and some were brown like the bark of her trees. And some heads were golden. Like the color of the sun reflecting off the pale stones by the streams in her forest. Cut close to the scalp or long down the back or no hair at all. She especially liked the hair that looked like another creature living on top.

Meg looked ahead at the steep mountains. Buildings now barred her view of the castle, but she knew the mountains would guide her. She straightened her shoulders and began making her way. What she planned to do once she reached the castle she didn't really know. But she could not very well turn around and go home now.

As she walked through the streets, Meg found herself looking down at the women she passed. The men were more varying in size, but she guessed she was taller than most of them, too. She suddenly became conscious of all the eyes drawn toward her.

"Meg, you should have worn something to hide yourself," she whispered to herself as she neared a group of staring men.

She felt the scrape in her stomach anew and ducked her head to hurry past.

She wandered and weaved, wishing the bricks would fade into bark and the roofs into boughs. The deeper she went into the city, the more frequently she passed men with pointed sticks and strange plates and bowls covering their bodies. And the streets became more hushed. Her senses sharpened. But she continued to move.

Her goal was now in view, towering magnificently just ahead. She was near enough now her sharp eyes could see the lines between the dark stones and the delicate patterns of colorful cut glass in the windows—blue, white, and green. The panes gleamed in the sunlight like jewels laying against coal. The castle seemed to mock the modest structures below.

Almost there.

Meg's gaze fell to her immediate surroundings again and rested on a man sitting up against the wall, a wavy clump of hair on his head. He nodded kindly and did not look away, so she matched his stare, tempted to approach him and ask some of her questions.

Suddenly a ruckus broke through the stifled streets. She turned to see a group of men and women, some clothed in bright colors, others in metal plates. All of their faces clean. A man dressed in a blue vest and long fur cloak held a small human by his shirt, his feet dangling below. A woman rushed in from the side and fell to her knees before them, her cries pleading. Meg watched as the man tossed the child to the ground and struck the woman with the back of his hand.

Meg stood frozen and alone in the street, unable to look away.

The robed man must have felt her gaze. He looked up to meet it and straightened. "You," he called. "Come here."

Meg swallowed and glanced around to be sure he spoke to her. Her feet wanted to run away but something heavy inside rooted them in place. She didn't move.

"My lady, I asked you to come to me."

"I am not called Milady," Meg replied.

The man looked at her in some confusion. His eyes flickered to the men at his side, then his shoulders began to shake. Meg realized he was laughing. Soon the whole group was laughing. He held out his hand to her.

"Well, if you are not Milady, then tell me. Who are you?"

His face was young. His hair short and dark, neatly trimmed. His eyes like hers. She liked his looks.

Humans are wicked. Warily, she approached him. He stepped back slightly once she was near enough to see the gold, leaf-shaped buttons on his vest. His eyes were lower than hers. She looked at his hand still extended, and he moved it closer to her.

"Come now," he coaxed softly, "give me your hand and tell me your name."

Slowly, she placed her hand in his, but when he clasped his fingers around it, she jerked it back. The women behind him whispered to one another.

A slow smile came to his lips, but it didn't make Meg feel warm like Mickelby's smile. It was cold. Like his hand. "If you won't give me your hand, at least give me your name."

"Megnolia. My name is Megnolia. But I like it Meg."

"Well, Meg." In one smooth motion, he flicked his robe and placed both hands on his hips, revealing a small, jeweled ax, molded of gleaming silver, hanging from his belt. Meg watched his hand, but he made no move to grab it. "You looked disturbed. I am curious, then, to know your opinion. What shall I do with this boy? He has crossed me numerous times. He is a known thief."

There were a number of words from his mouth she had never heard before, but the last one she knew well. Thief. The boy was a thief. All humans were thieves. Mother had said so—many times.

"Thieves should be punished," Meg whispered.

"Yes," replied the young man, his handsome face smiling. "I agree."

She looked at the cluster behind him, sneers stuck on their faces. She glanced at the woman still on the ground and the child under her arm. Suddenly, the man issued a swift kick to the young one. The boy gasped and curled sideways. Another kick and the boy cried out in pain. His cry stirred something in Meg, but her feet still wouldn't move. He needed his punishment. Just as the robed man reeled his boot back for a second kick, the woman moved in to shield him.

"No more, Your Highness!" she pleaded.

The man faltered, hopping on his still grounded foot, before setting the other on the ground. Then he reeled back again and gave her the punishment. And another. The stirring rose into Meg's chest and burst from her mouth.

"Stop!" she cried, nearly placing herself between them. "Stop."

The men in the circle stiffened and the women gasped. One of the armored men stepped forward with his hand raised, but the cloaked man blocked him with his arm.

He tilted his head back and rolled his tongue in his mouth. "Go home with your mother, boy," he said without looking away from Meg. "Do not cross my path again."

The boy, holding his stomach, nodded fearfully and looked at Meg with the same uncertainty. With the woman's arm wrapped around him, he hurried away and disappeared between homes.

The robed man turned his head slightly, but his eyes held Meg's fast. Then they moved swiftly about her face. His hand reached up to push back her hair. She flinched under his touch.

"That's an interesting piece in your ear. What is it made of?"

Meg remained still, pretending not to know. After a moment's pause, he held out his arm.

"I think I shall return home," he drawled. "But I would like to better know the sort of girl who bursts in on another's punishment. You will accompany me, my Lady Meg."

She looked at his arm offered to her in the same way Mickelby always did, but she didn't want to take it. She shook her head.

His lips slipped from a smile to a twisted, pained expression. "You will not come with me then?" With a *tsk*, he looked at the women behind him. "She does not want to come to the castle."

"The castle?" Meg blurted out.

He turned back to her, surprised. "Yes. I am Herrick the Fourth. King of Davare. That is my home you see behind me." He looked her up and down again. "Where are you from, Lady Meg?"

"I am from…the middle castle." She carried on with the same lie she told the woman with the round birds.

He eyed her suspiciously. "The middle castle? I have never heard it called that, but I suppose you mean Roshton Castle?"

"Yes, Roshton. Castle. Yes, there."

The suspicion disappeared from his face and he nodded, but Meg noticed two of the women behind him exchange looks. King Herrick held out his arm again. Still, she kept hers back. Suddenly his hand shot forward and warning flooded her stomach. She jumped away from his reaching grasp.

"Seize her!" he commanded.

Before the others moved, Meg was in a dead run through the cleared street. Recalling the way she had come as quick as her steps, soon she was weaving through humans and carts. The shouts from behind haunted her ears, seeming to never cease or grow faint. Once she hazarded a glance back. A look at the faces pursuing her and her legs received an extra jolt.

"Stay, stay, stay," she begged herself, willing her body to stay in elfin form.

In what seemed like an entire day of running, she reached the trees—shouts still chasing her. After the first bend in the road, she took a sharp, hoping to throw the humans off her course. She zigged and zagged through the trees, always heading in the direction of her forest. Soon the only sounds she heard were twigs snapping under her own feet. She slowed, then slumped against a tree, forcing her heaving chest to calm.

"Foolish!" she whispered to herself. "What a foolish thing you have done, Meg."

The thudding in her chest subsided and her frantic mind settled. She had been so close to the castle. If she had scattered like the others in the street, she might have made it. She laughed despite herself, remembering she had no idea what to do once she reached the castle.

"A worm-eaten plan from the start. Foolish, Meg." And through it all, she had forgotten to listen for what she had come for. She rubbed a hand across her damp forehead.

She must never tell Mother. Never.

But Mickelby. She might tell him. If she ever made it out of this wretched place. It was ugly and sad. A deserved world for wicked creatures. The image of the little, dirty one who had drawn a smile from her fluttered through her mind. She forced it out as quickly as it had come.

The sun was now descending. She pulled herself to her feet and began to jog toward her forest. She was sorry for the trees here. They could not lift their roots and escape with her. As she easily made her way, she sifted through what she had seen. The animals. The homes. And the faces—so many faces. The happiness, sadness, anger, fear. All mixed together.

Her heart picked up as she recalled her escape. It had been close. Those chasing men had wanted to harm her. Like they did the mother and child. But something struck her. She had passed dozens of humans, feeling at any moment a hand would reach out and grab her. But none had. In fact, the plain humans seemed to part for her. As if they had not wanted her to be caught.

Humans were strange. She was further from understanding them than she had been when she woke. And the question that bothered her most was why she even wanted to.

She stopped again to shake her head and throw the largest rock she could find.

Chapter Four

THE sun was behind the mountains when Meg returned home. Her castle was dark except for a small glow in the window of the kitchen door. She shifted, landing on her elfin feet in the yard, and quietly jogged up the steps. When she entered the room, Mickelby started, then jumped from his seat at the table to take her hand.

"I am fine. I am home, Mickelby," she whispered. "Is mother still asleep?"

The old man nodded.

Meg breathed a sigh of relief. She hadn't anticipated Mother waking on the first night, but the thought had still worried her. Now she wouldn't need to make up an excuse for being so late or need to hide her feelings.

"Mickelby, I must tell you something." The uneventful flight home had removed her reserve and replaced it with excitement. "Come."

She pulled him by the hand out the door and across the yard to their path.

"I went to the humans," she whispered with her eyes wide and something near a smile on her lips.

He started for the second time and shook his head.

"Yes, I did!"

He closed his eyes, his face blank.

When he didn't move to silence her, she hurried to explain. "I could not help it. I needed to see the castle. The big one. You would not believe all the faces I saw. More to look at than I can remember. I did not know humans were so dirty. You are not dirty, Mickelby."

He shook his head without opening his eyes.

"I saw some round birds and talked to several humans. Kind ones. And one with a knife. And one who tried to capture my arm. He named himself to me. What was it? Herr...no, *King* Herrick the Fourth." She shuddered.

Mickelby's eyes popped open, and his hand flew up to cover her mouth, a flicker of anger in his eyes. Startled, Meg stilled. She had never seen that before. Anger was something only for Mother's eyes. She chewed her lip under his hand. She should not have told him. But she brushed his hand aside and went on recklessly anyway.

"Listen to me. He tried to capture me, but I ran. He sent others after me. I had to run and run. I knew I could not shift. I knew that. So they do not know what I am. We are still safe."

Mickelby shook his head and rubbed a hand wearily over his face.

"I know I should not have gone. I know that now. But I..." She couldn't explain it to him. The curiosity. The need to know. To see. He was happy to just do as Mother bid. To stay about the castle forever. She stepped away from him and turned to go inside.

"Never mind it all. Mother is always right, is she not?"

She left him standing by the wall. As she ran up the steps of her tower, a churning feeling moved about in her chest. Mickelby didn't understand. There was no one to understand. It was just like the sky and the ground to her. Among the humans she wanted to be in her forest, but when she was in her forest, she wanted nothing more than to go beyond.

Meg threw herself onto her bed. The churning flattened into a hollowness in her heart.

"I cannot spend day after day searching," she whispered to the dark. "I must start finding."

She reached up to feel the Imperald piece in her ear—broken from the mother crystal. The heart of her forest. Her heart. The human king had been interested in it. She rolled over and hugged her folded blanket. Perhaps she should have kept her ear hidden. But it was no matter. She would never see him again.

When sunlight touched Meg's face, she stretched her long body, then lay still. Another day of searching loomed before her. She could not pass on her duties today. Going deep into her forest alone had seemed a gift at first. Protecting it and discovering it. But the gleam of false freedom had dimmed some time ago.

For a moment she thought of leaving without seeing Mickelby. She didn't want to explain herself today. She didn't want to give reasons for what she had done. She didn't want to see his face. But he would be hurt if she didn't eat breakfast with him. Meg rolled off the bed and trudged down the steps.

She found him in the kitchen and greeted him with a wink. He halfheartedly returned the wink. His fingers drummed against the table, rather than in their usual slow, smooth rhythm.

She had been too tired and put out to start breakfast the night before, so she grabbed a few pears from a basket to peel and mash. When she finished that, she went to the storeroom and came out with a few pieces of dried fish.

They ate in silence, and Meg really began to feel the extent of her regret confiding in Mickelby. Not only had he not understood, now he was upset. She shifted in her seat several times, uncomfortable no matter how she sat. Finally, the meal was over and both moved to clear the plates.

"I am off to search then. Mother should sleep until tomorrow evening, but if she wakes tonight and I am still gone, tell her I am searching near the Great Mountains."

Mickelby pushed his cheek out with his tongue and nodded.

"I am off then," she said again.

She turned to go to her tower, but Mickelby placed a hand on her shoulder. He glanced at the doorway that led to the main hall, then grabbed a satchel from beside his chair and pushed Meg out the door into the yard.

"Mickelby, what is it?"

He pressed a finger to his lips and continued to lead her away from the castle. Meg let out a chirp of surprise when he pulled her through the gate and into the trees. When the castle was no longer visible, he stopped and glanced around.

Meg did the same. "Mickelby, you are not supposed to leave—"

He pressed his finger to his lips again. When she nodded, he reached into his satchel and pulled out a rectangular piece of brown leather.

"A book," she whispered. Long ago, when she was no taller than Mother's hip, she had found a book similar to the one he held hidden in the unused tower. She had flipped through its leaves, wondering at the beautiful markings. When she had shown it to Mother and asked what it was, Mother had thrown it into the fire. "Books are for humans," she had said. Meg had held back tears as she watched the treasure curl into black ash.

Mickelby placed the unburned book in her hands.

She flipped through its leaves. "Where did you—how do you have this?"

He held out his hands and drew them to his chest.

"Someone gave it to you."

He nodded.

"Who? When?"

He swooped his hand indicating a long time ago. He pointed to her, then folded his arms and swung them back and forth. Meg pinched her eyebrows together, and he repeated the action.

"I did?"

He shook his head. She waved a hand.

"Never mind. Never mind that." She pointed to the marks on one of the pages. "I like how these look. Different sizes and ways. We must keep this safe. Mother cannot see it."

He nodded in agreement. She held it out to him. He shook his white head and pushed it back to her.

"No, Mickelby, I cannot take this from you."

He nodded again. Keeping the book in her hand, he opened it and pointed at the markings.

"Yes, I already said I like them."

He pointed at them again, more intently. Then he traced his finger along the lines. He put a hand up to his open mouth and dropped it several inches. She shook her head. He repeated the action, alternately pointing to the markings on the book.

"Out of your mouth? The book comes out of your mouth? I do not understand."

He pointed to her mouth, then the page.

"The marks come out of *my* mouth?" She laughed lightly. "My mouth? What do you mean? I...they are...sounds?"

He nodded, his smile very pleased. It slipped away as quickly as it had come, and he glanced back toward their castle.

"These marks are sounds," Meg said. "What do they mean?"

He shrugged.

"You do not know. Hm." She had a book full of markings that neither of them knew what they meant. "I—I like it just the same. Looking at it."

He pushed the book up to her chest and pointed. She followed his finger. When she asked if he meant take it home, he shook his head and pointed another direction. Then he marched back and forth, in all directions, and pointed to himself.

"Take it...to the humans?"

He nodded vigorously. She was certain last night he had been angry with her for going. Now he was encouraging her to go. Telling her to go, even.

He knelt down on the ground and brushed away the pine needles and pebbles. She watched as he placed a trembling finger in the dirt and made one large shape, then three circles below it. He pointed to the large shape. Meg shook her head. He sighed, paused for a moment, then made some straight lines with little lines coming out from the sides.

She circled around to look over his shoulder. "They look like trees."

He nodded and traced around the large shape again. After a moment of thinking and Mickelby dragging his finger through the dirt some more and pointing, she realized it was her forest and the three castles. He pointed to the far castle.

"You want me to take this there?"

He nodded.

"And someone will tell me what these mean?"

He shrugged and waggled his head back and forth. He pointed at the first circle, the largest, and shook his head with a grave look. He motioned his hands back and forth over one another, and she knew he meant for her not to go back to the nearest castle.

He handed her the satchel, and she gently placed the book back inside. The far castle was a good distance away, but if she left now, she would reach that side of her forest soon after the sun was mid-sky. It was very likely Mother would not wake until tomorrow evening. Meg would have plenty of time to find someone to help her.

"I will go today. If Mother wakes, tell her I planned to sleep in the forest." She looked into his light eyes, seeing what he tried to conceal. She looped the strap over the back of her neck. "And do not worry about me. I will be safe."

She moved away from him, jumped, and took to the sky. Two days in a row she would walk with humans. The satchel hung from her feathered neck, reminding her of the treasure inside.

After what seemed like a never-ending distance, the far end of her forest came, and she selected a safe place to land. The third castle was set further from the forest than the one in Davare. She would not go all that way if she could help it.

In her flight she had spotted streams of smoke flowing out of the dwarf trees and determined she would try there first. She shifted and made her way to The Edge. With little hesitation, she crossed the line out of her giants. Instinctively, Meg looked down to her ankle only to realize she had not strapped on her knife. She hadn't been planning to leave her forest when she had left her tower.

She paused only a moment before looping her arm through the bag and slinging it around with the strap across her chest. Mickelby had sent her here. He would not send her into danger.

As she beat her own path through the forest, she listened to the trees, speaking to her in their own way. The feeling she gathered was neither despair nor sadness. She was surprised to sense these trees had a keeper. Frequently, she touched the satchel to make sure her book was still there. *Books are for humans,* she reasoned. *It will not be difficult to find someone to tell me what the marks mean.*

"I will return to my forest before dark," she said, comforting herself with a smile.

Soon, she happened upon a wide path and, as it seemed to follow her course, stayed with it. A small while afterward, she caught pleasant whiffs of smoke that clung to the air in patches. Then came the strange sounds of bustling life.

When the village came into view, Meg paused. Earthen colors were not favored here. The structures were clean and orderly, made up of warm-colored bricks—red, orange, and cream. Doors were splashed with bright colors, though strips of weathered wood peeked through, and the streets were cobbled with smooth, round stones, making movement noisy.

The humans varied in shapes, sizes, and colors just like in Davare, but there was something different in this little village. As she stepped onto the nearest street, the feeling was almost palpable to her heart. Among the laughter and shouts, there were a few voices that sounded disgruntled. But there was no looming sadness. No heavy depression.

She pulled her book from her satchel and stepped up to a group of chatting women. One talked on for a moment until a companion gave her a nudge. Her mouth snapped shut and each face turned toward Meg. She winked at them, but no one winked back.

Meg held out the book, the pages flipped open. "Tell me what these mean."

The women exchanged looks and in unison shook their heads. With a stab of disappointment, Meg nodded and moved on. She waded through flows of people, holding her book out to anyone who acknowledged her. Each gave her the same flat refusal in varying ways. Uncomfortable looks and whispers trailed behind her.

In a short time, after passing through crowds and once a cluster of strange, fluffy white animals, she came to the center of the village. From where she stood, nine streets converged on a circular common area with a pool of water in the middle.

Meg stared at the little pond. It was surrounded by a pretty stone ledge and in the center was a tree unlike any she had ever seen—made of stone and spouting water from the top. It made a slurpy, bubbly noise that would have made her laugh on a different day. She sagged onto the lip of the fountain and placed her chin in her hand.

This was not going as planned. She gripped the book cover tightly in her other hand, wishing she could just understand the markings on her own.

Slowly, she straightened. She thumbed through the pages. Maybe there were too many markings. No one wanted to go through and tell her what all of them meant. But she noticed they repeated in different arrangements. If she asked someone to teach her what each individual mark meant, then she could go through the leaves herself.

Meg glanced around and selected a different street to try. It was the most crowded, with tented carts and propped open doors. She did not dare enter any of the buildings—sturdy traps—but moved from person to person in the open, asking if he or she could teach her to understand the markings. Again, she received the same responses—a gruff no, a shake of the head, an apology but no. Near the end of the street she approached a large man with spools of colorful string.

"Show me how to understand these."

The man peered at her book from under two clear circles perched on his nose.

"Sorry, miss. Can't read."

"Read?"

He squinted at her. "Yes, read." He looked up and down the street and let out a husky laugh. "Isn't anyone here to do that for you, miss. You're in the wrong place."

The book slowly lowered to her side. *The wrong place.* She had spent all this time in the wrong place.

"Where do I go then?"

The man laughed again. "You backward girl. You're fresh out of luck. There isn't anyone within miles to teach the likes of you. And even if there was, they wouldn't. It's forbidden."

Forbidden. Meg knew that word well.

She nodded and stepped away from the man, dropping her book back into the bag. Why had Mickelby told her to come here if it was forbidden to *read*?

The sun was well past its midpoint in the sky. Her stomach rumbled, and she realized how hungry she was. A tray of carrots rested across the way from the string man. She grabbed one and turned to leave the village behind.

"You better pay for that, miss," a voice said. "Miss. Miss!"

A hand grabbed her shoulder. Meg whirled around and jumped away.

"Easy, friend," said a young boy. "I was just saying you forgot to pay for that."

"Pay?"

"Yes. With coin. A turny will do," he held out his hand.

Meg stared at it and then the carrot. "I do not have a…turny."

"Then you'll have to give it back." He pushed his hand toward her and raised his eyebrows.

Mickelby had never asked Meg to give him anything for a carrot. Reluctantly, Meg returned it. The boy shrugged apologetically and returned to his stand. With nothing in hand or stomach but much in her mind, Meg trudged away from the silly gathering of humans.

"What helpless things," she muttered. "Cannot understand markings. And wicked, wanting something for their food."

"Wait," another voice called from the wretched village. "Wait!"

Meg stopped and turned, hoping to meet at least one human who would prove Mother wrong.

Chapter Five

A girl with two thick, honey-colored braids briskly walked up to her. "Here," she said breathlessly, as she placed a carrot in Meg's hand. She glanced quickly at Meg's bare feet. "Fenn should have let you have it. His mother would have if she had been at the cart today."

Meg nodded gratefully to her.

The girl swallowed and licked her lips. Then she placed a hand on her chest. "Um, I'm Serah. Serah Snofam."

"Meg."

"It's nice to meet you, Meg. I...I couldn't help noticing—ha! or hearing rather—that you have a book you are wanting to read."

Meg felt a spark of hope and reached into her satchel. "Yes." She held her book out to Serah.

Serah giggled, a pretty jingling sound. "Oh, not me. I can't help you. Well, I can, but not by myself. What I mean is, I know someone who can. I..." She hesitated. "I can take you to him if you want."

"Serah!" Another girl with the same color of hair as Serah strode up hefting a large, soft basket. "Here you are. You wandered away again."

"I did wander away, didn't I?" Serah said. "But it's a good thing I did because I found this poor, hungry—Fenn wouldn't give her a carrot, but I bought her one. And now we are friends. So..." She turned back to Meg and gestured toward the other girl. "This is my sister."

"Sister?" Meg was trying to keep up with so many new words and had pieced together the meaning of some. But this one she couldn't.

Serah's throat jingled again. "Yes, my sister. We are sisters. Don't you think we look alike? She must not think we look alike, which I guess we don't have to to be sisters. I know several sets that don't look much like one another. Lots of reasons for that I suppose, some we probably shouldn't talk about, right? Embarrassing for everyone. But everyone says we do so…"

The second girl placed a hand on her chest with a small roll of her eyes. "Lezah."

"Meg."

"Pleasant. If you'll excuse us now, we're late going home." She nudged her sister with the basket.

Serah pushed back. "Oh, but Meg is coming with us. I told her she may. Right, Meg?" She lowered her voice. "She has a book and wants to know what it says."

Lezah stared at Serah for a moment. "We can help her no more than anyone else, Serah," she said through her teeth. She looked at Meg. "Sorry, but I must rescind my sister's offer. We need to be on our way."

Meg felt her grip tighten on the book. For a few breaths she had found help. She wished this Lezah had not found them.

But Serah did not move with her sister's prodding.

"Lezah, you cannot take back my offer. I've told Meg that I might be able to help her and try to help I will. She obviously came a good distance—I've never seen you, you see, so I can tell that you came from quite a ways. And your bare feet! And, well…"

"Excuse us a minute." Lezah dropped her basket and pulled Serah enough paces away that Meg could not hear their whispers.

She watched their mouths form words and hands wave a few times. Lezah's face turned an interesting red once, but Serah's remained calm and determined. Finally, Lezah marched back to her basket, yanked it up from the ground, and trudged toward a nearby road. Serah stood in place and waited for distance to grow between her and the angry girl. Then, slowly, she returned to Meg.

"Sorry you had to see that. Lezah isn't usually angry, but she is always stubborn. Sometimes I find it easier to take along Robie—that's our mule—than I do her. I can at least get a ride from him, besides. But I suppose there would be no trouble if I didn't have a stripe of stubborn in me, too. Which Mama always says is a surprise because I was such an easy little babe. 'Just like a kitten,' she says. But when I have a mind to do something, there's no way around it. So come, let's follow that stormy little cloud of a girl."

Eventually, Lezah slackened her pace and allowed the other two girls to catch her. The path narrowed after a time but remained wide enough they could walk side by side. Lezah insisted on keeping the heavy basket to herself, and Serah had not stopped talking since the walk began.

"So then she said, 'Well, if you had your way Serah Snofam, we'd eat cake every meal.' And I said, 'That's not so Milta Rezfam. For breakfast, we'd have pie. The rest of the meals would be cake.' Ha! I showed her, what a pig that girl. All the Rezfams are. They root their noses through everyone else's you know what and then roll in it. Don't realize they're the ones who end up reeking." She sighed a sweet, little breath.

Meg smiled at her new *friend*. She liked to hear her chatter and laugh. It reminded her of the birds in her forest after a good rain. She also liked the way Serah's eyebrows bounced and her hands made motions for nearly everything she said. She noticed Serah had begun to walk differently, one leg taking shorter steps. It made her move in a mild jerking kind of way.

"Why do you walk like that?" Meg blurted out.

Lezah halted and deepened her glower at Meg.

Serah only smiled. "Noticed, did you?" She lifted the fabric around her legs. "I'm getting better at walking on this, but on longer treks, it gets a little sore."

Meg leaned forward to see that Serah had one leg like hers and one leg made of smooth wood starting just below the knee. A jointed piece was attached at the bottom in place of a foot.

The look on Lezah's face made Meg wish she hadn't noticed. "Oh," was all she could think to say.

"What's the matter? Haven't you ever seen someone missing a limb?"

"No, I—I—," Meg stammered.

"Oh hush, Lezah," Serah said. She shrugged. "A tree was felled, I was under it. That's that. But not many are lucky enough to have so fine a replacement leg as this. My papa had it specially made in the City of Turron," she added proudly.

Meg didn't admit she was struggling to understand much of what Serah said. Lezah was already making her feel fidgety. So many words. Lucky. Papa. Citiovturron. And she didn't know anyone could live without a part of their body.

Serah moved to walk again and was already on to another topic. "Don't you just love spring, Lezah? Meg? Just look at that field. It's growing as we walk. I've never seen anything so beautiful. Oh, look!" Meg followed Serah's pointing finger to a group of the small, white animals moving through a gate. A young man walked in the middle. "There's Jem Yulfam. Doesn't he have a cute little flock?" She waved her hand overhead. "Jem! Jem!"

He looked up and a wide smile spread over his face when he spotted Serah. He returned the wave but cut it short when his fluffy followers crowded into him from behind, nearly knocking him over.

Serah giggled, a glowing flash in her eyes. "What a goose."

Meg smiled to herself. *Goose.* The way Serah said it sounded soft and sweet. Goose Jem was someone to Serah. Meg put "goose" on her list of favorite new words.

"We're near now," Serah said with a sunny smile. "I'm so glad you found us, Meg. The village is busy this time of year with everyone getting their stuff growing. It was lucky, too, since Lezah and I weren't even supposed to be there today. But Mama sent us to get yarn for some stockings for Papa because his are worn right through, and then we picked out a few things on our own since we were already there. Lezah, you are a workhorse to have carried that basket all this way. I could carry some—I still have two arms, you know." For the first time, Meg heard some real bite in Serah's voice. But it only lasted seven words, which Lezah little noticed. "Anyway, it was lucky we found you, besides, Meg. So...you know, you don't talk very much."

"When is she supposed to?" Lezah muttered. "You do the talking for everyone within a shout's reach."

"That's true I do," Serah said reasonably. She glanced back at Meg. "I hope you don't mind."

Meg shook her head.

"See, Lezah? She doesn't mind." Serah turned back to Meg. "Lezah thinks anyone who talks too much only has nonsense to say. Because she is so silent all the time, she thinks she speaks only wisdom."

"I do not," Lezah said, bumping her sister with the basket.

Serah smiled playfully. "She hasn't taken to speaking in rhymes and riddles yet, but I expect it any day." She straightened her shoulders and lifted her chin, looking more like her sister. " 'A chicken may speak too oft, but the rabbit speaks only when he is being eaten.' Look out!" Serah laughed as she jumped out of the way of Lezah's swinging basket. "When you—Oh! There's the man we're looking for. Don't stare too hard at that ax swing, Lezah," she said with a larky laugh.

Meg followed Serah's gaze to a young man further up the gentle slope. He was turned away from them, but Meg could see his hair was light, like a buck's coat. His shoulders were broad and something about the way he swung the ax in his hands made her feel very curious to see his face.

When she pulled her eyes away from him, she took in the rest of their destination. A structure sat not far from them with happy round-birds pecking the ground around it. Sounds from inside told her other animals lived there, too. At the top of the hill, a proud little home stood framed in trees. It was pretty but not like the cottages in the village. It had a wide porch in front trimmed with thick logs and steps leading up to a pale blue painted door. The roof was newly thatched, looking neat and tidy.

Before they reached the young man, something leaped out from the long grass and bounded toward the girls. It stopped short when it spotted Meg and let out a snort before it growled, leaned forward, and tucked one leg.

"Wolf!" shouted Meg, stepping back.

Serah laughed. "Hardly. That's Riff. Gregry's dog. A wolf!" and she laughed again.

Meg felt her cheeks redden as she looked at the dog. It really wasn't much like a wolf, with floppy ears and white fur patched with liver-brown on its face and back. And it was kind of small. But she hadn't known what else to call it.

"Go on, Riff. That's no way to greet our new friend."

Riff darted away to his master and sat down, his hairy tail sweeping the dirt. The one named Gregry looked over his shoulder. Meg caught just a glimpse of his face before he turned back to his chopping stump and drove the ax in with one solid swing. Without another glance, he strode toward the house.

"Gregry!" Serah called after him. "Wait!"

He didn't stop.

"I told you we shouldn't have brought her," Lezah snapped. "He isn't pleased. Let's take her back."

"No!" Meg said desperately. "I cannot go back without knowing what is in this." She held up the book. "That is the hu…*man* you said can help me read it?"

Lezah put her hands on her hips. "He *can,* but clearly he doesn't want to."

"I have not even asked him," Meg said taking several steps toward the cottage.

Lezah put out a hand to stop her. "Sorry, you're not going to. I should have said clearly he doesn't even want to see you."

Meg's eyes narrowed at the irritating girl. What harm could it be for him to look at her?

"Don't worry," Serah said. "Let me go talk to him. And I'll make sure it's all right with Papa." She hiked up her skirts and dashed the rest of the way up the path to the door.

Lezah stood between Meg and the cottage with her arms crossed. Meg checked to make sure her hair still covered her ear and adjusted her tunic with her free hand. She clutched the book tighter in her fingers and took a deep breath.

"It's important to you, isn't it?" Lezah said, losing some of the chill in her voice. "How did you come by it if you can't even read?"

Meg shrugged her shoulders. "It was given to me."

"Couldn't the person who gave it to you read it?"

"No." Meg didn't want to say anymore. She didn't like answering questions. Or talking to this girl.

"Do you know whose writing it is?" Lezah continued.

"Writing?"

Lezah squinted one eye. "Yes, obviously someone wrote on those pages."

Meg hadn't thought of that. Someone *wrote* on the leaves. On the *pages*. Who had made the markings in her book? Mickelby would have told her if he had made them.

A door slammed. The young man moved down the path in long strides, Serah meekly following behind him. As he neared, Meg took in the features of his face. His nose was slender and straight but not too small nor too big for his face. A strong jaw tapered nicely into his chin, both shadowed by short whiskers a shade darker than his hair. Below a thick but not unlikable pair of eyebrows were a set of eyes made of an undefinable color. Meg couldn't decide if they should be called blue or green. But there was no mistaking the anger smoldering within them.

He shot Lezah a dark look when he reached them before looking at Meg. "Yes?"

Meg didn't like the way he spoke. The *sound* of his voice was nice, but there was something not nice in it. It reminded her of the way Mother spoke when Meg did something to displease her. Though she was his same height, she suddenly felt small standing before him. She stared into his eyes, wishing she knew as many words as Serah.

He raised his eyebrows, impatient for a response, and seemed to consider her for the first time. His face softened, just slightly, but he crossed his arms over his chest, still waiting for her to speak.

Lezah nudged her with an elbow.

"I have this," Meg said holding out the book. "And I do not know how to…read it. I want to know what the markings mean."

He looked down at it, then back at her. "I'm sorry you've come all this way for nothing. I can't help you."

"But Serah said you can read."

It was Serah's turn to receive the darkling glance now, and she ducked her head.

"I'm sorry," he said to Meg, his tone a little softer. "She shouldn't have told you that…she is mistaken. I can't read it."

Meg tucked the book back into her folded arms, against her chest. She looked at Serah, but the girl would not look up. She glanced at Lezah and thought she could see a trace of pity in her eyes.

"Do you know anyone who *can* help me read it?"

He tightened his lips and bounced his eyebrows. "No. I'm sorry, I don't."

Meg's face fell. She would have to continue searching. But where? She could only think of one place. She would have to go to the castle. That decision made, Meg lifted her chin and turned to leave.

"Wait!" Serah called out. "It will be dark soon. You won't make it back to the village before nightfall. Why don't you stay the night? You can have supper with us and everything."

"Serah!" Lezah scolded.

"No, a girl should not be walking about the paths alone in the dark.

And what if she gets lost."

"Papa won't allow it, Serah." Lezah turned to Meg. "It's better if you continue on your way. The sooner you leave the sooner you might find someone to help you."

Serah snorted. "You know as well as I do there isn't anyone in the village who can read it. Don't send her on a fool's errand. I'll go ask Mama. She won't send her away." With determined steps, Serah marched away.

Meg smiled as she watched the girl go. She knew she should leave, it would be unwise to stay a night. Serah didn't know Meg could easily head north a small distance and be in her forest. But the truth was, Meg didn't want to leave. Her smile lingered until she looked at Lezah. Her brown eyes were aflame and her face tight as if she were holding back a scream. Meg ventured a glimpse at Gregry. He had half turned away from her, his hands clasped behind his head.

"I do not mean any harm," Meg said quietly. "I would be pleased to stay. Just one night."

Lezah made a derisive sound. "You shouldn't even be here. Gregry, I'm sorry. I tried to tell Serah no. She wouldn't listen. Really I—"

"It's done, Lezah," Gregry said. "Say no more about it." He looked Meg up and down again. "Where are you from anyway?"

"Roshton," she replied.

He stiffened. "Roshton? What is your family's name?"

She hadn't needed a lie for that question yet. She didn't even know what a reasonable name would be for a family. "I...I do not have one."

He and Lezah exchanged a look.

"You should go."

But as he said the words, Serah crowed from the porch. "You can stay, Meg! Come in, you can stay!"

Gregry loudly exhaled and looked into the forest.

"Don't worry," Lezah said. "When Papa gets back, he'll not let her stay."

Gregry nodded but didn't reply. As the girls walked up the path to the cottage, he returned to his chopping block. Meg jumped at the loud crack of his swinging ax.

Chapter Six

SERAH led Meg through the cottage door and into a cozy room. In the center was a long, knotty-pine table with a bench on either side and a high-backed chair at one end. On the right was a fireplace with a stone hearth and a beautiful mantel of carved wood. Three chairs gathered around the fire, with a large woven rug of bright colors on the floor. A kitchen of sorts was in the back right corner, and in the left corner, underneath an open staircase, was a narrow bed with a little table beside the head.

Meg narrowed her eyes at the two books stacked upon it.

Feet shuffled on the floor above them. Serah invited her to sit in one of the chairs while Lezah hurried to the corner bed. From behind, Meg heard the scrape of a drawer open and close. Serah sat down on the rug at Meg's feet.

"This will be fun," she said. "We've never had a friend stay over." She swayed her outstretched prosthetic leg back and forth. "I'm glad we found you, you poor thing. Not even shoes on your feet. I don't think any of mine would fit you, but maybe a pair of Lezah's—"

A cough came from the kitchen, and Serah closed her lips and sank her head into her shoulders for a moment. Meg was learning new words all the time from Serah and hoped she wouldn't be quiet long.

Shoes. That's what they had on their feet. Mickelby was always bare-foot, just like her and Mother.

Serah licked her lips and looked about the room. "Mama is upstairs fixing up your bed. I hope you don't mind sleeping up there with all of us. Papa snores like thunder, but I'm so used to it, I never even think about it. But now I'm worried it might keep you up, but Gregry sleeps there." She pointed to the bed. Meg looked at the corner again and noticed the books were gone. "So you can't sleep down here." She laughed her chirpy laugh. "No, Mama would never allow that."

Mama. The name reminded her of Mother. Meg hoped Mother was still asleep. She almost asked Serah what she meant by *snores* but decided to wait and find out.

Lezah busied herself with slicing potatoes, loudly thumping each victim onto her block and hacking at it with astounding force. Meg would have preferred the girl leave the house.

"I am pleased to stay, Serah," she said loudly for all to hear. "I vow I do not mean any harm. I will leave when the sun first rises." *After I have asked Gregry once more,* she added just to herself. Aloud she said, "I like your home. It is so small."

Serah wrinkled her forehead and looked around. "I always thought our cottage to be one of the larger ones. Do you come from a big home, then?"

Meg realized her mistake by the look on Serah's face. "I mean it is very comfortable. It feels like a good place." She also needed to be careful not to say anything more to prompt questions.

Serah lightened. "I give you my thanks, Meg. It is a happy place. Just the five of us, mostly. Jem comes to supper sometimes and brings his sister. It's always nice to have other people to talk to. Usually, Mama and I chat away like chickens while Papa, Lezah, and Gregry sit like snails on a rock. Though I don't mean stupidly, just quietly. Not one of them is much for chatter." She leaned closer with one hand cupped to the side of her mouth. "Between you and me, I think all three of them could use visitors more often. I think they've all quite forgotten how to be friendly."

Meg concentrated on Serah's every word. She understood these humans didn't have others in their home often. That wasn't strange. Never had anyone besides Mother, Mickelby, and herself placed a foot in her castle.

"Why do you not have other hu—visitors in your home more?"

Serah looked carefully at Lezah, then leaned forward again. "I can't really say. We used to when I was a little sprout, but not anymore. Papa doesn't like outsiders. Especially ones not from Turron."

"Turron?"

Serah cocked her head. "Yes, you chirp. That is where you are. Turron. Surely you knew that."

Meg let out a little laugh. "Oh, yes. Turron. Where I come from we…said it wrong. So I did not know it."

Serah smiled. "Well, now that we've sat a bit, would you like to go on a walk?"

Walk. Meg knew what that was. "Yes, that would be…fun." She watched Serah's face to see if that was the correct word. Serah's happy expression didn't change as she got to her feet. Meg was pleased she had gotten it right.

Just as the girls reached the door, the stairs squeaked and a woman in thick skirts and a dusty apron descended. Her nose was a little small for her round face, Meg thought, and some of her eyebrows seemed to be missing. But there was a pretty color in her cheeks and her smile was genuine and serene.

"Hello, Meg. We're so happy to have you with us." The woman placed a hand on her chest. "Ida. I've made up a bed that I hope you will find acceptable."

"I am sure it will be…acceptable," Meg replied. She felt her whole body relax under the soothing sound of Ida's voice and realized how taut her muscles had been. Everything was so new.

"We're going out for a walk," Serah informed her. "Maybe we'll find Papa for you."

"He has never been lost before, but perhaps he will need to be found today." Ida shooed the girls out the door and before it shut called, "Send Gregry in for me, please."

The girls tromped down the path toward the chopping block. Gregry sat hunched forward with his elbows on his knees and his hands clasped. Riff sat before him with his nose pointed toward Gregry's head. When the dog caught wind of their scent, he stood with his head low and barked defensively. Meg smiled at the animal, thinking of the time she had surprised a pack of wolves by shifting from girl to giant, taloned bird. This little dog would not be so fierce with his bark if he saw her as falcon.

Serah scolded Riff into silence and ruffled his head. "Mama would like to see you," she said to the sullen master.

Gregry nodded and stood. Without a word, he stalked up to the house.

When he was out of earshot, Serah whispered, "He's not always a grouch. He's actually kind of fun to be around when you get him going. I shouldn't have surprised him by bringing you home. That's the problem. Not that it's your fault he's acting like a wet cat. It's mine. So don't worry about it."

"Why should my being here upset him?"

"Oh, you know. Several reasons. That is, he…well he doesn't really care much for surprises. Or strangers. That's all."

"But I am not a stranger," Meg said. At least, she didn't think she was one of those. Maybe that was the human word for Raparean. She checked to make sure her hair still covered her ears.

Serah looked at her confusedly for a moment, then linked their arms together.

"That's true. You aren't a stranger to us anymore."

Meg felt her shoulders loosen again. She wished she could talk to Serah as freely as the girl talked to her. As she prattled on while they walked, Meg tried to think of something she could say that wouldn't put her forest or Mother or Mickelby or anything else she cared for in danger. When Serah mentioned she was glad Lezah was helping with supper because it wasn't her favorite thing to do, Meg perked up.

"Oh, I love making food. I always do for Mickelby and me."

"Who's Mickelby?"

"He is a…um…he lives with Mother and me. He is old."

Serah jingled. "He's old, huh? How would he feel if he heard you describe him as only that?"

Meg was perplexed by that question. "He would not feel anything about it," she replied. "I think he knows he is old."

"Well, anyway, you like to cook. What's your favorite thing to make?"

"Um, I like to make…I do not know if the words are the same for you…but I like to make fish." She looked at Serah, who didn't look a bit confused. "Cooked little birds. And…oh! and cooked pears. Sometimes I…" She pulled her arm free of Serah's and pushed her fist into her other open hand.

"Smash?" Serah tried.

"Yes, I smash—that is a funny word—smash the pears. Mother hates those, but Mickelby and I like them. Mickelby showed me how to do that. And I like to make eggs when we can find them. I like to cook them, but Mother likes them just how they are found. And I like potatoes cut and cooked on the cook pan in the...water? It is not water, but what is left after cooking the fish."

"Grease?"

"Yes, grease. And I put all the leaves and some pieces of fish into a big cooking pan and cook that. We have a lot of leaves that I put in food. They make everything better. Mickelby showed me how to make most of what I do. But he likes me to do it. Says it is better."

She looked at her new friend and grinned. She had done it! Said a whole lot of words to Serah. Mother used to talk more, but she was too tired now. Even so, she never talked like this. Talk that had no purpose other than to say what was in your head. Meg talked like this to Mickelby and understood his motions and his expressions, but it was different talking with Serah. Someone who matched her energy and fed her curiosity. And she liked the new words. Sister. Goose. Smash. Grease. Others she couldn't remember but would know if she heard them again.

"Well, you'll have to cook for us next time you come."

Meg looked at Serah with her eyebrows pinched together, and she seemed to understand.

"You will come, again, now that we're friends, won't you, Meg?"

Meg nodded, unsure if that was the truth.

Ahead Meg heard the knocking of an ax, the rhythmic sound echoing through the trees. Serah got a little skip in her step as they neared the sound. They rounded a bend in the path and discovered a good-sized animal—bigger than a deer—with tall ears and large, round eyes. Ropes linked it to a heavy cloth weighed down by several trees, stripped of their branches.

Serah patted the animal. "Hello, Robie. Papa! It's time to be done. Supper is early tonight. It's a special occasion." Serah tucked her shoulders up to ears and looked at Meg with a giddy smile.

Through the trees, Meg spotted a man swinging his ax at the trunk of a tree. He was large, and Meg felt a little bit of fun drain from her. Lezah had told Gregry Papa would not let her stay. What if the big human sent her away?

"Papa! I said put down your ax! It's time to be finished. We have a visitor!"

The ax froze mid-swing. "Jem back already?" he hollered, a hint of merriment in his voice.

"No, Papa. Not Jem! Don't tease me. Lezah and I made a friend in the village, and she's come to stay a night."

His face snapped in their direction.

"If you'd come here to meet her, we would not need to shout!"

Before she had finished her sentence, he was barreling through the trees toward them. Instinctively, Meg took a step back. He was not more than her height, she could tell, but from one of his shoulders to the other, she could fit hers in twice. The look on his heavily bearded face made her wish he had dropped his ax.

Serah's smile disappeared, and she stepped in front of her friend. "Great mountains, Papa, you'll frighten her coming at us that way!"

"What's this?!" he thundered. "You finding a stranger and bringing her home?" He looked over his daughter's head and eyed Meg darkly.

Stranger. Meg wanted to correct this Papa and tell him she was no such thing. But she kept still and let Serah talk.

"Papa," she said, squaring her shoulders. "This is my *friend*, Meg.

54

She was in need of a place to sleep tonight, and Mama said she may stay. Her bed is already fixed up and extra potatoes have been sliced. Mama said she may stay," she repeated, emphasizing each word.

Meg watched the man deflate a bit. It seemed the Mama woman had some pull on this beast. He swiped a hand over his mouth, sucked in a deep breath, and muttered words Meg couldn't make out.

Serah gasped, looped her arm back into Meg's, and began pulling her away, her face bright red.

"We'll turn back now," she squeaked out. "But supper is near ready so don't dawdle."

When they went around the bend again, Serah apologized for her father's welcome.

"I told you he's forgotten how to be friendly," she said with a forced laugh. She was quiet the rest of the walk back to the house.

When they reached it, Serah asked Meg to wait outside for just a minute. She scurried away, and through the crack in the door, Meg heard hushed voices. She sank down onto a step, a keen stab in her stomach. She should not have stayed.

Mother was right. Humans should be left to themselves. They were strange, wicked beings.

Ida opened the door and swept past Meg to the path they had just come from. Serah took a seat next to Meg and tried to chat in her sweet way, but her face told the truth. She was not pleased. The smell from the little kitchen eased out onto the porch. Part of the scent she recognized but mostly it was like so many of the words Meg had heard today—foreign and unclear.

After a short time, Ida appeared at the mouth of the path soon followed by her husband and the mule. Gregry stepped out of the cottage door and went down to meet them. Ida returned to the cottage and smiled reassuringly at Serah, while the other two mechanically went about getting the stack of lumber stored and the mule back in the barn before approaching the porch.

Papa cleared his throat. "I apologize for the greeting I gave earlier," he grumbled. He placed a hand on his chest like the others had done. "Frelick."

So Papa was not his name, but Frelick. Just as Mama was really Ida. Why these people had two names Meg couldn't guess.

"Ahem-hm. And you are welcome in our home."

"I am not a stranger, so you need not be frightened," Meg said with a nod. There. She had corrected all of them at once.

Frelick looked away and rolled his tongue across his teeth before he climbed the steps and entered his home.

When all were gathered around the table, Meg picked up her fork and poked it into a potato. Serah nudged her with an elbow. Her hands were still in her lap, and she shook her head at Meg and looked at Frelick. He looked from face to face around the table and smiled at each one, though Meg noticed the smile for her was not quite right. Then he looked to Ida, who picked up her fork and took a bite. The rest of the family followed and began to eat. Meg looked at Serah for direction and received a nod.

Meg raised her fork and put her mouth around the potato. The warm food was like comfort moving down her throat, filling her chest. Chatter began, Frelick asking his daughters how their trip to the village went, his wife informing him that the family stores still looked comfortable, and Gregry reporting how much wood he had split and how his carving was progressing.

A basket was passed around, beginning with Ida. When the basket came to her, Meg took out a soft little ball like the others had done.

She watched Gregry use a knife to spread a pale yellow glob he had scooped from a bowl onto his ball. Lezah did the same, so Meg did, too.

When she took a nibble, she was surprised by the taste. The thing didn't look like much, but the flavor made her feel homesick for something she couldn't figure out. And she quickly realized she hadn't put nearly enough of the yellow on it. When she dipped her knife into the bowl for a second scoop, she looked up to see Gregry watching her. She glanced at Serah who was too focused on her own plate to worry about what Meg was doing. Without further hesitation, Meg spread more stuff on her fluffy ball and devoured the rest.

"Pass the roll basket, please?" Ida asked her husband.

Roll. As the basket crossed Meg's face, she snatched another one. Across the table, Gregry still watched, a twitch at the corner of his mouth. Meg looked at the little ball and decided roll was a sensible name for such a thing. It looked like it might roll.

Before the meal was finished, Meg had eaten nine rolls, all slathered with butter, as she found it was called. She wished she could tuck a few into her pockets for Mickelby. He would like them, too.

When every plate was empty and each belly full, the dishes were cleared and washed. Meg helped dry and put them away even though Ida insisted a guest should not. It was clear to Meg that Frelick and Lezah wanted her gone, but Ida was pleased with her. Gregry seemed somewhere in between. He never spoke to her, but once she caught him nearly smiling at something she had said.

With supper things put away, the family gathered around the fire. Ida, Frelick, and Lezah each sat in a chair, while Serah and Meg sat on the woven rug and Gregry seated himself on the raised hearth, whittling a piece of wood with a small knife.

"Papa, why don't you tell us a tale," Ida prompted.

"I am out of tales, my love," he said with a haggard face.

Serah put a hand on his boot. "Just one, Papa. No one tells a tale better than you. It's all right if we've heard it a hundred times."

He smiled at his daughter. "All right, which one would you like?"

She thought for a moment. "How about the Tale of the Kingdoms. Do you know that one, Meg?"

Meg shook her head.

Frelick's eyes widened. "All right. The Tale of the Kingdoms it is." He sat forward on his chair and cleared his throat. "Long, long ago, before there were fields, villages, and castles, forest covered all the land below the Great Mountains. But the forest was not without life. No, it was full of creatures of all kinds. Ones your eyes would not believe. Stags with horns made of crystal, rabbits with fur so soft it melted at a touch, and birds with a song that made men forget where they were and listen until they died."

Meg looked at the others. Ida was busy pulling a needle through a worn shirt. Lezah sat glaring at the fire with her arms tightly crossed, and Serah dreamily watched her father. Gregry stared at the wood in his hand, his knife still.

"But the greatest of all the creatures were the elves. The Raparean."

Meg straightened. She glanced at each face again, but none paid her any mind. She slumped forward and tucked her legs tighter to her chest.

"They were not elves like the ugly, small, mischievous ones found north of the mountains. They were tall and beautiful and many in number. They ruled the mountaintops and watched over the forest below. But the Raparean were not peaceful creatures—always at war among themselves. Battling for power. Their shrieks and screams

58

from the mountains could be heard over great distances." He paused. Meg's heart pounded in her chest. Frelick continued.

"Until one day the mountains fell silent. The forest, too, grew still. The great elves as well as the wondrous creatures that roamed wildly were no more. The land grew lonely. One fine day, three noble men entered the forest—one from the south, one from the east, and one from the west. It was the most beautiful land any had ever seen, and each created his own kingdom after his name. Turron, Roshton, and—the greatest—Davare.

"The kingdoms prospered and many happy years passed for the people of The Three Kingdoms—the open land allowing them to grow what they needed, the forest providing the rest. Then one dreadful day, a young king of Davare betrayed the Great Forest. It revolted—forbidding man's boots to touch its soil and keeping a vicious, taloned beast to guard its trees. No snow falls in the deep woods, no sun shines, and no wind blows. But The Three Kingdoms thrive yet, as there is naught to douse the stalwart strength of the human race."

The room was still when Frelick finished. Meg didn't dare look up from her knees. She had never heard such a history. Had never heard about the end of her kind. It was strange to hear Frelick talk of her race and her forest. And what would these people do if they discovered the taloned beast was sitting on their hearth rug.

"I love that story!" Serah said with a sigh. "Did you like it, Meg?"

Meg nodded without raising her head.

"And nobody tells it like you, Papa."

The family remained around the fire for another hour until Frelick declared it was time for sleep. As Meg laid in her bed listening to the sound from Frelick's throat that must be snoring, she wondered if these humans would allow her to return so she could learn more words and more stories. But what if she said or did the wrong thing and they found out what she was? Or, worse, what if Mother found out?

She rolled over and hugged the quilt tighter over her shoulders. She pictured each of her new friends' faces in her mind and remembered how they spoke to one another when they forgot she was there.

"These humans are good," she whispered into the dark.

Chapter Seven

MEG thought she was the first to stir in the morning, but when she sat up to peek at the other beds, she found all of them empty except Lezah's. She inhaled a deep breath, taking in the scent of something delicious with it. Quietly, she slid her legs out from under her covers and folded the quilts into a neat pile. She combed her fingers through her hair, making sure her ears were covered, and with book in hand went down the stairs, not a board squeaking underfoot.

Serah and Ida were busy in the kitchen, one shuffling something around a pan on the wood stove and the other slicing something like big rolls.

"May I do that?"

Serah startled and turned the rest of the way around with a smile. "You scared me! I didn't hear you come down. Are you any good making toast? We are making a special breakfast in your honor."

Meg shook her head. "I do not know what toast is. But if you show me, I will do it."

Serah put both hands on her hips. "Never even heard of toast. One would think you came straight out of the forest or something." She laughed.

Meg forced a laugh with her. "The forest. Ha. No."

Serah finished slicing the bread, then gathered up some forked sticks. She opened the stove door and motioned for Meg to join her. Ida stepped aside to make room in the small space.

"It's simple. Just put a slice of bread on a fork like this and hold it near the flame. See, like this. Check it every so often to make sure it's not getting too dark. Then when it's browned like this, turn it over and do the other side. Got it?"

"Got what?"

The corner of Serah's mouth turned up. "The idea. How to do it."

"Oh," said Meg. "Yes. Simple." Serah put the stick in Meg's hand.

"If you can manage it, do two at a time. We're running a little late," Ida added.

"Two at one time. I can…manage."

Meg placed another slice of bread on the fork, covering the half-toasted piece. Serah quietly picked up another fork, reached out, and plucked the second slice from Meg's. She handed a newly loaded fork to Meg with a smile and let Meg set to toasting.

"I'm going out to tell Papa and Gregry breakfast is nearly ready." Serah wrapped herself in a cloak, and as she pulled the door closed, Lezah plunked down the stairs.

Ida turned from her pan. "Lezah, you slept in. Gregry is already doing the milking for you."

"He is?" Lezah reached for her own cloak, a scowl pinching her face. "I'll go help him. Why didn't you wake me?"

"You looked so sound, and that boy wakes up before the chickens. He didn't mind when I asked him. I'm sure he's almost done by now. Serah's just gone to fetch him."

Lezah dropped her hand and stomped to her chair by the hearth to sulk. Meg continued making toast while Ida stood over her, scraping and stirring the pan, sprinkling in seasonings. Meg watched her sure movements and peeked into the pan several times. Some sort of crumbled meat popped and simmered with sliced onion and cabbage. The stack of bread had become a perfectly golden tower by the time the other three came inside.

"Meg! So many pieces of toast done so evenly!" Serah exclaimed. "Are you sure you've never made it before?"

Meg grinned. "I'm sure I never have," she said, combining the words 'I' and 'am' like Serah did. "I only did as you showed me."

"Well, I must be better at teaching than I am at doing it. Hoorah for no burnt toast! Are we ready? I'm famished."

"We are ready," Ida said, dumping her pan into a wooden bowl and placing it on the table with a plate of boiled eggs.

Gregry set a tin pitcher next to the toast, sloshing out a dribble of thick, white liquid, while Serah added bowls, forks, and butter to the table. Then everyone took the same seats as the night before.

No one moved to fill a bowl, so Meg waited with her hands in her lap and looked at Frelick. Starting with his wife, he smiled and nodded his head at each member of the family. Meg thought his smile for her came more naturally this time. Then Ida dished her meal before passing the bowl to Lezah. When everyone's bowl was filled, Ida took the first bite and the rest of the family followed.

Meg watched Gregry spread a generous amount of butter onto his toast, the knife scratching pleasantly over the surface. Then he pushed the butter bowl toward her, his face impassive aside from a tiny bounce of his eyebrows. She took up the knife and coated her piece. With a small glance at Gregry, she took a mouth-filling bite. The bread was crisp instead of soft like the rolls, but she liked how the fire had changed the taste—a light smoky flavor woven through the crumbs. And the white water—milk! She was sad the pitcher only lasted long enough to fill each person's cup once.

Over the scraping of forks against wooden bowls, the family talked through the day's plan. As Meg listened, everything felt normal. Comfortable. It was fascinating how at ease everyone moved and spoke. A rhythm she had never seen before. *It must be like this every morning,* she thought. How happy they seemed. Her mind conjured up an image of Mickelby sitting by himself at their table. She felt a prick in her heart. How lonely he must be.

"Will you be staying with us another day, Meg?" Ida asked, breaking into her thoughts.

All eyes turned toward her and half the family seemed to stiffen waiting for her response.

"No. I must leave today."

The table relaxed again, but she noticed Serah's disappointed face. Inside, Meg felt the way Serah looked.

"But I would like to come back. If I may."

"Oh yes, you must!" Serah said quickly. "We are always happy to see a friend, aren't we Lezah? Gregry?"

Lezah nodded but didn't smile or speak. Meg peeked at Gregry, but his expression was unreadable as he continued to draw bites from his bowl, his eyes cast down.

When the meal finished, everyone but Ida readied to go out into the cool morning. The sisters were going out to sort and stack wood, while Frelick and Gregry were going into the woods to cut more trees. Meg decided it was time and announced her departure. Ida and Serah each took a turn wrapping their arms around her, wishing her well and mumbling her praises. And each time Meg kept her arms pressed to her sides, waiting to be released. To her relief, Frelick just gave her a nod and wished her a good journey, and Gregry and Lezah nodded with him.

Meg picked up her satchel and joined them out the door, itching for a chance to speak to Gregry. Lezah's waspish demeanor made her nervous and seemed to encourage Gregry against her. And Frelick didn't make her feel any more confident. She needed to catch Gregry alone. With relief, she watched Frelick turn toward the barn and the sisters stop at the chopping block. Gregry continued down the path, an ax over his shoulder. After she rounded the first bend and the cottage was out of sight, Meg jogged until she was beside him.

"Teach me to read."

His countenance darkened. "I told you yesterday. I don't know how. I can't help you." He quickened his steps, but she easily kept pace.

"If you cannot read, why do you keep books by your bed?"

He glanced at her and scratched the side of his scruffy jaw with his free hand. "I…I like to look at the pictures in them. And I draw."

Frustration swelled in her chest. She hated having to ask what everything meant but knew no other way to understand. "Pictures? Draw?"

"Yes, you know. With a pencil. I draw. And some books have pictures printed in them. I like to look at those."

Still unsure, Meg pulled her book out from her satchel and flipped through the thin leaves. "Is this drawing?"

He stopped and gave her an odd look. "No. Those are words. Making letters into words and sentences is writing. Drawing makes pictures. Images of…" His tone hardened. "I can't tell whether you're gaming me or you've really never seen a picture. Where are you from? Who sent you here?"

"Who sent me? No one. I mean I did. I came myself."

"And where did you come from?"

"Roshton."

"You did not come from Roshton. That's a lie." He turned away from her and strode into the forest.

Meg looked at her book. Letters. And sentences. How did anyone make sense of them? With a determined huff, she marched after him.

"I just want to know who made these…letters. Can you at least tell me that?"

"I can't tell you anything about it if I can't read," he called back without turning around.

She caught up to him and grabbed his empty arm.

"I do not know why you are afraid of me—"

He stopped and quickly turned to face her, pulling his arm from her grip. "I am not afraid of you."

She swallowed hard. "Then I do not know why you are afraid to help me. But just look at it." She held her book out and softened her voice. "Tell me anything you can about it. I will bring you no harm."

He studied her face for a minute, then slowly set down his ax with the handle resting against his leg and took the book from her hands. "I can't read."

She nodded.

He looked the book over and flipped through the pages before handing it back. "That book is very old. How old, I can't say. But see how yellow the pages are? And the binding is rotting. The style of it tells me that it's the book of a lady and someone took great care in making it for her. That's all I can tell you."

Meg turned the book over in her hands and fingered the gilded symbol on the cover.

"I wish I could know what the marks mean. But you have made me feel content for now."

She looked up to find him regarding her curiously. He tilted his head. "What is that in your ear?"

"What?" Meg reached up and covered her Imperald piercing. Without another word, she turned away and quickened her feet into a run. She tripped onto the path, colliding with Frelick and the mule. Frelick caught her by the shoulders and stared at her wide eyed.

Flustered, she choked out the words, "I did not mean…I must go."

She yelped as his grip tightened. "Gregry!" he bellowed.

When Gregry answered, Frelick's grip loosened enough for Meg to tear free. She bolted down the path without a backward glance. A good distance away, she turned and ran north through the trees and didn't stop until she reached her giants. With a leap and swoop of her arm, she shifted and launched out of the trees.

Calm filled her chest. The very deepest part of her knew she was safe. She glided through the air for a time, just for comfort's sake. Then she moved to the ground and shifted. She found a seat on a gnarled tree and sat down to think about all she had experienced. The humans. Their words and the things they do. Her book. She recalled and pondered and considered every detail. Frelick's deep voice giving life to the story. The soft quilt around her shoulders. The creak of the steps. The scrape of a knife over toast.

Finally, a wave of exhaustion swept over her. She leaned back against the rough bark and closed her eyes. The air was still aside from a few birds flitting about overhead, and the quiet trees whispered peace into her ears.

****

When Meg woke, the sun was on its descent. How had she slept so long? She scrambled back into the air and made her way to her castle, weaving a zigzag course, feebly hoping she'd hear something and could take Mother good news. She looked toward The Edge on her left and flapped backward.

Smoke.

The thin shaft twisting upward in the windless space above the trees meant one thing. A human was in her forest. Maybe more than one. She bobbed her head, trying to make a decision. It had been a great while since the last time she had this problem. Should she leave it be? Or attack? She knew the answer, of course. It wasn't safe for any human to be in her forest. Wasn't safe for her or for Mother. Maybe even for Mickelby. Mother would have her attack, and she had already disobeyed enough.

She landed on a treetop, ducked her head to loop her satchel around the tip, then threw herself upward toward the clouds. The higher point she began her stoop, the more force and speed she could render, but too much and she would lose control in her attack. When the angle was right, she began the dive.

As she neared, her eyes found at least three humans. She kept her body straight and sleek.

Before any of the intruders looked up, she was upon them. Working as Mickelby had instructed years ago, her first strike aimed for the small fire, grabbing a burning log and releasing it a second later to land at one of the men's feet. As she shot back into the air, shouts erupted. She arched her back, flipped, and darted back down. She swooped low this time, scraping a talon over the other man's head, removing his cap. The third was a woman. And they were all scrambling for their weapons.

Annoyance flashed through Meg. They were not frightened yet. She let out several sharp shrieks in quick succession, forcing them to cover their ears. If she disarmed them, they wouldn't be so brave. She dove again and screamed just before dropping through the trees.

As predicted, they lowered their guard for the sake of their ears, and she brought herself down on the first man, pinning him to the ground and cracking his spear. An arrow sliced through the air, nicking the top of her head. Before the woman could nock another arrow, Meg dived at her, catching the bow in her foot and crushing it. The woman stared up from her back, and for extra effect Meg shrieked in her face.

Meg glanced at the third and discovered his hands empty. At some point he had thrown his spear and missed. Meg spotted it driven into a nearby log, took it up in her beak, and snapped its thick shaft as if it were no more than a pine needle. She faced the three humans and let out more shrill warnings. They heeded her call this time and fled, leaving behind their nets and shredded gear. She screamed again and after a great while flew after them to be sure they moved in the right direction.

Thank the heart of the Great Mountains, they were not far from The Edge and needed only a little corralling to get out. She had hated the time she had been forced to pick up a human and carry him toward the line because he kept running the wrong way. And the cut on her head stung. She wanted to be home.

She retrieved her satchel and reached her castle just before it was fully dark. When her scaled feet touched the roof, she realized she had forgotten to find something for supper. She flung her satchel through her window, glided toward the grassy yard, and flipped just before landing, shifting into her elfin form. Mickelby instantly appeared from the kitchen door, with more than the usual questions on his face.

She smiled for quick reassurance all was well and ran to him, taking up his hand. He returned the smile, then took her by the shoulders and quickly ran his eyes over her. He stepped back, scrutinizing her injury.

"Is it bad?" she asked, reaching her hand up to feel the cut.

He turned her head, then pulled her into the kitchen. She sat down as he scrounged around for a cloth, filled a small bowl with water from the old kettle, and set to work cleaning the wound. It didn't feel very large to her fingers, but there was plenty of sticky blood in her hair. He wiped small sections at a time, then dabbed at the actual wound. He seemed less concerned by the time he finished.

He took the seat next to her and shrugged his shoulders.

"I am not going back. To Turron," she whispered. "It is unwise. No one can teach me—" she glanced around and lowered her voice even more, "—to read. And I did not find anything either. And I came upon three humans in the forest on my way back. They were not easily frightened. I do not know what that means." It all felt like time misspent. Nothing had gone as she had planned. A friendship with Serah was the only worthwhile thing that had happened. And even that she couldn't keep. She leaned forward and rested her chin on her folded arms. "I did not bring anything for supper. Do you have anything for Mother if she wakes?"

He shook his head and shrugged apologetically.

"I better go fetch something then."

She left him and went to the nearest stream. She didn't feel like hunting down a rabbit or a pile of birds. Fishing was easiest. She walked along the water until she came to a wider section where the flow wasn't as swift. She spotted a number of long, shadowy figures and snatched one up before it knew she was there.

Mother came down from her room just as Meg lifted the fillets from the pan.

"Your search, Meg?" Her voice was raspy and harsh, but no more stern than usual. Mother did not know Meg had left the forest.

Meg breathed a sigh of relief. "Nothing, Mother. Forgive me." She felt a sting knowing she hadn't even looked. She glanced at Mother's slight frame, then kept her head down pretending to focus on supper.

They ate in silence.

After the meal, Meg and Mickelby went on their walk about the yard. She whispered to him more details of her visit, and he was clearly disappointed she hadn't found anyone to help her. She offered to give the book back to him, but he waved his hands insisting she keep it. With a thin finger pointing to Mother's tower and a shake of his head, she knew he meant for her to keep it secret, too.

While sitting at Mother's knee near the fire, Meg's questions stayed at the forefront of her thoughts. She looked up at Mother, whose pretty but worn face held a slight look of contentment. She had been in a good mood since waking. Meg decided to risk spoiling it and ask one of her questions again.

"Mother, how do you know humans are wicked?"

Mother smoothed her forehead with her fingers. "Feel the mark on your head. They are dangerous thieves. They only want to harm you and steal our Imperald."

Meg shifted her position and tucked her legs further under her body. Mother's answer did not satisfy.

"But how do you *know*? And if you or I cannot find it, how could a human?"

"Humans are devious beings, Megnolia. They will steal it. They always steal." A pained expression crossed her face. "Thank the heart of the Great Mountains, the Imperald keeps our forest from wherever it is hidden."

Encouraged by her current willingness to answer questions, even though vaguely, Meg continued. "And what if neither of us find the Imperald?"

"Then all is lost." She placed a hand on Meg's head. "Megnolia, I am aging quickly now. I can feel it. My need for the Imperald grows. If we do not find it soon, I will die. And you will be alone."

"I will have Mickelby."

Mother's voice rose. "Mickelby? Take the place of a mother? Of one of your own kind! You will be alone, Megnolia." Her shoulders dropped and her voice softened. "I will die, and you will be alone."

Meg nodded submissively, feeling guilty for suggesting Mickelby's company would be enough for her. "Forgive me, Mother. I will work harder."

"I want you to search the far forest again." She slumped deeper into her chair. "I searched it over and over long ago, but you have not done it near enough." She inhaled a deep breath. "I do not believe it is likely to be so far, but perhaps I have been mistaken. Begin your search there tomorrow."

"Yes, Mother."

Meg went to sleep that night with renewed determination. Mother had not allowed her to go to the far forest before she was tall, and even now only rarely. She was growing desperate.

"Mother is close to passing," she whispered into her pillow. "And I must save her so I am not alone."

Chapter Eight

DAYS passed, giving nothing but routine and lonely hours. Meg had dutifully begun her search of the far forest, only to return nightly with empty hands.

One morning, as she prepared breakfast for two, Meg wished once again she had been able to bring home some bread to make Mickelby toast. Maybe she could have learned to make bread on her own. But she wouldn't go back to Serah's. If the one called Gregry wouldn't help, there was no use in it.

After finishing the quiet meal, Meg bid the old man goodbye and climbed her tower stairs. She had decided she wouldn't be returning until the following evening. It always made Mickelby anxious when she stayed out alone. She smiled thinking of his attempt to dissuade her. Or convince her to at least sleep as falcon. But she would not be dissuaded. And while she could sleep as falcon, she always found it more comfortable to sleep in elfin form. It wasn't without risk—if anyone happened upon her in her more defenseless state. But no one ever had, deep as she stayed in her forest.

To prepare for a night among the giants, Meg carefully rolled a couple pears in her cloak and stuffed the precious bundle into her satchel. She could always find mushrooms, wild onions, and eggs. But pears were something her forest didn't provide. Only Mickelby did that. Just before ducking out her window, she tucked her book into the satchel as well. *If no one will teach me to read it*, she thought with a lift of her chin, *I will learn on my own.* She shook her head at herself.

"Meg. How would you ever make sense of it?"

But she kept the book in her bag just the same. She looped the strap around her neck and climbed onto the ledge and to the roof. The warming sun bid her good morning as she prepared herself for the flight. With a fearless leap and a twist, the elfin girl disappeared, and the great bird left its castle behind.

As she glided over the trees, the itch for speed tingled in her bones, eventually giving way to a burning. She moved swiftly as it was, but sometimes it wasn't enough.

Mother says stay low, she reminded herself. *Stay low.* She sliced her wings through the air several times. *But Mother is asleep.* Meg angled her wings and shot away from the trees toward the open air.

Memory of the rush took over her thoughts. Higher and higher she climbed. When she reached the peak of her mountain in the sky, she allowed herself just a moment. Wings stretching to their greatest length. Wind threading through her feathers. Everything was easy at this height. Nothing but freedom above her and a land seemingly empty below. No one to please, no one to save, no one to hide from.

She ducked her head and dove into a stoop, finding the right position for her wings—the angle that allowed the air to flow the freest around her. She cut through the space like an arrow, the forest her target. At the very last second, she pulled out of the teardrop shape, caught air under her wings, and raked the top of a tree with her talons. When she reached the middle of the far forest, she dropped her feathered body into the trees and shifted.

The far forest was comfortingly the same as every other part of her forest. Bracken and wildflowers sprouted wildly from the soft earth, and moss filled the spaces they forgot to claim. Dark pines loomed overhead, trunks so thick two men could hide behind one. The younger trees twisted and arched, searching for the sun.

She inhaled deeply the joy of life within her trees. They were happy to have her as their keeper. With her toes digging into the soil, she slipped one arm through the satchel loop and slung it across her chest.

"Listen for the Imperald," she told herself. "I am listening, Mother."

She closed her eyes to open her ears. She listened for something different. Something she had never heard before. But all sounds were familiar. The distant babbling of a stream. The occasional call from a songbird. A woodpecker's drill. And stillness. Always a stillness. A scene from the cottage floated into her thoughts. The family sitting around the table, talking and laughing, and Serah passing her the roll basket. She smiled in response to the imaginary Serah.

Meg opened her eyes and looked up. The sun was not quite above her yet, the day still new. She had time to venture out of her forest to pay her friends a visit. Then she remembered the fright she felt when Herrick's men had chased her. Or when Frelick had briefly gripped her shoulders. She had been lucky to get away at all the first time and so easily the second. And Mother.

"No. I must stay."

She walked among her trees, brushing over bark with her fingertips, allowing pine needles to rake through her short hair, all the while listening for something new.

She had asked Mother many times what she was listening for. 'You will know when you hear it.' Meg could never understand what that meant. How can one recognize something without ever meeting it?

The longer she walked, the more her thoughts wandered. She felt her steps grow lighter as she pretended Serah was walking with her, chattering away about nothing important. That is, nothing important to Serah. Every word was important to Meg.

"Snore. Toast. Realize," she said to herself as she walked. "Shoes. Fun. Pages. Dog. Papa. Goose." Her smile widened at that last word. "Goose," she said again.

For several hours she meandered, her feet moving a fraction of the speed her wings would have carried her. When she finally stopped to determine where she was, she was surprised to find herself so near The Edge. She pursed her lips and chided herself for wandering so close. And somewhere along the way she had become so wrapped up in her thoughts, she had stopped listening.

She turned in another direction and rounded out her path, moving away from the forbidden line. She strode up a short incline and leaped down the other side, landing with her hands on the ground. A low growl made her freeze. She looked up to see a white animal with dark brown patches not twenty paces away.

"Riff?" she whispered.

The dog cut his growl but kept his head low. A snapping twig turned Meg's attention to her right just as Gregry appeared on top of another incline. He cocked his head.

"Meg?"

Run. It was the first reaction that popped into her head and she took it. Like a rabbit fleeing a fox, Meg sprinted and weaved a course away from him. How had he found her?

"Wait! Wait, Meg!" She could hear him shouting for her, but she didn't slow.

She glanced over her shoulder to see how close he was and was pleased to see him so far behind. He lumbered and struggled over the debris and undergrowth while she bounded over it all like a deer. But she wasn't out of sight yet. Shifting was too risky. She glanced back again and realized the dog was also in pursuit. Her lungs were starting to burn, but she could not slow. Riff would surely catch her.

She caught the sound of rushing water and cut sharply to one side.

The calls echoed from somewhere behind. "Meg! Stop!"

Riff's bark disturbed the trees.

Hide! The wide stream came into view. Not far was a small falls flanked by boulders. She kicked in one final effort to the safety of the rocks and tucked into a tight gap. Breaths came sharply in her throat, and her heart wouldn't settle in its cage. She closed her eyes and tried to listen for any signs of someone approaching, but the water moved so noisily over the rocks, nothing else could be heard. She tucked her head lower and curled into a tighter ball.

"Do not see me, do not see me, *don't* see me." *Mother will be so angry. What is he doing here?*

He needed to leave. Leave and forget ever seeing her. Time passed with nothing but rocks and water to see her in her hiding spot. Her legs cramped from the sudden crumpled position but still she stayed. She would stay all day until she was sure he was gone.

Then she felt them.

Eyes watching her from above. Slowly Meg raised her head and found Riff, one leg tucked up, head low, and nose pointing directly at her.

"Go away, Riff. Go away!" She swatted a hand at him, but he didn't move. She looked around for a stick, planning to poke him in the eye, but found none.

Before she could come up with another means of escape, Gregry appeared over her.

Puffing, he leaned forward to put his hands on his knees. "Good boy…Riff. Good boy." He ruffled one hand on the dog's head and looked down at Meg. "What…are you doing?"

She shrugged.

"You don't know." He nodded and straightened. "Right." He stood for a moment, his chest still heaving, then held one hand down to her. "Don't run again. Please."

Meg hesitated. She looked at his hand stretched out to her, then up at his face. He gave a slight nod but waited patiently. There was no flash of danger. He was not going to force her. Meg relaxed. She reached up and took his strong hand.

He pulled her from her hiding place and released her hand only to hold her gaze, a puzzled furrow between his brows. "Why are you here? In the Death Woods. Are you lost?"

She suppressed a smile. How could anyone call her beautiful forest the Death Woods? And lost? "No, I am not lost."

"Then what are you doing here?" he repeated.

She looked at him pointedly. "What are *you* doing here?"

He stiffened. "I will answer you if you will answer me."

She nodded.

"I am hunting."

"I live here."

His eyes widened, and he looked around. "Here? I told you the truth."

"And you think I lie? I live here." She flourished a hand indicating her forest.

He stepped back. "All right, then. You live in the Great Forest.

Here." Mockingly, he moved his hand just as she had done. "Do you live here alone?"

She shifted her weight and smoothed her fingers over the hair covering her ear. She should not answer any more of his questions. "I have to go."

"Wait!" Gregry reached behind his back and pulled something from his belt. "You dropped this," he said, holding out her book.

Meg's cheeks flushed. She reached for it. He jerked it back and waved it teasingly.

"Uh-uh. You have to answer my questions."

She lunged for it, but he spun away from her. She hadn't thought him so agile the way he stumbled after her minutes ago. But each time she reached, he easily ducked away and kept the book out of her grasp.

"Give it to me!"

"Just answer my questions."

"I will not!" She swallowed the urge to shift and make him sorry.

When he started laughing at her failed attempts, she had had enough. She ducked and pushed off both feet, throwing her shoulder into his gut. A surprised *oomph* issued from his throat as they both tumbled to the ground. She quickly adjusted herself and placed both knees on his chest, leaning forward to dig them in as hard as she could. He seemed temporarily paralyzed as he tried to catch his breath.

She snatched the book from his hand. "Mine."

His mouth twitched, ghosting a smile. "Yours," he conceded in a wheeze.

She pushed off her hands and got to her feet. "I'm going that way." She pointed toward the Great Mountains. "Do not follow me again. And do not tell anyone you have seen me."

He sat up but didn't rise to his feet or speak. Meg glanced at Riff still sitting on a rock, his hairy tail sweeping it clean. She looked at Gregry once more before taking several backward steps, then turning the direction she had indicated.

"I'll teach you to read it."

Meg stopped.

"If you will help me, I will teach you how to read your book."

Keeping her back to him, she asked, "What do you want?"

She heard stirring and knew he was on his feet now. "Have you ever seen the Rathern?" When she didn't say anything, he went on. "You know. A great winged beast the size of ten men, with eyes that glow like fire, claws like a bear. And teeth as sharp as a king's sword. They say it's hideous, though I've never seen it."

She was glad he still looked at her back, so she didn't have to hide the smile on her face. It was strain enough holding back a laugh. Eyes of fire and *teeth*—Ha! She looked down at the book in her hands.

"Yes, I have seen it."

He gave a little cough. "You have, have you? Hm. All right, then if you will help me hunt it, I will teach you to read."

She considered the proposal for a minute and turned to face him. "You said you cannot read."

"I lied," he said unapologetically.

She squinted one eye at him. *All humans are liars,* Mother said. But she couldn't really be upset with him for lying, as she had lied, too. About several things. If she took his offer, she would continue to lie to him. She knew he would never capture the *Rathern* as he called it. She would never allow him to succeed. But she needed to make sense of the marks on the leaves of the book. She needed to know what they could tell her.

"I will help you." She held out her book. "We can begin now."

80

He smiled and closed the distance between them. "I can't read *that*. It's a lady's book. A man should never read a lady's book. But," he looked up at the sky uneasily, "since you are anxious to get going, we will work on my end of the bargain first. Come, let's go where it's quieter."

They walked away from the river until they came to a log that looked like a welcome seat. He took the book from her hand and flipped through the pages again and settled on the last page.

"This is the back of the book. Normally one begins at the front, here. But we are going to use these pages that are blank, so I can write the letters for you to learn."

"What do you write with?"

"Well, normally I would have a quill and ink." He looked at her perplexed face. "A sharpened feather, using the tip of course, and ink is the liquid…stuff that makes the mark. But I have neither so…" He looked around. "Can we build a fire? Men have said fires draw the beast in, but you would know."

She bit her lip. Mother did not like fires in the forest. "Yes. If we need to. A very small one."

Gregry set to work. Meg watched him and was pleased to note he built fires the same way Mickelby had taught her, by gathering small pieces under several larger pieces. Using two bits of flint from his pocket, he ignited the kindling. When his fire was going strong, he took up several dried twigs and used his knife to form the tips into points. Then he put the tips into the fire.

They didn't speak as he worked, but Meg watched his every move, memorizing him. His hands were clean though the grooves in his skin were etched with stains and calluses covered the pads below his fingers. The skin at the corner of each eye was smooth, the crinkles she noticed on Ida and Frelick and Serah absent on his face. One of his eyebrows was slightly wilder than the other. The side he slept on maybe? His shirt tie was looped in a neat knot, and he turned his head to the side a little when he focused on something. She tilted her head when he did.

With charred sticks in hand, he sat next to Meg and took up the book again. "Each letter has a name and a sound or two. That's where we'll start."

He drew several symbols and said the name and sound of each one. Meg repeated after him. Then he drew several more. She liked the scratching sound of char against paper and the way he made the neat marks, his hand movements sure. It was fascinating to watch the page fill with strong lines. When he had written all the letters of language and Meg had said them all three times, he snapped the book closed.

"All right now it's your turn to help me."

"That's all I need to know?" Meg opened to the first page with the lady's writing. She recognized the symbols but couldn't make them into any words.

He breathed something near a laugh. "No. Reading takes time to learn. You have to practice. It takes some people months and months to learn. You'll need more than one lesson."

Meg's shoulders sagged. "Oh. How many lessons?"

He looked sideways at her. "I can't be sure, but I don't think it will take *you* months and months. Now, what can you tell me about this forest. This is my first time here, and until you came along, I was lost. And, as I won't own to being afraid, we'll say excessively nervous." He smiled. "Now I'm just lost."

She returned the smile. Talking to him now felt like talking to Serah or Mickelby. She was fairly sure they were friends.

"Well, the Great Mountains are that way." She pointed for him. "And the three castles are that way. Then there is forest this way and forest that way."

"Uh-huh," he said after looking all the directions she had indicated. "Well, I must be thickheaded because I'm still lost. How do you keep your direction?"

"I…" She almost slipped and told him she can see everything when she's above the trees. Trying to think how she keeps her way on foot, she said, "I know my giants."

"Giants?"

She laughed at herself. "Yes, the trees. I know many of the trees. Or rocks and streams. I have been all through my forest—many, many times. So I guess I just remember. And the sun. I track its path."

He looked up. "You can see the sun?"

She scrunched her face and looked up, too. "It is right there."

Gregry shook his head. "I can't see it. You know, people come into these woods and get lost. They used to come anyway. Nobody tries anymore. There have been many people who have entered and never come out." He cleared his throat. "Eaten by the beast or swallowed up by carnivorous mudholes or burned to a crisp by fire-breathing deer and—" He stopped talking as Meg whooped with laughter. "Well, that's what they say!" he said defensively but not without a smile. "How else should it be explained when skilled huntsmen do not return? There have been a small few who only by sheer luck found their way out. Men who talk of wandering these woods for days with nothing to eat or drink but what they took with them."

She grinned at him. "My forest is full of things to eat."

He looked at her as if her arms had just sprouted feathers. "No one can eat here. The water, the animals. Everything is poisoned."

"It is not," she said with a laugh woven into her words. "If it were, I would be long dead."

His expression turned thoughtful. "How long have you lived here, Meg?"

"All my life." She looked at Riff lying on the ground at their feet. "So, you are hunting the...Rathern? Why?"

He picked up a charred stick and began swiping it across a smooth stone. "I have my reasons. What can you tell me about it?"

She leaned nearer to watch him scratch out a tree. It was like what Mickelby had done in the dirt. "Is that drawing? A picture?"

His hands dropped into his lap. "Yes, but you already had your lesson today."

She sat back and thought a moment. "I have only seen it a few times." This was true, as she had seldom seen her reflection as falcon. "But it does not have teeth. It is a bird." She stopped, wondering if she had said too much.

"A bird?"

"Yes, you know feathers and—" she flapped her arms.

"I know what a bird is."

"But it is a very large bird. Not like the little birds. Or your round birds. Maybe like me or a little larger. It makes a sound like—" She unleashed her best shriek but had never tried it in elfin form. Rather than terrorizing, it sounded more like dying. "And...it does have big claws."

They were both silent for a moment.

"Is that it?" he asked, slightly amused, his wild eyebrow quirked.

"Yes. That's it."

"Well, someone is getting a good deal more than the other in this arrangement. Can't you tell me where it lives?"

"No!" she shouted. She lowered her voice. "No, I cannot. Um…I do not know. Where it lives."

He eyed her doubtfully. "Right." He stood. "Well, I got you started with the letters. I'm sure you can figure out the rest. It was, uh… pleasant running into you again, Meg. I feel sufficiently stupid now. If you'll just point me in the direction I should go, I'll be on my way."

"You are going? But what about more lessons?"

"I gave you one lesson, and you kind of reciprocated. I would say we are even."

She was getting annoyed with all the new words. "What do you mean?"

"I mean clearly you are not interested in helping me. I see no reason to continue taking time from my hunts to teach you when you have nothing more to pay me with. If it's a bird as you say, Riff will be more help than you."

She looked at the dog and remembered how easily he had found her in the rocks. She swallowed. A twinge of panic turned in her chest. Gregry took several steps one way and looked around, then up at the sky. He muttered something about the stream and turned back toward the water, sidestepping a patch of mud. Meg looked at Riff again, who was still on his haunches across from her watching his master blunder around. A small whine escaped the dog's throat, and he looked at her with his head cocked in confusion. She felt the panic thin and her amusement thicken.

"You need to go that way."

Gregry turned in the direction she pointed. "Right. This way to the three castles."

"And you will never catch the Rathern, as you call it. It is too clever for you. It's too strong. Your time is wasted."

He turned and flashed her a smile that she liked very much until he ruined it by speaking.

"I don't want to capture it. I want to kill it. Good day to you, my lady." Before he was too far away, he called back, "Serah is hoping to see you again. I won't tell her I met you here, but if you would like to come by the cottage again, I promise I won't act like a wet cat."

Meg watched him make his way through the trees in a fairly straight line. Thank the heart of the Great Mountains The Edge wasn't too far. She felt sure he would make it out fine.

When she could no longer see him or Riff, she picked up her book again and looked at the letters. She repeated to herself the names and sounds. Then she flipped to a page with the lady's writing and tried to make sense of it. When she finished all the sounds in a line, she couldn't decide what the word was supposed to be. It just didn't sound like anything. She tried again with the same result. Frustration nearly made her throw the book into the river. Instead, she set it down at her feet.

"*Hmph.*" She put her chin in her hand. Reading was stupid. And hard. The charred sticks Gregry had left caught her eye. She picked one up and looked at the tree he had drawn on the rock. She found a larger stone and scratched the charred stick against it, leaving one long streak. Her eyebrows bounced. She scratched some more, trying to draw the things she saw—rocks, trees, ferns, her book.

Then she found another rock and tried to draw things from her mind—birds, a bucket, a pear. She tried Mickelby's face and had to laugh at the blobby shape with eyes far too big and a crooked mouth. What fun it was to draw. She liked it very much. She could see why Gregry had a book just for drawing. Maybe someday she could have a book for drawing, too.

She drew for a while longer until her hand cramped from gripping the stick. Feeling restless, she tucked the charred sticks into her book and set off toward the Great Mountains—the opposite direction Gregry had gone. She glanced back a few times to see if he was following her but saw no sign of him. She hoped he had left her forest. A tiny part of her worried whatever happened to the men he talked about would happen to him, even though she knew it all to be human nonsense.

She decided she would search this area tomorrow to make sure he wasn't still wandering about. Or harmed.

The rest of her afternoon was spent swinging from low branches, hurdling fallen trees, and scaling small cliffs. Nothing but familiar sounds drifted to her ears. By nightfall, her unbeaten path had snaked its way back toward where Gregry had left her. A peculiar gathering of rocks reminded her of a nearby cave. Meg moved through the trees until she came to the small ridge she was looking for. She skipped to the rubble hole and slipped in.

The cave was shallow and still warm from the day's rays. She unrolled her cloak and spread it out near a little pool. Then she hiked up her leggings and sat down to dangle her feet in the water and eat a pear. From the darkness that had spread outside came the comforting hoot of an owl. Her forest was busier at night. She liked not feeling alone.

Chapter Nine

A warm, wet something rubbed across Meg's cheek and tickled her ear. Before her eyes fully opened to the threat, she scrambled away, pushing her back against the cave wall.

"Oh good, you're awake." Gregry sat on his heels a few paces away while Riff continued to investigate the hideout.

"You—" she gasped. "You should not be here!"

Gregry picked up a pebble and lobbed it into the little pool. "I've given it some heavy consideration and decided I'll give you another reading lesson."

Meg narrowed her eyes. "How did you find me?"

"I didn't. Riff found you. He seems to have a knack for picking up your scent." He looked the small cavern over. "Is this where you live?"

"No," she snapped. A peculiar uneasiness swept over her. He had found her again. "You should go. You should not be in my forest."

"*Your* forest?" He seemed amused by her possessive claim. He stood up and cleared his throat. "Truth is, I tried to leave. But I couldn't." He scrunched his face. "I'm still lost."

"Lost?"

"Yes, lost," he said ruefully. He scratched his jaw. "I tried to go the direction you said but somehow came to that stream again. I followed it hoping it would lead me out, but it just led to a pond. It must have an outlet somewhere, but I couldn't find it. From there, I went in what I thought was the right direction. Before long it was dark, and after leaving a few markers, found I was going in circles. Riff here was no help at all until he caught a scent trail and took off again. Found him pointing down your little rabbit hole. I couldn't see anything, so we camped out there—a little ways off. When it was light enough, we came in and..." He shrugged.

Meg couldn't help her twitching lips. She almost felt sorry for him.

When she didn't say anything, he continued, "I don't know how you find your way around. Honestly I don't. So if you'll lead me out, I'll give you another lesson. I don't believe it would be fair otherwise."

"Fair?"

"Just. Honorable? The right thing."

Meg understood. She thought of Mother. She should be searching, not wasting time. But she could search while she walked with Gregry. She had never really searched near The Edge, so it actually would be a good thing to do. Gregry's expression begged for an answer. She really did like to look at his face.

"Yes, I will help you. But you should not hunt the bird. Leave it and my forest be."

"I won't make a promise I know I won't keep."

Meg pursed her lips. She would just have to keep her distance from him. And others of his kind. She was beginning to understand why Mother wanted her to stay away from humans.

Meg grabbed her book and held it out to him. He took it and walked into the broadening beam of light coming through the cave opening. She followed, and they sat down together, ferns and Riff curled at their feet. They went over the names and sounds of the letters again. The first lesson had thrived in her mind, and Gregry seemed surprised at her retention.

"It took me weeks to know this much." He thumbed through the pages. "Though I was just a small boy," he added quickly.

He continued to teach—letter pairings, rules that made letters have particular sounds, words that were common. She concentrated on each bit of knowledge he gave to her, repeating it in her mind, often saying it aloud. This lesson lasted longer than the first. When Meg's stomach grumbled its hunger, Gregry grabbed his own pack.

"I do not need to eat your food," Meg protested. "I can find something."

"It's all right. I have plenty. And I have one of these." He produced a roll from inside his bag.

Meg's mouth watered but still she resisted. After a couple failed attempts to get her to take it, he grabbed her hand and placed the roll in it. She relented with a grin and began nibbling her prize. It was not quite as soft and a little smashed, but still wonderful. He watched her take a few bites with a half smile, then looked out into the forest.

"How did you come to live here, Meg?"

"I told you, I don't live *here*."

He chuckled. A very merry, pleasant sound that made her want to laugh, too.

"I know. I mean here in the forest." His face lost some of its humor. "Do you live alone?"

She looked away. Just like it had been hard for her to avoid Serah's questions, she found she had to almost bite her tongue. She *wanted* to be honest. She *wanted* to answer his questions and tell him all about herself.

"No." She had to speak slowly to ensure the wrong words or too many words didn't spill out. "I live with Mother. And Mickelby." That was safe. She had told Serah that much.

"Mickelby?"

"He is a...friend." Yes, that was a good word for Mickelby. It meant someone good to be with.

Gregry nodded. "And where exactly do you, Mother, and Mickelby live?"

"In the forest."

His face cracked into another one of his smiles. *Goose,* she thought. Meg swallowed. He seemed to sense that was all she wanted to say and didn't ask any more about it. She felt relieved, but also strangely disappointed he didn't want to know more about her. Since she had answered a few of his questions, she decided to ask him some of hers.

"How did you learn to read?"

He leaned back on his hands. She watched his face turn thoughtful as memories floated in his eyes. "My father taught me."

"Father. Frelick?"

"No, not Frelick," he replied quietly. He smiled a little. "Though he is like a father to me now. No, my blood father taught me. Where I was raised, it is usually the mother's responsibility to teach reading. But my mother died when I was very small, so my father had to." His words were carefully measured, just like hers had been.

"And now you are not with your blood father. Why?"

He inhaled a deep breath and leaned forward again. He picked up a rock and threw it. "My father died." As he spoke his words became hard, heavy with anger. "My home became no longer safe. I had to leave it." He was quiet for a minute and during the silence Meg wondered what it would feel like for her home to be unsafe. "The Snofams took me in. I've lived with them since I was ten years."

Ten years didn't mean anything to Meg, but she guessed it meant he had lived with them for some time. Instinctively, she reached out a hand and placed it over his.

"I am grieved for you, Gregry. It is hard to have lost your first home."

He looked down at their hands but didn't move his. "Meg, I need you to help me hunt the Rathern. It's the reason my father is dead, and I—"

She pulled her hand away. The Rathern was the reason his father was dead? How could that be? She thought back to the times humans had entered her forest. She had burned their goods, scratched at their backs, screamed in their faces. But she had never killed anyone.

"You should go," she said rising to her feet.

He nodded and followed her lead. Riff circled inside the cave for one final sniff before he bounded out of the dark and into the bracken. The first little ways they walked in silence, the energetic dog the only disturbance in the stillness. Gregry didn't seem inclined to speak, and Meg wanted to think.

She wanted to keep Gregry as her friend, but he was dangerous. What would Mother say if she knew Meg was walking through their forest with a human hunter? What would it feel like to not be nicked by an arrow but to have one slice through her heart?

She shuddered. She could not take the turmoil of her own mind any longer.

"What do you draw?" she blurted out.

"Hm? Oh, well, I'm certainly not an accomplished artist. But I like to draw trees and lakes. Sometimes animals. Sometimes things from my home in Roshton."

Meg looked at him in surprise and caught his wince. "You come from Roshton? Is that how you knew my home was not there?"

He gave her a crooked smile. "Yes. All people in Roshton have a surname. And know what drawing is. We're kind of known for that. And woodworking."

"Oh. Is that why you cut so many trees? To work them?"

They stepped over a log together.

"Yes, 'to work them.' Most of what we cut is for craft—for making things of wood. We send a lot to Roshton. Good timber is hard to find there."

"Why?" She stopped to pluck a handful of golden raspberries from a cane.

He shrugged. "Much of the Roshton forest is dying, the trees are rotting from the inside out." He shook his head when she offered him a few berries.

Meg remembered the despair she sensed in the trees of Davare. Roshton's trees must be suffering the same. "It is sad to cut down so many content trees."

He kicked over a rock with the toe of his boot. "I don't think a tree really knows whether it is happy or sad."

Meg stopped. "But it does." He looked skeptical. "Trees really do, Gregry. Not in the way you feel, but in their own way. Mother told me once that trees used to speak to many creatures—elves, gnomes, raccoons, birds. They could speak to everything and could understand every feeling, every touch. Over much time, they have forgotten how to speak, but they have not forgotten how to feel." She looked up and around at her giants. "These trees and your trees, all of them take in the feelings from the creatures around them. I did not know it before, but I think they grow strong when they have keepers who are good and weak when there is suffering. Can you not feel it?"

Gregry swallowed hard and met her gaze, his face intense and uncertain. "No, I can't." He glanced around, and she watched him trade his expression for one less heavy. "It's a good thing they don't speak anymore. Imagine the noise if they all tried to be heard at once."

Meg had never thought of it, and the idea made her laugh. He joined in, and they continued walking, joking about what the trees might say. Riff, padding along beside them, suddenly darted into a thicket. A rustling produced a deer, flushed from its afternoon bed. Gregry jumped in front of Meg, bravely putting himself in harm's way, but the animal merely bounded away, silently disappearing into the forest. Meg hid her smile as best she could when he sheepishly looked over his shoulder. She pushed past him and decided to ask a question rather than roast him about fire-breathing bucks.

"What else do they do in Roshton?"

He cleared his throat. "Well, we do what most people do I suppose. Work. As I said, Roshton is known for woodworking—furniture, carving, cabinetry. And art. We used to have a festival in the autumn to celebrate the animals in our forests. Everyone made a mask and dressed up—as deer or raccoons or foxes. I was a skunk once. My father thought that was appropriate for me."

"Why?"

"Because skunks stink," he said with a wink.

"Oh." When he wasn't looking, Meg leaned toward him and sniffed. She knew she did not like the smell of skunks, but she did not mind the smell of Gregry.

The further they moved together the more natural it felt. Like walking with Mickelby or Serah. Meg smiled as she realized Gregry was stepping around every patch of mud and began doing the same. He might have realized the deer were harmless, but it would be good

if he remained afraid of being swallowed by mud. He might stay away.
She sighed. "You said you *used* to have the—what is it? Where you
would be animals?"

"Festival."

"Yes, festival. Why do you not have it anymore?"

He drew in a deep breath. "I guess I'm not certain they don't but
if the rumors are to be believed, many things changed when the king
of Davare took the throne of Roshton."

"King of Davare," Meg said recalling with a shudder the man who
had tried to grab her. "That is Herrick the Fourth. I like the gold
leaves he wears, but I do not like him."

Gregry looked at her sharply. "You know him?"

She blinked, surprised by his reaction. "I saw him. Once. When I
tried to go to the first castle." His face didn't relax. "I was curious
what the...people were like. I can see the castle when I..." Meg was
finding it harder to lie the more she spoke. "Climb some of my giants.
So I was curious. I thought it would be...fun." Then she thought of
a better lie. "And I wanted to learn how to read my book. I went there
first. For that. No one helped me."

He still eyed her warily.

"I did not like Herrick the Fourth," she repeated for good measure.

He was quiet. After a few minutes, Meg asked a question and they
picked up their conversation about Roshton again. It was covered in
forests, like the edges of Turron. The people had been happy when he
lived among them, enjoying celebrations and plays. Gregry explained
each kingdom was known for something. Roshton its woodworking
and art. Turron its farming and inventions. And Davare its hunting
and mining. The kingdoms used to trade and sell freely, but King
Herrick had implemented strict rules for movement of goods between

Turron and the two kingdoms under his rule. He didn't say it, but Meg understood this angered Gregry. His shoulders tensed and his replies became short and quiet.

She didn't like him withdrawing, so she changed the subject again. She told him how interesting she found Turron, her thoughts about the people and the homes they lived in. He listened intently as she described the houses in the village that she liked most, how she felt in the Snofam's home, how different it was from her own. She described some of the new animals she had seen—he told her the names of each one—and faces she liked, describing them in detail.

"And my face?" he asked with a grin. "What have your keen eyes found about it?"

Meg shrugged one shoulder. "Oh, a few things. Your nose is the size I think it should be, and this eyebrow," she pointed with her finger, "is not smooth like the other. You have a patch of hair here that is lighter than the rest, and your eyes are not the same color they were when I first saw you. You have a white spot on this tooth, and when you think hard about something you hold your mouth like this." She pulled the left side of her lower lip between her teeth, then tilted her head. "And your head like this."

This made him laugh. "I do? No one has ever told me."

Meg nodded. "I like to watch your face. Very much." It felt good to tell him something so true when much of what she said was not. And he was amused by it, which made her want to say more.

But they had reached The Edge.

Gregry turned to face her. "Well, I give you my thanks for being my guide—helping me through your forest. And for allowing me to talk so much of my homeland. I haven't done that for a long time."

Meg bobbed her head. Then neither moved. He seemed to be

waiting for something, but Meg couldn't think what. She rubbed her fingers on the frayed edge of her tunic.

He smiled. "When someone says 'I give you my thanks,' it is proper to reply 'I receive your thanks.' "

More odd human customs. But she didn't wish to offend him. "I receive your thanks, Gregry. And...I give you my thanks for helping me read." She hoped she had used the words correctly.

His nod reassured her. "I receive your thanks, Meg."

He called out to Riff, and a rustling echoed through the hush until the bright-eyed dog arrived at Gregry's heels. Before they stepped over the border into Turron, Gregry reminded her Serah wished to see her again. And after a pause added he would be happy to see her again, as well. Meg watched him until she could no longer see his form through the trees.

And as soon as he disappeared, the blanket of loneliness wrapped around her. She spent the rest of her day searching for the Imperald and thinking about her new friend, replaying their conversations in her mind. She was anxious to tell Mickelby all he had taught her.

When the sun dipped into the western horizon, she determined it was time to return home. Her flight went quickly, her long shadow flickering over the miles of forest. The late hours passed without any stirring from Mother, and Meg was able to tell Mickelby about her friend and lessons without interruption as they walked on their path. He was pleased with her success. She decided against telling him Gregry's purpose. There was no need to make the old man worry.

The night was spent in peaceful slumber, followed by a morning of easy routine. Meg spent the day searching a nearby section, and in the evening returned for supper as expected.

Mother woke ready for her meal, which was prepared and plated.

They ate in near silence after Meg gave her report. Her replies to Mother's questions were rigid, as she concentrated on hiding the most significant events of her time in the forest. One slip of the tongue, and Mother would soon know everything.

When the frail woman was comfortable by her fire, Mickelby and Meg went out for their walk.

"Mickelby," Meg whispered. "Have you been to Roshton?"

The man's white head bobbed several times, then flicked to the castle. Meg didn't want to make him more nervous than he was but needed to say one more thing.

"My new friend is from Roshton, but he says Roshton is no longer safe for him to live in. It is hard for him." She exhaled a deep breath. "And something else I do not understand. Gregry says Roshton has been taken by the King of Davare." Her memory revived Herrick punishing the little boy for being a thief. "Herrick is the king. But he has stolen something."

They walked in silence a little further, an owl announcing himself awake and the mist rolling just outside the wall. She looked sideways at her friend. His face was so wrinkled it reminded her of the bark on the trees. A new question came into her mind.

"Which of the three kingdoms did you come from?"

He looked at the castle again. Slowly, he rolled his head from side to side, debating whether or not he should answer.

"Roshton?"

He paused, then shook his head.

"Turron then?"

He shook his head again.

"So Davare."

Mickelby nodded and a smile almost touched his face. He looked up at the trees on the other side of the wall and lifted his hand, waving it once, almost a swatting movement.

"Far away?"

He shrugged a little and repeated the motion with a bigger sweep of his hand.

"Long ago." Meg thought of the many days he had been with her. Sometime before, he had left his home just like Gregry had. "Long ago," she repeated. She would not ask what life he had left behind.

They finished their walk, and Meg went to Mother's knee before the great fireplace. She watched the flames devour the wood, still thinking of Mickelby. How had he come to live here with them? She had wondered before, but never this deeply. She had never considered that he may have fled from danger. That he may have left a home and lost people he knew and loved.

When Mother released her late in the night, she went to bed with a troubled heart. From its hiding place under her mattress, Meg took out her book. She fingered the gilded symbol pressed into the leather. Questions were growing thick like the forest mist outside. What Mother said had satisfied her for much of her life. But now having seen beyond her forest, there seemed to be much more to know. Meg needed to broaden her search.

She went to sleep with the book underneath her mattress, the lump keeping her from restful slumber until early in the morning. After breakfast, she and Mickelby walked together to the small orchard in the northwest corner. She talked to him about some of the animals she had recently seen while searching and imitated her favorite bird calls. When he was completely at ease, she pounced. With nervous looks but less hesitation, he answered her questions.

Why couldn't he read the book? Hands on his head with his

thumbs forward and palms facing up. Deer? No. Heavy on your head? No. Never mind that. How did he come to live with them? Long ago. On a funny walk? No. Never mind that, as well. She needed to know more of the human world for his responses to make sense. Why didn't he go back to Davare? A hand on her shoulder.

Warmth spread from his hand to her heart. This answer she understood. He stayed for *her*. She didn't know what to call what she felt for the old man, but she could see in his eyes he felt the same for her.

When it came time for her to go into the forest, she stood on her tower for just a moment. She flipped through the pages of her book until she came to Gregry's writing. She traced her fingers lightly over the letters, saying the names of each one. Before she closed it, she determined she would not be going into the forest to search for the Imperald. She was going to the cottage on the far edge of Turron to find answers.

Chapter Ten

THE miles skipped below Meg, all the while her mind busy with thoughts. She came to the Far Forest sooner than expected and The Edge sooner than expected after that. With little more than an adjustment of her tunic and hair, she walked beyond her border, excitement fluttering in her stomach.

She easily found the path she sought and jogged along, admiring each cultivated field that peeped through stretches of forest. She had told Mickelby she would be gone three days and hoped the Snofams would allow her to stay that long. She could have a lot of lessons in that amount of time.

A sudden thought slowed her pace. Gregry had said it wasn't right to receive something for nothing. Three days of lessons was a lot to receive. What could she give him? This time it had to be useful.

Satisfied with a small list of vague things to tell him about her forest and the great beast, she sped up. When the fields stopped coming so frequently, she knew she was getting close. She passed Serah's Jem with his flock and waved to him as Serah had. He returned the wave, though not as exuberantly and his face not a little confused.

"Maybe one only waves like that to their goose," she whispered under her measured breaths.

She shrugged and kept jogging until the cottage nestled in the hills came into view. No one was outside, and in her excitement to find the house, she had not looked in the forest for Frelick or Gregry. She reached the steps and slowly moved up to the door.

And stood there.

It didn't feel right to just open the door and walk in. It was not her home, after all. She looked around, hoping to see someone, then leaned her ear against the door. All was quiet.

"Hello?" she said finally. Then a little louder. "Hello?"

Steps inside neared the door. When it opened, Ida stood before her. She smiled once recognition set in.

"Meg! You've found your way back to us. Come in, come in." She took Meg's hand and pulled her inside. "Everyone is out doing their chores but should return soon for their midday meal. Serah will be so excited to see you."

They chatted for a minute—how have you been and anything new. Ida asked Meg what brought her back this way, and she replied she had missed them. Ida assured her she was just as welcome this time as she had been the first visit. In her heart, Meg hoped she would be more welcomed. By everyone. When conversation completely dried up, Ida invited Meg to help her prepare the meal.

Frelick and Gregry were the first to return. When Gregry entered the house and met Meg's gaze, he looked both surprised and pleased. As if they had never met in the forest, he greeted her with a nod of his head. Frelick's welcome was gruff, but he didn't threaten to toss her out. Both men sat down at the table.

"I'm sure we'll make good," Frelick was saying. "Seasons like this, you've proved to be a great help to our family, Gregry."

"We have done well this month. I hope it is enough."

"If only we had access to them trees a little further north. Just one would equal four of what we have here. One day I'll be brave enough to try, but it's not today. If them animals are poisoned, I'd bet my left hand them trees are, too."

Instinctively, Meg felt Gregry watching her. The knife in her hand stilled over the bread she was slicing.

"I agree," he said after a pause. "We had better not try it. The forest is protected by both enchantment and creature. I would not risk it." His words seemed honest, no hint of hiding any other feelings. He still thought the forest cursed. Meg exhaled and sliced another piece of bread.

"But like I said," Frelick added, "we'll make good this month. We'll make good."

Just then his two daughters bustled in, Serah talking animatedly and Lezah carrying a bag full of wild onion greens. Serah let out a squeal mid-sentence. She skipped to Meg, her wooden foot knocking against the floor, and enveloped her in a great hug. Meg returned it this time, feeling as though they had embraced a hundred times. Lezah dropped her bag and went back out the door.

Over the next several hours a complication arose in Meg's plan. Serah and Lezah knew about her quest to read, but she did not know what Frelick and Ida would think of it. It seemed likely to Meg they would forbid it. But if they didn't know about the lessons, how could they put them to an end?

The problem was she had not anticipated how difficult it would be to catch Gregry alone. After the meal, he worked the rest of the afternoon with Frelick and did not return until supper. After that, the family gathered around the fire like the time before, each in his or her particular place. Meg tried to catch Gregry's eye—waving her hand low or giving him a hard, determined stare—but he never looked her direction.

When everyone turned in for the night, Meg found herself lying on the same quilted bed made up on the floor near Serah. Frelick's snores were punctuated with the soft, steady breathing of his family. Her first day had been wasted. *Everyone else is asleep and here I am, eyes wide awake,* Meg thought. She sat up. *Everyone is asleep.*

Slowly, she got to her feet and stood still, waiting to see if anyone noticed. No one stirred. No one spoke. Silently, she made her way to the staircase and down.

The room below was dark, only faint blue light reaching through the cloths over the windows. Meg tiptoed to Gregry's corner and smiled. She had not been able to hear his quiet snores over the choking din upstairs. She leaned down until her nose almost touched his.

"Gregry?" she whispered.

He didn't stir. She reached out a pointed finger but pulled it back. She didn't want to startle him awake. He might make a noise. Bent on getting a lesson before the night's end, she blew softly in his face. He twitched a hand over his nose. She did it again, a little harder.

With a snort, his eyes opened wild and wide and his hand swatted at her face. She jumped back, stifling a laugh.

"Meg?!" he whispered. "What are you—?"

She leaned back into his face. "Gregry. I need you to teach me."

He rolled onto his back and put his hands in his hair. "You shouldn't wake someone like that. Blowing in faces. You're lucky you didn't get a fist to the nose."

"I tried to wake you with your name, but it didn't work. Get up. I still cannot read anything. I will tell you more about my forest. I will answer your questions better than I did before."

He didn't move, but she heard the hint of a smile in his voice. "You are persistent, I'll give you that. I thought you were going to bore a hole into me with your stares earlier."

He turned his face back to hers, their noses a finger-length apart. She blinked at him.

"All right," he said. He gave her forehead a little nudge with two fingers. "But only for a little bit. Frelick expects me to work. I can't put in a good day if I don't have a good night." He sat up and proceeded to pull his trousers on over his underclothes and put on his boots. "We'll go to the barn where we won't have to whisper." He handed her an oil lamp, loaded an arm with his quilt, then opened the drawer of his table and grabbed his books.

As silently as they could, they slipped out the door and scurried to the barn. When Gregry lifted the latch and the hinges creaked, the animals merely rolled their eyes and returned to sleep in their neat stalls, unconcerned with the midnight intruders.

Gregry lit the lamp and placed it on the dirt floor, pushing away any stray bits of straw. The flame cast a warm glow against the bare wooden walls, transforming the cool barn into a cozy study. In the corner, Meg noticed a half-built chair with tools and wood shavings scattered about.

They sat down side by side with the quilt over their laps. Gregry handed a book to Meg. When she flipped open the cover, a piece of soft leather slipped out and fell to the ground. Meg picked it up and turned it over to see a wreath embossed in gold.

"What is this?"

"What?" Gregry turned from the pile of straw he was arranging into a pillow. "Oh. Nothing." He snatched the leather from her hand and tucked it into his pocket. "Just a token from an old friend. I forgot it was in there." He flipped past several pages. "Here now. A book must always be read from front to back. Never skip. Let's start here."

They went through the letters and sounds. Meg remembered all of them. Then he began helping her put the sounds together to form words. Sentences came together slowly, but Meg couldn't keep a smile from her face as a story of a young man and a troll slowly unraveled from the pages. Gregry took a turn reading whenever she tired.

Frequently, they came across words she didn't understand. He clearly explained them, and she repeated each one hoping to use them later. She liked sitting in the dim barn with Gregry. It was easy to ask him questions. Easy to smile at him. Easy to feel comfortable.

"The troll grabbed…Descinda by the thr…o-at."

"Throat. Right here." He pointed to his neck.

"Throat. Well, then she cannot breathe! Oh, that wicked beast. Will Brando save her?"

Gregry smiled. "Can't spoil it. You'll have to keep reading."

Meg wiped her palms across her leggings. "I don't like not knowing what will happen." She swallowed, trying to get rid of the dryness in her own throat, grateful no one's green hand was around it.

"By the throat. Swift as the river, Brando raaa…raced into the cave, braaand-ish-ing —what?"

"Brandishing. Waving it like this."

"Brandishing his great sword. Oh good! I am so glad he brought his troll killer." She heaved a breath of relief. *"His great sword. The troll hissed and rel…re-leased the faa…ih-r—"*

"Fair maiden."

"Fair maiden. I'm glad she is honorable."

"What?"

"She is fair. In my forest you said fair means honorable."

"No, no. In this case it means beautiful."

"Well why not just say beautiful? *Fair maiden. The wicked creat...creature grabbed his dagger with his big, green hand.* Oh, I am too slow. I feel so nervous for them. Read it to me. I cannot do it."

Gregry laughed. "I've read this one so many times, I've forgotten what it was like to not know the ending. This is a book from my boyhood. My favorite bedtime storybook. And now the only one I have."

"Why?"

"It was all I could bring with me. But here. Now for the ending." He leaned his shoulder against hers, leaving the book in her hands, and read the rest of the story. Meg closed her eyes as she listened to Gregry's voice and imagined the characters acting out the scene—the battle between Brando's sword and the troll's dagger, and Brando's victory over the creature. She could see them so clearly, almost hear the clang of metal against metal. The story ended with Brando and Descinda exchanging a kiss—which Gregry had to awkwardly explain—and riding off into the sunset on a white horse.

"The End." He reached over and closed the book. "Of that story anyway. There are about thirty more."

"Let's read another."

"No, it's late. We should turn in."

"What about your lesson from me?"

He dropped back into the straw with his hands behind his head. "All right then. What have you got?" He sounded doubtful she could tell him anything useful.

Meg straightened. "The Rathern is a bird, like I said before. It lives mostly on the other side of my forest." Knowing he'd never make it that far, she felt safe saying that much. "I have seen it attack humans before. It can snap a thick stick with its beak and escape arrows. It is smart. Thinks like you and me." She glanced at him and could tell he was gaining interest. "When it makes its sound, they have to cover their ears. And if there is a fire, it will use that to frighten them."

"So it does use fire." He sat up. "You say if there is a fire, but the stories I hear say it breathes fire."

"It does no such thing. It is just like a little bird only much bigger."

"You've only seen it a few times. How do you know everything it can and cannot do?"

She shrugged. "I just do."

"You underestimate it. If you heard the stories—"

"I do not need stories."

"Men shredded by its claws. It's attacking more and more."

"If you'd just leave it alone!"

A nasty feeling swelled from her gut to her throat, and she turned her whole body away from him. He was not listening. He refused to let her teach him. A long, tense silence passed.

"Meg?" Gregry was first to speak. "I'm sorry if I've upset you. Please turn around."

She ducked her head lower pretending not to hear him.

"I should go in," he said quietly, but he didn't move. Minutes passed. "Would you like to see some of my drawings?"

Meg raised her head a little. She could hear pages turning. She turned just enough to see the little brown leather book he held, no bigger than his hand.

She inched around a little. "I don't want to talk about the *Rathern*."

"I don't either. But I also don't want to go in."

Their eyes met. With her lower lip pinched between her teeth, she scooted herself back around. He handed her the book and let her look at it herself. Small, colorless sketches of trees around a pond or the cottage. A few drawings of the barn animals. And birds. Numerous pages of songbirds, forest birds, and one owl. She liked the way he had drawn them.

"This bird. It makes a sound like this." She whistled the little songbird's tune. "I like when it wakes me. You are very good at drawing. And carving." She looked at the ax hanging on the wall. The handle had been carved with vines and swirls. "Did you do that?"

"Yes. A hobby. I learned some before I came here, but mostly I've taught myself. There are many—even children—who would put my work to shame." He picked at his shirt. "But it gives me control over something. Even if it is just a piece of wood."

"You like to have control then?"

"Yes. I've only lately realized that. I'm past what is considered of age. And yet here I am, in another man's home. Unable to go forward or backward without permission. I like the Snofams. Like my own family. But..."

Meg compared the life Gregry described to her own. They were much the same. "I live with Mother. But I can't do as I want either. Mother needs me—she is very ill. But I like it here, out of my forest. I like it there, and I like it here. If I could make them one place instead of two..."

"Your mother is ill?"

"Yes, life is leaving her. She is very weak, and unless I find—" *the Imperald.* She almost slipped. "Food for her, she will die."

"Why do you stay in the forest?"

"Because it is our home. And because Mother says that the people of the kingdoms are dangerous. To us. You and the Snofams have been kind. But the people in Davare. They would hurt me."

He cocked his head. "Why would they hurt you?"

She shrugged. She didn't want to think about her encounter with Herrick again. "Your drawings make me smile. I wish I could draw like this, too."

"You'll have to think of some other way to pay me if you want drawing lessons."

She looked up at his face. Seriousness lingered only a second before he smiled, little creases forming around his eyes and a few underneath the scruff around his mouth. A wisp moved inside of her. She nervously tucked her hair behind her ear and looked back at his book.

Suddenly he lifted a hand and tapped her ear with his finger. "What is this, Meg?"

She jerked away and moved to get up.

"Sorry." He caught her wrist, and she allowed him to pull her back down. "Last time I asked, you ran away as well. I won't ask again. I've just never seen anything like it."

How could she let him see her ear again? Mother would be furious if she knew. But Meg couldn't remove the crystal to keep it hidden. Mother forbade that, too. She forbade everything. Meg puffed out a loud breath. "It's a piece of the Imperald. Given to me by Mother."

"Hm," he replied, a little distant. He didn't understand, which pleased her a little. She had confused him with her words for once.

"The Imperald is the heart of the forest. It is my heart, too. This," she touched the piece in her ear, "keeps me strong. I mustn't ever take it out." But after saying that much, she was afraid to say more. Her determination to defy Mother had already burned out.

She picked at her tunic. "We should go in. I should let you sleep."

He sat forward again, bits of straw tousled with his hair. "I'm glad you woke me. It's nice to do something different from routine."

"Why have you not taught Lezah or Serah to read?" she asked, absently plucking a few stowaways from his hair.

"It's not right for them to read. It's not even right for you to read. But I need your help." He paused. "And I can tell it means a lot to you."

She smiled. "It does. I give you my thanks, Gregry."

He stood and held out his hand for her. She took it, and he pulled her up in one easy motion.

"I receive it."

He picked up the lamp and blew out the little flame.

Chapter Eleven

AFTER another week away, Meg returned to the Snofams. Her days spent searching and evenings at Mother's knee had been uneventful. Only her walks with Mickelby saved her from lapsing into a severe state of boredom. He had become more animated in his conversation and made her laugh more than she did him.

She felt content when she was with him. But when she was not, as she coasted over giants or sat before a roaring fire, she continually struggled against the pull of the far end of her forest.

As she approached the warm homestead, she found Serah in the garden, pulling a hoe over the soil just like Mickelby.

"Hello!" Meg called from halfway up the path.

Serah straightened and turned toward her. "Meg! Hello!" She dropped the hoe in the dirt and walked to meet her friend. "I was hoping you would come to us again. I'm so glad it is so soon!"

Meg instantly noticed her labored gait. "You are walking heavily. Are you hurting? Let me carry you."

Serah let out an exasperated breath and lifted both hands to stop Meg from scooping her up. "Oh great mountains, not you, too! Carry me! You chirp. I'm fine, really I am. I'm only a little sore because yesterday I stacked wood and carried a few things to Jem—er—the

Yulfams. And the hen-witted thing I am, didn't realize how little cloth I had packed between my leg and…my leg." She let out a little jingle. "So it's just a little sore today. That's all. Mama tried to keep me in the house resting, but I wouldn't do it. Such nonsense."

"Will it not get worse?" Meg asked.

"It won't get better, is the thing," Serah replied, grabbing a wad of her apron and crushing it in her hands to wipe away the dirt. "No one seems to understand this. The accident was not so long ago. I haven't always been like this, you know. But since it happened, everyone seems to think I need to sit. All day. Mama and Lezah have left me for town, saying I shouldn't go more than once every few weeks because it is so far. But I will go mad if I stay in all day. I might have broken under that tree, but I'm not a little feather that will blow away in the wind!"

She dropped the fabric clenched in her hands and clucked her tongue. "Sorry, Meg. Never one to keep anything in my head. I know they mean well. And sometimes I do need help or rest. But Jem is the only soul I know who treats me just the same as he did before. So I would like it if you would, too. Even though you didn't exactly know me before, so you can't really treat me how you have if…never mind. Rambles. Come, Papa and Gregry will be coming in for their midday meal soon. They will be pleased to see you I think."

As Meg followed her friend to the house and helped put together the meal, she wondered what it would be like to be Serah. Though not without restrictions, Mother sent her out on her own every day. Trusting she would work. Confident in her ability to care for herself. If Mother lost that confidence and kept her under watch continually, Meg would whither. She suddenly felt a heavier feeling of dread. Mother must never discover her secret.

When the men stepped across the threshold, Meg was pleased to receive a warm welcome from Frelick. He even greeted them with "Hello, my girls," just as if it had been Lezah standing with Serah. Gregry greeted Meg with a polite 'Hello, how are you?' and they sat down to eat before going out for more chores.

Later, as the sun drew closer to the horizon, Ida and Lezah came tromping up the path. Serah was struggling toward the house with a pail of milk she had assured Meg she could manage. Meg watched from the barn as Lezah set down her basket and ran up the hill toward her sister. She reached for the bucket, but Serah resisted. Lezah tried again and successfully yanked the thin handle from Serah's hands. White cream sloshed over the sides, but Lezah paid no mind and hurried up to the cottage.

Meg crossed the way to pick up the basket Lezah had dropped and watched Ida approach the still Serah where Lezah had left her. After a few words murmured to her by her mama, Serah nodded and moved with her up the path and into the cottage.

Meg set the basket by the door and jogged back down the steps toward the barn to think. Minutes later, Lezah stormed into the little sanctuary.

"So you're here again, I see. Haven't you got a home, or do you just travel around intruding on others?"

Meg didn't feel like having a round with the girl but thought better of running away. "I have a home. But I was told I am welcome here."

Lezah raised her eyebrows and ran the tip of her tongue over her teeth. "Well, if you're going to continue to come, you'll need to pull some weight. Help out. We don't take kindly to scavengers."

"Yes, I know. I will not be a burden."

"Is that why I returned to find my sister stumbling with a bucket you easily could have carried? I saw you standing in here watching her. She—"

Meg cut her off. "She told me she could carry it."

"Well, she's stubborn and sometimes you have to make her listen to reason. You should not have allowed it, Meg. If you were any kind of friend to her, you would not have allowed it."

Meg straightened. She was a friend to Serah. A good friend. "I should not like to tear the bucket from her hands as I saw you do. She does not like the way you help her. She told me so. You hurt her with your words and your doings."

She watched Lezah's face change colors from her neck to the roots of her hair. The girl let out a wild, exasperated cry and stomped away. A moment later she reappeared and shrieked, "I love my sister!" Then was gone again.

A cow bellowed, as if seconding Lezah. Meg sat down on the straw-covered ground feeling more perplexed than when she had come into the barn. She thought of Serah struggling up the path, determined to make it to the house. She thought of Lezah taking away her struggle. And Ida rubbing her hand across Serah's back, telling her she should have just let Lezah help.

Meg had not liked the unsmiling look on Ida's face when she had turned to see her following with the basket.

She could not decide who was right and who was wrong. They could not all be right, but somehow it seemed so. The sound of slow clopping hooves neared the barn. Robie appeared at the door with Gregry at his side.

Gregry looked around. "Waiting for someone to throw you some hay?" His smile failed when she did not return it. "Why are you sitting here?"

She shrugged. "Lezah is angry."

He coaxed Robie into his stall and bolted the gate. "About?" he prodded, as he picked up the pitchfork and began throwing flakes of hay to the mule.

Meg picked up a piece of straw to shred into strips. "Serah says she can do things. And Lezah is angry I let her. And I think Ida is, too."

He leaned the pitchfork against the wall and sat down beside her with his legs stretched out long in front of him. "Don't be bothered by Lezah. She doesn't talk much and when she does, it's usually rooster spurs."

"But should I have carried the bucket?"

He shrugged and leaned back on his hands.

Meg answered her own question. "No, I do not think I should have. I think Lezah just wants her not to hurt."

Gregry tapped the heel of his boot on the ground, loosening some of the caked-on mud. "Lezah was protective of Serah before the accident. Now she can hardly stand letting her out of her sight. She's calmed down some, but…"

"Humans are strange," Meg muttered under her breath.

"Humans? Yes, humans are strange." He nudged her with his shoulder. "And what are you then?"

She swallowed hard and turned her head away, trying to laugh with him. "Uh, hungry. I'm hungry. Should we go in?"

He got to his feet and held out his hand. She took it, and he pulled her up, giving her hand a reassuring squeeze.

"Gregry, can we read here again?"

He agreed to another lesson and together they walked to the cottage for supper.

****

The sun continued to move across the sky and Meg fell into a new routine, spending three days with the Snofams, then three days searching, and returning to her castle just as Mother woke in between. Soon it became easy to conceal her double life from Mother, and she had no difficulty giving false reports. She didn't really consider it lying since she truly had found nothing.

It was a little more difficult to hide her forest life from the Snofams. They talked far more than Mother, and Meg continually felt impulses to relate her own experiences and things of her life. She and Serah had become thick as molasses, yet Serah paid little attention to the many things about her friend she didn't know, which Meg was grateful for.

Throughout Meg's visits, Lezah warmed some but rarely spoke directly to Meg. Meg didn't let the chill from the girl seep into her bones. She considered herself part of the family. She had learned to do many of the chores—including making bread—and none would claim she didn't pull her weight around the homestead.

Gregry wiped his napkin across his mouth and dropped it onto his plate. "I think they ought to let the old man hang."

Lezah nodded. "I agree with Gregry."

"You always agree with Gregry," Serah pointed out.

Lezah reddened and looked down at her plate.

Meg listened intently from her seat at the dinner table as the family discussed some gossip from the village. An old man who had been caught stealing another man's chicken was currently in the stocks, what Gregry had already explained to her as a trap for the hands and neck.

"This isn't the first time," Frelick chimed in, stabbing his knife into a potato. "Likely not the last."

"Why did he steal the chicken?" Meg asked.

"Old Man Bertfam lives in a hut just outside the village," Frelick answered. "He keeps to himself, peddlin' wood scraps he carves into spoons, so it's hard to say why he continues to do what he done. First it was apples. Now chickens. Hang him and he'll not do it again."

"Why?"

"He'll be dead, my girl."

Meg shifted in her seat. Stealing was wicked. Mother had said so. But she remembered when she was hungry and didn't have the coin to pay for her carrot. Serah had bought it and given it to her.

"Mistress Hersfam told me he has been tending two children for some time now," Ida said. "His daughter's children, but no one has seen her for months."

"Well, perhaps he was only trying to find food for them," Meg suggested.

"Doesn't matter," Gregry answered. "Let him hang."

"I do not agree!" Meg said with more force than she intended. The table grew still, and all eyes turned toward her. She met Gregry's gaze and shook her head. "To make the man dead does not seem fair. What of the children? Who will care for them if he is dead? Why was the man so hungry he had to steal to eat? Was there no one who had food to give him? He is already receiving punishment in the trap. Let that be it, and the other humans around him see that his family has food. Then he'll not need to steal again."

Gregry listened to her speech with interest. Everyone turned to him for a response, but it was Ida who spoke first.

"I agree with Meg. Mercy is what Mister Bertfam needs. He has never done anything like this until recently. He has always tried to make his way selling spoons. Perhaps we should buy a few more of them when all of this is over."

After a short pause, Frelick replied, "You reason well, my love. I will go in tomorrow to see if anything can be done for him."

The subject was dropped, and Ida moved the conversation to a recent village wedding. Still Gregry held Meg's gaze. She could not tell whether he was pleased with her or angry. She was surprised to realize she didn't care. Suddenly, Lezah's cup tipped over, spilling water across the table, and the trance was broken. Gregry jumped up to fetch a kitchen cloth, and the mess was sopped up while Lezah, red faced once again, begged an apology.

The gathering around the fire that evening was more subdued than usual, each member more inclined to inward contemplation. Even Serah had run out of things to say. While she repeated conversations in her mind, Meg watched Gregry's hands work a piece of wood with his knife. Just what he was shaping it into she couldn't yet tell. But watching the little scrap take on a form—a new life—pleased her.

He finished his work just as Frelick declared it was time to turn in for the night. A dog. *Riff?* Meg wondered. She watched Gregry cross the room and kneel at Lezah's chair, the little wooden figure held out as an offering. For the first time, Meg realized tears stained Lezah's cheeks. Quietly the girl reached out and took the dog. A small smile came to her lips. She glanced at Meg watching them, and the smile instantly vanished.

In the dark hours of night, two figures slipped away to the makeshift study in the barn. Meg's reading lessons had been moving along slowly, as it was difficult to find time for them. Both she and Gregry worked through the daylight hours and were tired at night. On a few of her visits, he had been away the entire time—fetching goods from a far-off town she was told. But every visit he was home, they found one night to go out to the barn and read. And sometimes they didn't read at all, spending the time talking about things of no significance to anyone but themselves.

Gregry pulled out his book to read another story, but Meg held out her own. After some pushing and pushback, she convinced him to read her book with her. She had tried reading the first page of her book on her own, but handwriting was more difficult to read than printed words. And the words in her book seemed more complicated. With Gregry reclined on the straw beside her, Meg began.

"Mas-a-beth Ard-ian Miri-cam… what does that mean?"

She held out the book, and he tipped his head forward to look at the page. "Looks like a name. That must be the lady's name. The lady whose diary this is."

"Masabeth. I wonder why she gave her book to Mickelby." Meg turned the page and right away hit a block. She held out the book again with her finger pointing at marks she did not know. A date, he told her. A date that over one-hundred-and-twenty-five years had passed—a very long time ago.

"This Masabeth probably didn't give the book to your Mickelby. More likely one of her descendants—someone in her family long after she was dead."

Meg nodded and continued.

"This book was given me by my love, Jonef. What a lovely gift it is. I shall be able to continue to wuh-rite…write…all my many thoughts, for I think about a great many things and work pit-if-uhlly to keep them in order. The forest is calm tonight. My little babe, Megnolia—"

Meg stopped. "That's my name."

Gregry kept still, his eyes closed. "Names are used over and over, Meg. I know of half a dozen before me with my name."

She nodded and continued reading.

"My little babe, Megnolia, is sound asleep in Torah's arms as I write. She is the sweetest babe, a reward for my long wait for a child. She has hair as black as a raven and eyes just like a doe." Meg shot Gregry a look—certainly that description confirmed it was her. But he remained unaffected. *"She has her looks from me, but I feel quite certain she takes after her father in all other ways. I had hoped to pass on more of me than my hair, but it was not to be. She is a playful little one, with a ready smile and a laugh that would make fairies dance."*

"That is kind of like you," Gregry interrupted without moving.

Meg moved her head back and forth, not certain she agreed, and continued. *"I sing to her all day long, songs of our kind. Little Meg loves it and so do I."*

Meg continued reading, Masabeth's words going on to describe the furnishings of her new home—the draperies and rugs she had picked out, the chairs and tables. She described the four towers and the location of her room. Meg read on, all the while struggling not to jump to her feet, her eyes moving quicker over the words. She felt sure she was the babe Megnolia and that Masabeth described her castle. Almost as sure as she knew she had ten fingers.

She finished two pages before a new date was at the top. Her head ached from struggling to recognize the symbols, understand the words, and reconcile her opinion with Gregry's. She set the book down and took a deep breath.

"I think this book is Mother's."

"Meg, it is very old. Your mother would have to be at least one hundred and forty. Probably older. No one lives that long."

"Maybe Mother has. You don't know."

A smile spread across his face. "Is her skin wrinkled like a prune and all her teeth rotten stubs from years of use?"

"No."

"How about her hearing?"

"It's very strong. She can hear me from my room."

"I very much doubt, then, that she is over one hundred and forty years. I once knew a man who lived to be eighty-two, and you could clearly see the years of life on his face. And he couldn't hear a rock dropped in a tin bucket right next to his head. It isn't possible, Meg."

Well, maybe Raparean live longer than humans, she retorted in her head. Then she remembered her ear. She reached up and touched the Imperald. The Imperald was life. Mother said Meg needed it for her strength. She said nothing more about it to Gregry.

Later, as she painstakingly began reading her book page by page from the beginning as Gregry had said to do, Meg learned many things about Mother. Little things, jotted down in short notes. Her dislike of being alone, her love of hiding things for others to find, her favorite color—purple, and her fondness of wading in streams. After reading of her love of flowers, Meg planted seeds from the village in the castle garden. The flowers grew rapidly, but Mother never seemed to notice, even when Meg placed the tender, purple blossoms in a cup on the table. Her stoic face always remained the same.

Chapter Twelve

ON a day when the sun felt unusually bright and a friendly breeze brushed over the hills, Meg arrived at the homestead and set right to work with Serah in the garden. This late in the summer season, the weeds were few, and it wasn't long before they moved on to the barn, mucking out one of the stalls.

When Meg commented she had hardly seen Lezah lately, Serah replied her own chatter probably had driven her sister into the forest more and more. She laughed good-naturedly and quickly carried on to another topic.

Much of Serah's talk on this particular day revolved around the festivities they would enjoy when the morning had been spent. It was the Queen's Holiday, and every village held their own celebration.

"I love to go for the music," Serah chimed away. "Not one of us in this family can play an instrument, including Gregry, which is strange given he…but none of us play anything. Jem plays the tamdar. Do you know what that is? Oh, well it's made of wood and has nine strings that you pick at with your fingers. Such a fun—it's a celebration in a sound. He is quite good—the best in the area. Lezah thinks I exaggerate, but I don't. He can play The Hunter's Tune, Clarie-Dear, the Elf Dance. Anything really.

"How many songs he must have in his head. Made up some even. You will hear him today. So…and then there's the food and the tournaments. Jem and I competed last year in the pair's—dead last. I don't care for competing myself, but I love to watch. Each team is made up of a boy and a girl, and you do three challenges. This year I think they are doing the chop, tied race, and the pies. Or maybe it was a rope climb. Or the roll. I guess I don't remember. I'm not good at any of them. Except maybe the pies. *Never* turn down a free pie!"

She paused for breath and grinned.

"You will go with us, won't you, Meg? Gregry won't go, but the rest of us will."

Meg dropped the tip of her shovel to the ground and straightened. "Why won't he go?"

"Oh, he never goes. Hates crowds and such. And some days I think he even hates fun. But you might as well—please come."

"I don't know. It does sound fun." Fun. She still liked that word. "But I shouldn't. I don't think Mother would be pleased."

"Mother? Well, she isn't here. And *my* mother would heartily approve of you going."

Meg thought a minute and felt inside she really did want to go. She had never seen anything like what Serah had described. "All right then. I will go."

Serah grinned even wider and assured her she wouldn't be sorry when she got a taste of sugared plum cake. The girls kept working until the sun said it was nearly midday. They had just finished washing up when the three who had gone into the woods returned.

"Meg is going with us!" Serah crowed. "Scoot, Lezah, and get yourself ready. Papa, Mama would not approve of your hands. To the wash!" she demanded, tugging at his arm.

Frelick chuckled and allowed her to drag him toward the house. Lezah lingered near Gregry as he studied Meg.

"You're going, then, are you?" he asked.

"Yes. I have never been, and Serah says it will be fun."

He nodded.

Lezah looked from Gregry to Meg. "I don't think I'll go this year. It's just the same old thing. I'll stay and help you finish the work we didn't get done this morning, Gregry."

He rocked on his heels. "I haven't been to a Turron celebration before either. Maybe I'll go this year."

Lezah stiffened. Meg could plainly see the hurt rolling in her eyes.

"Won't you come, Lezah?" she said, feeling a need to soften her friend's feelings. "Maybe there will be something new."

Gregry turned to her. "Yes, come, Lez. You shouldn't stay here alone."

Some of the coolness ebbed from her face, and she reached up and grabbed her braid. "All right. I'll go wash up." She strode toward the house, her shoulders stiff but her hands unclenched.

Gregry and Meg watched her go, then faced each other again. He smiled and she smiled back.

He ran a hand over his jaw and looked up at the sky. "I better go clean up, too, if I'm to be ready when everyone else is."

It wasn't long before the family was strolling down the trail, Frelick and Ida leading the way with Serah and Meg behind them, and Gregry and Lezah bringing up the rear. Serah talked enough for everyone the entire way. Meg found herself looking over her shoulder more than necessary.

Before she could see anything but trees, Meg heard the gathering already underway—laughter, shouts of greeting, and noises unlike any she had ever heard.

"That must be music," she said to herself.

"What? Oh yes, the musicians are starting up." Serah added a little skip to her step. "Pretty soon you'll be able to smell the meats roasting on the spits. Just a little further now."

The group rounded a bend and what had only hours earlier been a plain clearing opened before them. It was now a field of motion and noise, full of people, animals, and peddler stands. Triangular banners of purple and green dotted the field. And on a pole in the center of all the bustle, a rich purple flag embroidered with a bright green wreath flapped in the warm breeze.

As the Snofams waded through the crowd greeting their acquaintances, Meg could not help noticing the curious looks she received and the few even directed at Gregry. Serah introduced her as a friend from Roshton, which was more readily accepted by these people than it had been by Gregry. Most gave her pity-filled welcomes.

Soon, as Serah predicted, a smoky, savory scent wrapped itself around Meg's head. Her mouth watered, but when she asked, Serah said it would be a while yet before anything like that was ready for eating. But to hold her over, Serah used her own coin to buy Meg a sugared plum cake.

Meg felt a giddiness settle over her as she ate the dense cake with a sweet, grainy crust and watched the ever-growing crowd. Instead of focusing on hair and faces, Meg found herself studying movements. People stepping in to help assemble a large platform. A man calming a wailing child. A woman patting the hand of a very old man. Another straightening a crooked flag.

She watched children roll painted wooden balls across the dirt and chase each other through the crowd. Their shouts and laughter rivaled the music from the instruments, and she found herself laughing at the tiny imp of a girl chasing and catching one by one children nearly twice her size.

Not for the first time, Meg wished Mickelby was with her. It didn't seem fair. He should be among these people, not always alone in a lonely castle. It hadn't been possible so far to convince him to bend Mother's rules. Still, Meg felt determined to finagle a way to get Mickelby to a village celebration with her someday.

A young boy stopped to say hello to Serah and Lezah. Meg knew his face but could not place it.

"Fenn," Serah said, pulling Meg up beside her. "You remember my friend, Meg?"

The boy looked up at her. "Oh, yes, I remember you. Stolen any carrots lately?"

Meg blushed. The boy at the vegetable cart. She had almost been a thief. "No," she replied with a smile. "I have better things to eat." She held up her last bit of cake.

"Ah, well I hope you paid." He winked. "Enjoy the celebration, Serah. Lezah. Meg."

When the hour was deemed right, a woman climbed onto the platform and shouted a welcome to the Queen's Celebration. She offered thanks to the Noble Queen for her ever-watchful protection and for supplying the feast for the day. A boisterous cheer erupted from the crowd.

Serah leaned over, still clapping her hands, and whispered, "Queen Iril always supplies the celebration food. For *every* village. She is very generous. I know we are fortunate to live in Turron." She gave Meg a meaningful look. Roshton was a not so fortunate place to live.

"Let our celebration begin!"

First up were the children's races. As the woman on the platform announced the rules, several men began roping off a large square for the game ring. Then children of all sizes lined up near the flagpole. A few tears were shed by little ones whose bravery lasted only as long as it took to organize the chaos.

A foot race was run in three heats based on age. Then a log rolling race and finally a hopping challenge. The top five competitors were each awarded a purple ribbon tied to a stick and a basket of pears. Only one of the champions looked at his basket of fruit in dismay.

Next was the women's competition, sixteen years and up. Serah nudged Meg and dared her to step into the ring. For a second she considered it but held back, feeling like an intruder among friends. But Lezah strode into the ring at the last minute. Meg sized up the competition and beamed. Her friend seemed just as likely to be champion as any of the other women.

Their first challenge was a log toss. Lezah's log fell a hands-breadth short of another's. Meg, Gregry, and Serah cheered and chanted her name when it was announced she qualified for the second round.

Next, the women were challenged to complete a course of twelve upright log sections, hopping from one to another with only one foot touching at a time.

"Lezah has this one in the bag," Serah proclaimed. "I've never been able to push her from a log—she has the balance of a squirrel!"

"True, she does," Gregry agreed.

As predicted, Lezah completed the course in swift, easy movements. As the crowd cheered her performance, Meg itched to give it a go. If she could perch on a rooftop, she certainly could glide across blocks. But she remained rooted in place and watched the other women bounce or stumble from point to point.

Only four of ten successfully completed the course.

The last event was a knife throw. The crowd was cleared on one side as the targets were set.

"She has this one, too," Gregry said confidently. "I taught her everything I know about throwing."

Meg listened intently as the rules were explained. Each competitor would receive four knives to throw. The targets were painted with a hand-sized green circle. A blade in the green was worth three points and a blade outside worth one. A complete miss was awarded nothing.

The first two women threw, earning three points each. Then a girl with light wavy hair and long arms stepped up to the line. When her throws were finished, two blades rested in the outer circle and two in the green. The crowd cheered and chanted, obviously believing her not to be topped.

Lezah stepped up as the final thrower. Meg studied her stance, one foot placed in front. Her arm raised, and with a forward step of her back foot, she released the knife. With an awkward whack, the knife hit the outer circle and bounced to the ground.

"Oh, she's nervous!" cried Serah. "You can do it, Lezah! Forget the crowd!"

Lezah took a deep breath and threw her second knife, which sank solidly into the green circle's edge. Again she threw, the third blade settling neatly in the green. With her last knife and her score two points behind, she stepped forward and released the blade into the target. The crowd cheered at the score, nine to eight. Lezah was proclaimed the winner of the women's competition and received a purple-ribboned medal and a basket of pears.

Meg was satisfied to see her friend's rare smile. She couldn't remember ever seeing Lezah so happy. They eagerly welcomed her back into the crowd to watch the men's competition. Meg hoped Gregry would step out, but he did not. It was not as exciting to watch a competition of unknown faces, but Meg still found herself amused as the participants tossed logs, demolished pies, and wrestled.

Then the pair's competition was announced. Teams of two began making their way into the ring, about a dozen couples or so. Gregry stepped up beside Meg.

"Do you want to give it a go, Meg?"

"Me?" She craned her neck trying to study each set in the ring. "But I'm not from here. And I don't know who I would go with."

He cleared his throat. "I meant do you want to partner with *me*. I'm not from here either, but I will compete if you will."

Meg felt Serah and Lezah's attention turned toward them now. "What about Lezah?" she said encouragingly. "She can be your partner."

"I've already competed," said the champion dejectedly. "The rules forbid me to again."

"Serah?"

"I told you, I'm really not fond of competing. I want to keep my cake in my stomach, thank you very much."

Gregry looked at Meg with his clear eyes. The last call for competitors was made. A refusal was on her tongue, but instead, she found herself stepping into the ring. Her heart thudded inside her chest, but she felt like bouncing on her toes.

Baskets of scrubbed potatoes were lined up on one side of the square, one for each team. Then the same number of empty baskets were set out across the way.

"The Wheelbarrow Potato Mouth!" the mistress of ceremonies shouted.

The crowd erupted in whoops and hollers.

"Oh, no," Gregry groaned. "I've heard of this one."

Meg watched the young men drop to their stomachs as the rules were declared. Each team was to move as many potatoes as they could from one basket to the other using only the fellow's teeth. No hands allowed. And to move from side to side, the man was to walk on his hands while the woman "drove" him by holding onto his ankles.

Copying the others, Meg picked up Gregry's legs, and he pushed up onto his hands. When all teams were positioned, the race began!

The crowd rolled with laughter as thirteen teams struggled across the game ring. Potatoes and ankles dropped, and a few faces were smashed into the dirt. Gregry fought valiantly to keep himself up and each potato in his mouth. Once, his arms couldn't keep pace and gave out, sending Meg flying forward, tumbling over his legs and into the dust. Another team, whose wheelbarrow boy was easily twice the size of the driver girl, remained sitting in a heap in the middle of everything, laughing at the others.

A bell rang, and the race ended to the relief of everyone in the square. A point was awarded for each potato successfully moved, and when the potatoes were tallied, Meg and Gregry were announced as second place. Meg tried not to smile at the grumpy expression on her partner's face.

"I thought we had it," Gregry muttered, brushing dry grass from his chest.

"You should have taken potatoes two at a time," Meg snickered.

While the top six teams recovered, instructions for the next event were given. An egg toss. Each team was handed an egg. Once positioned opposite each other, one teammate tossed the egg to the other. If the egg was successfully caught, each team member took a step back.

If the toss was unsuccessful, either with a failed catch or a crushed egg, the team could progress no further. The three teams who stood the furthest apart by the end would move on to round three.

"Light fingers, Gregry!" Serah yelled from the sideline. "Pretend it's the only thing you'll get to eat all day—nobody wants a dirty egg!"

The signal was given, and the tosses began. At first it appeared the teams were merely handing the eggs back and forth, but quickly the challenge grew. Before very long, one team was finished, their egg a sad puddle at the boy's feet.

Gregry's tosses came easily, finding Meg's gentle hands. Her aim was not quite as true, and by the time they were five paces away, he had to do a little more work to safely catch the little, brown egg.

"Sorry!" she called when he had to slide onto his knees.

By ten paces, Meg's aim was improving. One more team lost their egg. With four teams left and the noise of the crowd all around, Meg wiped her palms over her leggings. Two more throws and they were the second furthest team apart.

A third team lost their egg. Meg and Gregry were certain to move on. But by the determined expression on his face, Meg could see Gregry was bent on winning. A fourth egg smashed during a catch. They stood neck and neck with one last team. The girl tossed their egg.

"Come on. Drop your egg," Meg whispered under her breath.

"Drop your egg, you looby!" Serah yelled, clearly not worried who heard.

The opposing man caught the egg easily, forcing Gregry into another throw. He lobbed their egg, and it sailed through the air in a perfect arc until it found Meg's waiting hands. The crowd cheered as they each took a step back, becoming the furthest team apart. The other man tossed again, but this time he misjudged the distance, and his teammate was forced to raise her hands above her head. The egg did not survive the clumsy catch.

Bouncing on her toes, Meg could hardly contain her excitement. "We won!" she nearly shouted when she was reunited with Gregry.

He grinned. "Shh. Yes, that round."

Meg couldn't shake the jittery feeling from her fingers but found she liked the wave of joy inside her chest. "What is next?"

Her stomach dropped when three green-circled targets were set up once again. But instead of knives, nine hatchets were set out, three for each team. As the first man threw, Meg studied his stance and motions. Gregry whispered in her ear the mistakes in his form, though Meg thought his throws were quite impressive. One hatchet on the outside and two hatchets in the green—one just barely.

Then it was Gregry's turn. As he stepped up to the line, Meg watched for the difference in his movements compared to the other man. Right away, she sensed his confidence and noticed his easy grip on the hatchet handle.

When he released the first ax, it stuck perfectly in the center of the green circle. Cheers sounded, and he stepped up to the second line. His movements were precise and sure, he didn't flinch as he stepped forward and sank the second ax into the center of the target. Another cheer, and a few cries of astonishment at the repeated perfect throw.

Then the third ax was thrown, perfectly mimicking the other two. The crowd whooped with delight. Meg glanced at their friends in the crowd. Frelick, who had joined his daughters with Ida, was receiving slaps on the back for his boy's performance.

Gregry returned to Meg's side, smiling ruefully at her expression.

"You have surprised me. I've never seen you…" She imitated a throw with her hand.

"I've thrown a time or two. Should I have missed one?"

She shook her head. "No. But I am sorry you chose so poorly in your companion. It should be Lezah here with you."

He said nothing and turned to watch their opponent.

The third man threw, failing to impress the crowd. Meg noticed his hand shaking each time he reached for an ax. He should have thrown first instead of after Gregry.

The women stepped up, each with the hope of building her team's score. Nine, seven, and one. As the first woman threw, Meg felt the sugared cake grow heavy in her stomach.

It had been one thing to compete side-by-side, but this time *she* would be the one out there on the line. Alone. All eyes looking at her. And she had never thrown a blade in her life. And what was more, Gregry was depending on her.

The first competitor's throws brought her team's score to fourteen. Meg acknowledged that team was well matched.

"Two," Gregry said quietly. "You must get two in the green."

She nodded and with a gulp, stepped up to the line. She had battled armed humans alone. Wandered dark forests and gone into strange kingdoms. Why should she be nervous? She rubbed her damp hands over her leggings.

Mimicking Gregry's stance, she placed her right foot a pace behind the line and raised the hatchet with the blade behind her shoulder. With an exhale, she stepped forward with her left foot and released. The ax struck the edge of the target and bounced to the ground. An audible noise of disappointment came from the crowd.

"More!" Gregry called. "Don't hold back, Meg!"

She nodded and got into her stance in front of the next target.

Recalling Gregry's throw, she stepped forward and released. The ax spun through the air and sank solidly into the green circle. A cheer erupted and carried her to the third and final target.

Trying to recall the feeling of her successful throw, she glanced at Gregry. He grinned and nodded encouragement. Something inside twinged. Feeling jittery again, Meg turned back to the target and tried to repeat her movement.

Before the ax bounced against the target below the green circle, she knew it was a failed throw. Cheers and cries of disappointment echoed from the crowd. They would end the throw with twelve.

"Next year," Gregry assured her when she returned to his side. "Next year the prize will be ours."

"I wish it had been roll eating," she replied. "Then you would have a basket of pears in your arms."

He laughed and together they watched the last thrower outshine her counterpart, scoring three. Medals and pears were awarded to the winning couple.

The meal of roasted pig, boiled potatoes, and corn cobs was served, and the air filled with jubilant chatter. Jem joined them, and as Meg chewed on a cob, she watched Jem fill Serah's cup when it was empty and Serah give him half of her corn. Their eyes sparkled whenever they looked at one another.

Suddenly she felt awkward seated between Lezah and Gregry. It didn't take much observation to see Lezah sometimes look at him the way Serah was looking at Jem. But Gregry didn't ever look at Lezah like that. He looked at her like he looked at Serah or Ida or any of the other girls she had seen him say hello to walking through the festival crowd.

Meg chewed her empty cob some more.

Had Gregry ever looked at her in a different, sparkling way, and she simply never noticed? The awkward feeling deepened. She stole a glance at him. He caught her movement and turned his face to look at her. He smiled with a cheek full of potatoes.

No, she thought. *He looks at me the same.* She felt relieved and disappointed at the same time. He made her feel that puzzling way often.

After the meal, a storyteller took to the platform. He shouted a tale of a boy lost at sea and found by a magical turtle that granted him four wishes. Then he told of an old woman who sewed quilts with her own hair and fed wild dogs carrot tops. Meg didn't understand that one at all. Finally, he told the Tale of the Kingdoms, and by the time he was through, she was happy to see him shut his mouth and dance into the crowd.

Serah was right. No one told that story as well as Frelick.

In the evening light, while festivities continued, the family plus Jem began their walk home. The square-faced, reserved young man took Meg's place next to Serah, and Meg found herself between Lezah and Gregry once again. The three of them were back far enough they couldn't make out any words spoken by the two ahead.

Meg watched Jem and Serah quickly press their lips together. *A kiss.*

"What is Jem to Serah?" she asked.

"Nothing yet," Lezah said with a sigh. "I am sure he hopes to marry her someday when they are both of age. I don't think she would mind one bit, though I think he's a bit of an oaf."

"Jem Yulfam is a good man," Gregry said thoughtfully. "I think they would be a good match. Serah is happy with just about anyone, but I would be very pleased if she were to marry someone who didn't make her work at it."

Lezah snorted. "Not that you should care any."

"And why shouldn't I?" he replied sharply. "Serah is like a sister to me. Both of you are."

Lezah set her jaw. "Never mind," she muttered. "I didn't mean anything by it."

They walked in heavy silence for a bit, the joyous mood having evaporated and been whipped away by the increasing wind. Meg picked at the edge of her tunic trying to think of something to say to ease the tension.

"Lezah, I was very proud of you in the competition."

Lezah forced a smile. "Yeah," was all she replied as she shifted the basket of pears in her arms.

Meg tried again. "When I go home, I will practice throwing logs."

Lezah smiled a little more naturally at that but said nothing.

"And also, I look forward to the next time I eat a nose of corn."

"Ear," Lezah said with a little laugh. "It's an ear of corn."

"Somehow neither sound appetizing to me," Gregry concluded.

Peace restored, they talked on until they reached home. With Riff gleefully bouncing up to his shoulders, Gregry went to the barn to check on the animals, and although he had a good walk to get back to the home he had passed, Jem lingered with Serah by the chopping block.

"I need to ask you something," Lezah said suddenly, grabbing Meg by the arm. "Do you...like Gregry?"

Meg shrugged her shoulders. "Yes. He is very kind."

Lezah rolled her eyes. "No, I mean do you *like* him. Like...like Serah likes Jem."

"Like to press my lips to his?"

Lezah scrunched one side of her face. "Sure."

"Oh." Meg chewed her lip and watched Serah and Jem a moment. She thought of her and Gregry's talks in the barn, specks of straw in his hair. How he helped her understand things. How his eyes always looked thoughtful and how he handled a knife, a pen, and a fork all the same way, with complete precision and control. She briefly envisioned him swinging his ax. The way he had looked at her when she hit the target.

Meg's stomach squeezed. "Um, no," she said slowly. "I don't think I do, Lezah."

"Good." Lezah bobbed her head once. "Because if you ever do, you'll be sorely disappointed. He has certain…qualities that he needs. Requirements. That you don't meet."

Meg did not understand what Lezah meant, but before she could ask her to explain, Ida called to them from the porch.

Looking out over the forest, she pointed. "What do you suppose that is over there?"

Far in the distance, a large figure floated just above the trees. Meg squinted at the dark silhouette in the dimming light. It glided gracefully back and forth—possibly in a circle—before disappearing. If they had not been on a hill, it would never have been in sight.

Lezah shrugged, unconcerned, and went into the house, but Ida's brow remained pinched as she and Meg stared at the location where the figure had disappeared. Then a thread of smoke appeared. Within minutes it stretched its weave and became a black cloud rising against the dusky sky.

"Frelick!" Ida shouted. "Frelick, quick!"

Frelick burst out the door, frantically looking for a threat, Lezah on his heels. Gregry hurried out of the barn. Ida pointed and both men looked toward the smoke.

"I saw something. Something flying just like a bird. But it was much too large. And now there's smoke."

"It looks to be near the Bilfam fields," Frelick said. "They've just been preparing to harvest their wheat. Gregry, get the shovels!"

"We can go the rest of the way on horseback once we get to my place," Jem called back, already having let go of Serah's hand and running down the path.

Gregry returned to the barn and reappeared in seconds with two shovels and an ax in his hands.

"I will come, too," Meg said. One look at Gregry and she knew what he was thinking. The Rathern.

"No, Meg," Frelick said. "You stay here. All of you. Stay put."

Before she could protest, they were off, jogging swiftly after Jem. The four left behind stood on the porch to watch them go. Ten minutes after the men had disappeared into the trees, as an orange glow grew on the horizon, Ida abruptly turned to go in, beckoning the girls to join her.

"They'll be hungry when they get back."

Serah and Lezah went in after their mother. Meg wondered when they would notice she was not behind them.

Chapter Thirteen

BRANCHES swept over Meg's hair like waves as her bare feet glided over the needle-littered ground. She could not have sat contently in the little cottage as a blaze grew and an impostor floated about—hovering in the sky pretending to be her. In all her life she had never seen anything like herself. Raparean. She and mother were the last two, and she had never even seen Mother shift.

A hot coal of anger fueled her legs, and her pace quickened. She hadn't wanted to overtake Gregry and Frelick on the path, fearing they would send her back, so she had chosen to move through the trees. The forest was growing dark, but she kept her heading. Soon she was certain she was beyond Jem's family homestead.

After covering a good distance, a deep breath drew in smoke. Not the comforting smell of pine smoke from a chimney but thick, black, ugly smoke that made her lungs burn. Shouts echoed from somewhere ahead, stopping Meg in her tracks. Standing still, she tried to make out Gregry or Frelick's voice without success. But off to the left, she could now see her destination.

At a quick pace but no longer running, Meg moved forward, an orange glow now her compass. It appeared the fire had started on the northwest end of the field, a barn already consumed down to a charred skeleton and the surrounding area the stippled remains of wheat shafts. She had passed fields just like this one on the way home from the festival. It was jarring how quickly so much hard work was lost. A good distance from the flames, a line of people worked frantically with shovels, attempting to dig a barrier to stop the fire's progression. She still could not make out whether or not any of the people gathered were Gregry, Frelick, or Jem.

Now that she was here, Meg wasn't sure what she thought she'd accomplish. Whoever was responsible for the blaze wasn't standing defiantly in the middle of the field, and she certainly couldn't take to the air to search. She scanned the outskirts of the field, the trees dark and suddenly forbidding. While she debated her next move, the billows of smoke continued to roll toward the sky and the burn moved toward the line. A better idea eluding her, she backed silently into the trees and began making a large circle around the field, hoping to find whatever was hoping not to be discovered. If only she had thought to bring Riff. He was good at finding things like that.

Away from the light of the fire, Meg's sight was diminished in the moonless night. Anything tucked in a dark corner could easily stay hidden. Perching on rocks or logs, she listened for any sign of disturbance. She had just noiselessly stepped off one of her lookouts when calls from a covey of birds made her freeze. The sound of alarm. She moved in that direction toward a grouping of large rocks. The snapping of twigs sounded from the other side. Meg's feet stealthily took her closer.

Another snap, then a quiet scrape against stone.

Seizing the moment, Meg bolted around the rocks. Her eyes took in the outline of a tall figure, and she dove, throwing her shoulder into the dark unknown being. With a muffled *oof,* she took it to the ground. A struggle ensued until her victim took her by surprise.

"Meg!" the figure wheezed. "What in Three Kingdoms are you doing?"

She popped her head up and looked down at the face below hers. "Gregry?"

He shoved her shoulder, pushing her aside to get to his feet.

"What are you doing here?" he loudly whispered.

"I..." she lowered her voice, too. "I came to discover what the flying thing was."

He shook his head. "Why didn't you stay where you were supposed to? If anything was here, it certainly isn't now."

She shot to her feet. "I didn't stay *where I was supposed to* because I wanted to find the flying thing. I thought everyone would be tending the fire. No one would think to look for the cause."

"I did, Meg. But I think we both know what did it. Do you believe me now? This is how—"

"No, it's not what you think. It's something else."

He heaved a big breath. "This is how it all started in Roshton. This is the third barn in four weeks. Soon children will start to disappear."

"Children? What—no, it's not—"

"People saw something ugly flying overhead. Then the fire. Ida saw it. You saw it. I heard a few others, too."

"Yes, I saw it, but it didn't look right. It wasn't the Rathern that I've seen. It was too..." she flapped her arms. "It didn't move right."

He shook his head and turned away from her. "I can't believe you are still arguing this. You *saw* it."

"I saw *something*. But I didn't see *the Rathern*." What a stupid name. She couldn't help saying it mockingly.

"You don't know what you saw, fine. I came from that direction, combed the woods as best I could. You must have come from that way?" he asked, pointing.

She nodded, not wanting to talk to him anymore.

"And the only thing you found was me." He looked around with his hands on his hips and muttered what Meg guessed were curses like Ida scolds Frelick for.

"It's too dark, we won't be able to find anything now." He snatched his ax out of the dirt. "Come on. Let's go back and help with the fire. We'll do more good there."

The blaze was mostly contained now, the waves of fire diminished to ripples across the field. About half of the grain had been preserved. The barn was a total loss. The skeleton had collapsed into rubble.

As Meg searched each face for the two she knew, her heart sank. These people were afraid. She could see it—feel it. Their words were quiet and fretful. A few laced with anger. Across the field, they found Frelick and Jem, preparing to mount the horses they had brought.

"Gregry!" Frelick said gruffly. "Where'd you disappear to? We could have used you on that trench."

Without a hint of penitence, Gregry replied, "Into the woods."

Frelick accepted that as if it explained everything, lashed the shovels to the saddle, and pulled his large frame onto the horse. He looked down and noticed Meg for the first time. "Is that you, Meg? By the...how did you get here?"

"My legs."

His mouth twitched a bit. "You ran all the way here? In the dark?"

"Yes. I...wanted to help."

"You should've just come with us then. We could've gotten you a horse at the Yulfam's."

She smiled nervously at the beast beneath him. She wouldn't have known what to do with one anyway. She watched Gregry and Jem mount their own beasts, one so dark it looked like only a shadow of the other in the light of the stars.

"Hop up there with Gregry, Meg," Frelick suggested. "No sense in your legs taking you all the way home, too."

Gregry looked down at her, his shadowed expression asking her acceptance.

Her legs did feel a little wobbly from all the excitement of the day. "All right. I've never been on a horse before, though."

Gregry removed his foot from the leather loop. "Put your foot in and give me your hand."

She did as he instructed and imitated the movements she had seen, kicking her leg over the horse's rump. Finding herself pressed up against Gregry, she tried to scoot back but slipped off the saddle and nearly off the horse. Gregry said she could hold onto him if she needed to. She clutched a fistful of the back of his vest.

He let out a small laugh. "Not what I meant, but that works, too."

He gave a gentle kick with his legs, and the horse jolted into motion. The sudden jerk startled Meg, and she instinctively threw her arms around Gregry's middle. The horse settled into a gentle walk, but Meg didn't feel comfortable sitting freely, with no place for her feet. So she kept her arms where they were, wrapped around her solid friend. Soon she relaxed her head and allowed it to rest against his back, whiffs of smoke still lingering on his clothes.

"You still awake back there?"

"Hm?" She pulled her head upright. "Oh, yes. I just did not know how tired I am. But I don't think I could fall asleep like this."

"That's good because you'd probably fall off. So stay awake, all right?"

"Mm-hm," she mumbled, placing her cheek against his back again.

That was the sum of their conversation the entire way back to Jem's barn. They helped him put the horses in their stalls, then Jem told them he'd take care of the saddles and brushing. Frelick thanked him for the loan, admitting he wouldn't have otherwise made it there in time to be any help.

As they walked home, Frelick and Gregry discussed the events in low voices. Both of them were convinced the Rathern was to blame.

"The Bilfams are lucky enough help came to dig that trench. And that the wind blew in their favor. The blaze would've taken the whole field."

"There's been three fires now, Frelick. Do you think Queen Iril will act soon?"

"I don't know what there is to do. No one will go into that forest. No one but you. You're the best hunter I've seen, and even you haven't had luck."

Gregry glanced at Meg. "No, I haven't." He adjusted the ax on his shoulder. "I just don't understand how Herrick is able to protect Davare and Roshton from attacks. It's almost as if he...do you think he controls the beast?"

Frelick laughed. "I don't think a beast like that could be trained. You know boy, your father did all he could. People don't always act wisely when they're frightened. Your father couldn't guide them any more than a gooseherd can keep his flock together when there's a wolf on the prowl."

Gregry glanced at Meg again, and Frelick did the same, looking somewhat abashed. She smiled weakly, having nothing to say, and repeated the conversation in her head trying to piece together why Frelick would look at her like that.

The men continued to talk about the attacks, and Meg found herself listening less and less, her own thoughts troubled. It had been one thing to be feared in her forest, but it was quite another for people to be afraid of her in their own homes. She pictured the children lined up for their festival race. And to be suspected of harming them—stealing the little creatures from their mothers—it almost made her stomach turn.

The three who stayed home were huddled around the fire and sat up anxiously when the door opened. The table was still set with bread and butter and a pot of stew sat warm on the stove. Over the meal, Frelick related a brief report of the loss. Ida was relieved no one had been hurt.

She asked if anyone else had seen what she had, and Frelick said one of the little Moorfams had seen something big flying overhead, and a few others thought they had seen it in the failing daylight. But no one was able to describe it in detail and no one knew what had become of it. Exhausted from a day of pleasantry turned sour, the family turned in for the night directly after finishing the meal.

As Meg laid in her bed on the floor waiting for sleep, she recalled the events of the day. She had felt so light and happy being among the people. It felt natural and right to return smiles and greetings. To tap her toes to the music and join in on the games. How would the villagers react if they knew the Rathern was among them, cheering for the competitors and sharing their food and drink? Her brow furrowed and her stomach lurched when she pictured the crowd turning on her with their pitchforks and axes. Or worse fleeing from her in pure terror.

She rolled over and pulled herself into a ball. No one must ever find out.

****

An hour passed tucked in bed, but Meg could not sleep. When she was sure the others had drifted off, she crept down the stairs to wake Gregry. She was surprised to find him sitting on his bed, ready to go to the barn with her.

"I knew you would come down tonight," he whispered. "I need to speak with you."

Something in his tone almost made her turn back for the stairs, but she followed him out the door instead. As soon as she crossed the threshold of the barn, he turned to face her.

"Meg, I need your help hunting the Rathern. I need you to guide me through the Death Woods."

She dug her nails into her palms. This was definitely not what she wanted to talk about.

"The Rathern is not as wicked as you think, Gregry. You need to leave it be."

He began to pace, his words rapidly filling her ears. "Are you sure there's only one? I can't be surprised. It must have a cave or a nest, some place it goes."

"I can't tell you. It—"

"Maybe we can bait it. Do you think that would work? Meat? Maybe a pile of fish?"

"Gregry, please."

"And arrows. I've been thinking arrows will probably work best."

"Listen to me."

"Spears would be difficult. But with a bow, we wouldn't have to get real close. I'd need practice, but—"

"No."

"Just one good shot through the heart—"

"Gregry, stop!"

He stopped pacing, a surprised look on his face, as if he'd forgotten she was with him.

Meg took a step forward. "You must leave it alone." Gregry pushed his hands through his hair and groaned, but Meg pressed on. "It is not causing any harm. It never tries to kill anyone. Only scare them away."

"You don't understand, Meg! This has to end. If Turron is to be saved, you must help me capture it at the very least."

"But why?" she cried. "It is only protective. Of the forest. Of its home. You could even say it's protective of me. I tell you it doesn't leave the forest!" Half true. "What has it ever done to you?"

A strange look flashed in his eyes. He opened his mouth to speak, but closed it again, shaking his head and turning away from her. Meg waited, suddenly aware of the cold dirt beneath her toes and the musty smell in the air. When the silence grew too long, she moved to sit by the pile of straw that so often served as their place for talking. A moment later, he sat down beside her, hunched forward with his eyes closed. After another long wait, he said suddenly, "Roshton used to have its own king, its own royal family. It used to be great."

Meg leaned forward. "What happened?"

Gregry shrugged. "It started years ago, long before I was born. There was a time when people reported sightings of something above the trees—across the Three Kingdoms. Always at night, so no one was sure what they had seen. And it seemed to disappear quicker than it came. Then one by one, fields were burned to stubble. The stories say some mornings after an attack, men were found dead, eviscerated." Meg looked at him with her head cocked to the side. "Gutted. All their insides on the outside."

Meg felt her face flush, imagining a human's insides pulled out like a fish's. "That's impossible. It would never do anything like that!"

Gregry laughed mirthlessly. "Whatever was attacking the people was doing a thorough job, Meg. And rumors said it came from the Death Woods. Obviously, people were terrified. Then the attacks stopped. Just…stopped. For years, nothing. But no one forgot. When I was about nine, the sightings in Roshton started up again, only this time the evil went into villages, too. Inns and taverns burned, children were snatched from their play. People grew angry at the royal family. Demanded protection. So the king sent hunters into the forest. Not one was successful. Some didn't even return."

Meg nodded, remembering a time Mother had been overwhelmed with the sense of a foreign presence in their forest. Meg, herself, had been young and, with Mickelby's guidance, had worked hard to rid her trees of them. But she hadn't always been so proficient at guiding them out.

"The King of Davare offered his assistance, but at a heavy price," Gregry continued, rubbing a thumb across the palm of his other hand. "He claimed his father had successfully defended Davare from similar attacks and that the beast never troubled his people. When King MarKus refused, an uprising gathered. Roshton is the smallest of the three kingdoms, you know. People were so afraid it wasn't difficult to stir them into revolt against their own king. King MarKus grew so desperate, he went after the beast himself.

"He never returned, nor any of the men who went with him. With no one to take the seat, King Herrick the Third claimed himself steward. The attacks from the Rathern ceased, but the king of Davare proved to be no more a savior of the people of Roshton than a wolf of his neighbor's pups. He has since died, but his son rules in his stead.

And if rumors are true, he is just as bad if not worse. The kingdoms of Davare and Roshton are failing. And now the attacks are increasing in Turron. It is the same all over again. Turron will fail, too."

Meg listened patiently to his story. She remembered the hungry look in the eyes of the people in Davare. There was no doubt that part of his story was true. But what of the attacks? Until recently, she had never even left the forest.

Meg shook her head and reached for his hand. He looked up, startled from his thoughts.

"I promise you," she said, "the Rathern had nothing to do with those attacks. It was something else."

He looked down at their clasped hands. Meg couldn't read the expression on his face, and it suddenly felt awkward to touch his skin. She withdrew her hand and tucked it safely away with the other.

"But what else would do such things?" he asked. "No, I think you underestimate the creature. Or creatures. We really can't be sure there is only one."

"No, I know—"

"And if I can rid the forest of it, the attacks will stop, and Turron will be safe."

"It won't!"

"Meg, you live apart from everything. You don't understand the ramifications of these things."

Heat burned from her throat to her cheeks. "Stop using words I don't understand!"

He took a deep breath. "The consequences. You don't understand the things that will happen if Turron and Queen Iril fall, too."

A nasty feeling exploded inside Meg. "I may not know every word, and I might live somewhere different than you, but I am not a stump in the forest. I can *understand* that King Herrick is not a good king. And I can *understand* what it means to be hungry and that people are unhappy. I saw all that when I went to the big castle. I could *feel* things are not right there. But hunting the Rathern is not going to fix these things. It is not going to stop what is happening."

"How do you know?"

"Because I..." Seconds passed. She dropped her eyes to the ground. "Because the problem is the king. The people should get rid of King Herrick."

Gregry laughed bitterly. "Get rid of King Herr—and how are the people who can barely manage their lives going to *get rid* of him? Protected as he is by thick walls and lines of soldiers? Men who are willing to lay down their own lives for him because he keeps their families fed. They're not. They can't. You really don't understand."

Meg uttered a strangled sound and turned her whole body away from him, arms crossed tightly against her chest. She did understand! What she did not understand was how killing her was going to solve all the problems in the kingdoms. He wasn't listening to her.

He is the one who does not understand. "Stump!" she seethed.

"What?"

She winced realizing she had spoken out loud. "Nothing! I do not like talking to you right now."

The dim barn was quiet, other than the low bellows from the cow and the scratching of mice running along the rafters. She wiggled her toes hoping to wring out some of the tension she felt. She wanted to leave. To run away. To shift and take to the sky where she wouldn't be bothered with humans and their stupid problems.

Gregry finally spoke. "So you won't help me?"

There was no mistaking the hurt in his voice.

She closed her eyes. There had to be something. *Anything* other than what he specifically asked. "I will help you," she said over her shoulder. "But my own way. Just be patient while I find out how." She turned a little more, to let him see her face, to see she meant it.

He nodded. She could see the muscles in his face drawn taut. He was angry. But there was nothing for it. She could not hand over what he sought. And she could not tell him why.

Any pleasure that might have been gained from their visit had been choked out. Wordlessly, she left him in the barn.

Chapter Fourteen

THE next morning Meg announced her departure. Serah was dismayed her visit was only to be one night and asked when she would be coming back their way. Meg truthfully replied she didn't know. During the course of the night, she determined it would be better if she left before anyone was able to guess where she came from or what she really was.

After breakfast was finished, Meg bid the Snofams good-bye for the last time, squeezing Serah extra hard in their hug, and began her trek down the now familiar path, though this time she walked. She felt too heavy inside for running. She worried once she got to her forest, she would be too heavy even for flying.

As she drifted down the path, the wind teased the tops of the trees, causing them to bend and sway. She snatched up a stick and swung it at the wildflowers like she had seen Gregry do once. She felt satisfied when she was able to lop off an entire bloom with one swoop rather than merely breaking it into parts, leaving lone petals behind.

Still, something was lacking. The path was lonely without anyone else. She had never minded being alone in her forest before, knowing Mickelby would be waiting for her when she returned home. But this new piece of her life, a wider circle of people she loved to be with, took up more room in her heart than she anticipated. It hurt to think she would not walk this path again, and yet it felt like the best thing.

"The Imperald is my heart. I must not fail." She repeated the words a few more times, then fell silent and continued her walk for some time, feeling the hole in her heart deepen with each step. "If I had just never left my forest…" she said bitterly.

For a few miles, she argued with herself whether or not her rebellion had been worth it. She thought of the peace she felt before knowing what the world was outside her forest. Before she knew hunger could be seen in someone's eyes or kings could fail. Not once had her giant, silent friends vexed her. Not once had they made her question her actions or think really hard. And she thought about gentle Mickelby and the comfort she felt in their routines.

But then she thought of Serah and her undying optimism. Lezah's quiet strength. Ida's patience and kindness, and Frelick's concern. Gregry's thoughtful conversation and easy temperament—most of the time. Even Riff had grown to be a furry friend. Her heart thumped peacefully thinking of her friends' faces. And she could read Mother's book now.

In the end, she came to a conclusion. "It was better to have come."

Even if there was a hole in her heart, it had been made larger by the Snofams. It could bear the wound.

Eventually, Meg soothed herself enough to increase her pace to a jog. It would take all day to reach her forest at the rate she had been moving. The jog lasted for a time, then quickened, and soon she bounded past The Edge into the company of her giants. A deep way in she shifted and launched herself above the tree line. She wove up and down and around the tops of the trees, creating a game to see if she could skim a tree with her talons without making it move. Her built-for-speed body cut through the still air, and she found peace in the self-created wind that thread its fingers through her feathers.

When she arrived at her castle, light rain began to fall. She threw her satchel through her window and landed in the yard. Mickelby stood alone in the orchard. Without pausing for a greeting, she strode right to him and threw her arms around his neck.

"I'm not going back," she whispered. He pushed her out an arm's length and studied her face. "It isn't safe."

He held out his hands, hinged together at his little fingers, a hopeful expression on his face.

"Yes, I still have it. And now that I can read well enough, I have no more reason to go."

He nodded, something of disappointment in his eyes. He moved as if to say something.

"Megnolia!"

They both jumped at Mother's voice and turned to see her standing in the doorway of the kitchen. Instantly, Meg thought through the words she had just spoken, wondering if Mother had heard.

"I am ready for my supper."

Relieved, Meg acknowledged her and left to find something even though supper time was hours away. When she returned in a full downpour from the sky, she was surprised to find Mother in the kitchen with Mickelby, waiting for her. The air was heavy as Meg shook out her hair and set to work preparing the meal. Wanting to ease the gloominess all three of them seemed to be feeling, she searched her memory for some of what she had read in the book and remembered Mother liked music.

As she sprinkled herbs in the pan, she began to hum a tune she had heard at the festival. It was one of the light tunes, simple and joyous, like a lark bouncing in the trees.

"Megnolia!" Mother's voice was sharp. "What is that sound you are making?"

Meg looked at her, shocked by the acid in her question. "It is just…a sound. That I made up. You do not like it?"

"No. I will not hear it again."

Meg turned back to the hot pan. Why didn't Mother like her humming? Serah hadn't seemed to mind it when she tried humming with her as they worked. She stole a glance at Mickelby, who only shook his head. His face alerted her to what her humming might have revealed.

After her false report, they ate the early meal in near silence, the rain relentlessly pounding against the castle. Afterward, Mother sent Meg to her fire and brusquely instructed Mickelby to clean up. There would be no more talking with Mickelby this evening.

Meg sat by Mother, the frail woman's hand stroking her head, for what felt like the longest hours she had ever endured in her spot. She tried, but she couldn't squelch the frustration she felt at Mother's response to her humming—at all her attempts to make Mother pleased. When Mother excused her to bed, Meg had never been so relieved to get away.

She darted up the steps of her tower and threw herself onto the bed, though too restless to sleep. The rain had finally ceased, and the dark pouring in from the window would soon hold traces of light.

Unable to even close her eyes, she found her flint and lit a candle. She searched over her room for the satchel and found it under her bed. The book's spine was looser than it had been. Next time she wouldn't be so careless when she tossed it through her window.

She opened to her page marker and began reading passages. Some words were still hard to sound out and others she didn't have any idea what they could mean. She wished for a fleeting moment that Gregry was sitting beside to her, helping her. She should have spent less time working and playing with the Snofams and more time reading. Serah could have helped her at least know the meaning of words.

As she read, she learned nothing important but many things she liked. Mother had never told her how she was as a child. She was grateful to have several pages of silly things she had done—sitting inside kitchen pots, trying to climb out high windows, rolling in mud-holes, and dancing around the room with Jonef. *Her* papa.

That was another thing she was grateful for. Until meeting the Snofams, it had never occurred to her that there had been someone else in her family besides Mother and Mickelby. Another someone who cared for her and played with her.

Her anger with Mother faded as she smiled at the little stories. Somehow reading Mother's words made Meg feel closer to her. She now knew Mother in a way she never had before. In her writing, she was typically lively and amusing. Even her more serious entries, when Meg was terribly sick or her father went away, showed more life than she did now. What had made her change?

Meg woke with sunlight streaming through her open window, having no inkling when she had drifted to sleep. As she stretched, a little songbird came to her window to wish her good morning.

"Good morning, little friend," she whispered with a half smile. "If you wait until you see me out in the yard, I will help you find some breakfast."

She lifted her book from her chest and carefully pushed it under the mattress. As she slowly made her way down the steps of her tower and ran her fingers over the cool, gray stone, she wondered again what had made the change in Mother. She was so weak, even her voice was losing its power. But there was more struggle than just weakness. Her eyes never smiled. Meg had never heard her laugh. The diary shed new light on everything. Meg shook her head at herself. How had she never realized Mother had been someone before their memories became shared? Where was her father now?

Mickelby was already in the kitchen stirring a pot of applesauce.

Not even taking a breath to wish him good morning, she blurted out, "Do you know what happened to Mother? And where my—"

Shocked, Mickelby's face flicked from her to the table. Mother sat in her chair, her hard, golden eyes fixed on Meg.

"Mother!" Meg's face flushed. "What are you—I mean—good morning, Mother."

"Sit, Megnolia," Mother said.

Meg sat.

Mother stared at her face for a long while, considering her in a peculiar way. The only sounds in the room came from Mickelby, awkwardly scraping the spoon against the pot.

"Do not ask the human to answer your questions. His answers are filthy. Do you understand?"

Meg nodded. Defending Mickelby would bring Mother's wrath down on them both.

"Megnolia, where have these questions come from?"

Meg swallowed. "I—I have been thinking that if I knew why you are...and what happened when the Imperald...I could..." She trailed off and glanced fleetingly at Mickelby, who refused to turn and look at either of them. "Why are you not sleeping, Mother?"

"There is something about you, my eyas," Mother said, ignoring her question. "You are changed."

Meg didn't dare move or speak. She felt her heartbeat quicken as she fought to hold Mother's gaze.

Finally, Mother spoke. "Your questions surprise me. Your curious nature will bring you harm, Megnolia, but my time is ending, and I know I cannot protect you from everything much longer. Perhaps you must have answers." She inhaled a deep breath. "Long ago, well before your birth, we were at war. A division among our own kind, beyond repair. As what I expect was the last battle began, your grandfather told five of us to flee from the mountain, entrusting us with the Imperald and the care of the trees. He vowed to send for us." She was quiet for a moment, her chest rising and falling with memories she didn't speak. "Eventually, one other and I were all that remained." Her voice softened. "It was just the two of us."

Meg leaned closer. *Jonef,* she almost said aloud.

Mother closed her eyes. "It is difficult for me to speak of all of this. I have wanted to forget. I tried to do my duty to my ancestors, but the Imperald was lost. I was deceived, my eyas."

"By whom?" Meg asked.

Mother shook her head. "He stole *everything* from me! When the Imperald returns to us, what should have been ours…all will be made right."

Meg swallowed trying to ease the dryness in her throat. "What if we do not get it back?"

"Understand—if we do not find it, my life. Our kind. Our forest. All will be lost!"

Meg touched her ear. "What if I give you mine?"

"No!" She clutched at Meg's hand. "No. I have told you. It is yours. Do not ever take it out." Mother held Meg's gaze, her weary eyes desperate to impart the importance of this instruction.

Meg squeezed Mother's hand to show she understood. She would not try her further with questions. She and Mickelby ate their break- fast. To please Mother, Meg didn't dawdle in leaving for her search. She bid the old man goodbye, and with a press on Mother's hand, she climbed her tower, gained her wings, and flew toward the north section of the forest to search.

A month passed, and the sun continued to shine over the undying forest. Meg had given all her focus to finding the Imperald. For Mother. For the trees. For her home. She wandered the forest in patterns known only to herself, paths that thoroughly covered the grounds. Every three days she flew home to check in with Mother, who was awake when Meg arrived and awake when she departed. Mother had even walked silently with Meg about the yard after supper on a few occasions. Meg noticed this attention with a pang. She knew Mother was using all the energy she could summon to spend time with her. The candle of Mother's life was burning low—the flame would extinguish soon. And she had not been faithful the days she had gone to Turron.

But within the boundaries her fervent efforts set, Meg felt her own spark diminishing. Flying, searching, walking. Her chest felt empty. The hole that had been burned weeks ago remained. She did not laugh and rarely felt a smile. Mickelby would have been a balm for her heart, but he kept away from her now that Mother was awake. Strangely, though walking beside Mother was lonely, reading her diary entries was the best company Meg could reach. Her love increased for Mother as she read through all the pages of her book, and she worked hard to reconcile the woman she called Mother with the woman she knew on page. Meg clung to the hope that if only she could give Mother what she needed, she would again be the bright being she was long ago.

Sitting on one of her fallen giants, resting from her search, Meg opened the book to reread the last page. Unlike the neat entries of random thoughts that came before, the last few were disjointed and difficult to make out. Splotches of ink covered the paper and the marks looked more like scratches. But the struggle to read the words was gone now—Meg had done all the deciphering a week ago and knew the words nearly by heart.

"Trouble has come upon us," she read aloud. It was much easier to concentrate when she did so. *"Jonef says we must go into hiding for a time until he is sure we are safe. I dislike it so. So many years I have spent hiding and now I am forced to again. But I have asked the forest to keep us. I saw Torah while I was out. I know why she is here. But she will not be rewarded for her betrayal. Jonef will be leaving me soon."*

She moved on to the next entry.

"It is dark out. I am not sure when Jonef will return. He has been gone three days longer than I expected. I wish he had never gone. He was not himself when he left. We did not part well. I will leave tonight to discover what has become of him. My eyas cries often. She senses something wicked is afoot. I fear she must sleep. I hear her now. I must go."

Meg paused and tried to remember, to unearth a memory—anything—of that time in her life. She thought she could remember Mother rocking her to sleep, but she wasn't sure if it was a real memory or one she had made up to match what she had read.

The entries ended there. Meg stared at the symbols, still amazed her mind could make them into words. She flipped through once again to make sure there were no undiscovered writings. When she came to Gregry's letters, she stopped. His writing was different than Mother's—tighter and more slanted. She traced a finger over several of the letters, careful to not smudge the char "ink."

A strange sound echoed through the trees and gave Meg a start. There had been several hunting parties in the forest recently, and a new anxiousness had settled under her skin. But this sound made her heart beat quickly for a different reason. It could be a welcome sound, if it came from the right creature.

Chapter Fifteen

MEG stood on the log and listened. Again, the bark came. She leaped to the ground and jogged toward it, her sharp eyes searching for a furry white creature with liver-colored spots, and even more eagerly, for a taller figure, with a pleasant-to-look-at face.

The forest was still again, and after covering a good distance, Meg's heart began to worry she had imagined the sound. And then far ahead, off to her right, Riff bounded over a mound. He seemed to be running loosely her way but had not actually spotted her yet.

"Riff!" she called. The dog stopped and snapped his head in her direction, one ear cocked. "I'm here. Come, boy!"

With a twitch, he sped toward her, tongue out, ears flapping. She squatted to meet him as he jumped his front paws onto her knees and put his nose to hers.

"You have found me again, haven't you?" Meg said, taking his head in her hands and rubbing his ears in just the way he liked. "Where is Gregry?" She looked back at the mound. "Is he with you? Or—?"

Just as the worst entered her mind, Gregry appeared over the hill. Even the distance between them did not hinder her from seeing his face light up when his eyes found her. Her heart tripped over itself once before it settled, and she calmly watched him jog toward her.

"I am pleased to see you," she called when he was near enough.

"I'm pleased we found you! Been in here a couple days searching."

She noticed the pack on his back. He slowed to a walk when he was ten paces away and stopped when he was only three.

"Good boy, Riff," he said, roughing up the dog's side. He looked up at Meg, and they reacquainted their smiles for a moment. Then Gregry's slipped away, and his brows pinched together as his eyes searched her over. "Why haven't you come to see us these last weeks? Are you all right?"

Meg bit her lip and bobbed her head in quick movements. "Yes, I'm fine. I…Mother has needed me. She doesn't have much time."

"Oh," he said with meaning, looking around at the unruly forest. "Is your home near then?"

"No. It's a good distance that way," she responded, motioning in an indistinct direction. "Very hard to find."

"Hm." He looked around again, thrumming his fingers on his thigh. "Well, I'm sorry your mother is so ill, but I'm glad you are all right. We have all worried. Riff and I tried your forest north of Turron several times with no luck. Obviously. I tied ribbons to trees every so often so I could find my own way out. But I was just south of here and—"

"You were that way? In Roshton?"

He seemed to hesitate, then said, "Yes, on an errand. Anyway, I decided to try for you from there. I knew Riff would sniff you out if I could just get him in the right area." He smiled, pleased with his success, then frowned and held out his hand. "Not that you smell bad. Or strongly. Or anything like that."

Meg smiled. "I must just smell like a bird."

"Yes, maybe that's what it is." He looked around, as if trying to find something to do or to occupy his hands and settled on just sitting down on a low rock.

She sat down beside him.

"How are my other friends?" Meg asked. "Everyone well?" She could always depend on him to give her accounts and explanations. He only pretended to be reserved.

"Yes, as of eight days ago when I left them. Frelick and I have gotten a good supply of wood built up. Found some really beautiful timber that will sell for a good price. He won't need to do much this winter if we can keep on it. Ida is keeping everything held together like she does." He rubbed Riff's ears some more. "Serah and Jem are coming right along. And Lezah…well, Lezah is just the same."

Meg looked sideways at him. There was an odd note in this last report. "Lezah is unhappy?"

He looked at her, surprise in his eyes. "You seem to always read my thoughts, Meg. Hear things I don't say. Yes. She is. I'm afraid she does not want me for just a brother-like friend."

Meg nodded. "I know. Lezah thinks you are a goose."

He laughed. "A goose? I might be a fool, but I don't think she sees me *that* way. She might now I suppose."

Meg chewed her lip and looked at her feet. "Lezah has thought you a goose for a long time. Like Serah thinks Jem a goose."

"Yes, but Serah means it nice when she says a goose. I am sure Lezah does not. At any rate, I don't return her…feelings."

"Why not? Lezah is a good girl. And she is strong."

Gregry glanced at her, a shade of annoyance on his face. "That's true." He picked up a stick and proceeded to demolish it. "But she's not the sort of girl for me."

Meg felt a nip of curiosity. "What sort of girl is for you then?"

He picked at a piece of dry sap and focused on his hands for a moment before throwing his handful of stick pieces. "I guess I want a girl who won't hide from me."

Their eyes met. *A girl who won't hide.* A wave of confusion washed over her. She knew he didn't mean behind a tree or in the rocks. He meant something more. But she *was* hiding from him. All the time. Even as they sat there together, she was hiding from him. A sudden wish to shed her Raparean skin and become human frightened her.

She jumped to her feet and began long strides to get away.

"Meg. Meg wait." Gregry scrambled to place himself in front of her, blocking her path. "I'm sorry if I said anything wrong. Don't run again."

She kept her face turned away from him.

"Meg, when you stopped coming, I lost something." He put both hands up in surrender. "Friends. That's all I want."

She still didn't want to look up.

"Riff is a good pal, but he's not much for conversation. I was hoping to have a good philosophical discussion with someone before I had to go wandering back through the forest with him." He placed a finger under her chin and forced her to look up at his playful, pleading face. "Don't send me away yet. Please."

Her lips cracked into a reluctant smile. "All right. But only as long as you don't insult Riff anymore. After all, he's the one who found me, not you." She noticed for the first time two hatchets hanging from his belt. "You have your hatchets."

He followed her gaze. "What? Oh. Are you up for some practice? There's a basket of pears I'm determined to win next year."

Throwing proved to be the distraction Meg needed to ease back into comfortable companionship with Gregry. As she watched him spin the hatchets into trees, Meg was once again amazed by his skill. Mimicking his motions, her own accuracy improved by the time their shoulders were worn out.

"A few more practices and you'll top Lezah. Perhaps we can arrange a mock competition before next Queen's Day."

Meg was pleased by his confidence, but somehow challenging Lezah did not sound like fun.

Hatchets away and Riff joyfully bounding in and out of sight, they walked through the forest together, conversation filling the empty spaces. Meg had not forgotten how easy it was to talk to Gregry. He explained things in a way that always made sense to her and was careful with the questions he asked. They laughed about a new pig getting out on a rainy day and the slippery pursuit that followed. They talked about Serah and Jem and the happiness they each hoped for their friends. They discussed the entries she had read since their last meeting and Mother and how much Meg wanted to heal her. They talked about the fiery attacks continuing in Turron and the three suspicious deaths.

This topic lit its own fire in Meg's chest. She again refuted his idea it was the Rathern and came within breaths of telling him how she knew. But she regained control of her tongue and kept that part of herself back. Gregry dropped the subject rather quickly.

In the pause of conversation, Meg realized she had forgotten to follow her pattern of search and looked around to get an idea of where they had wandered. A large stream was nearby.

"Come this way." She grabbed his hand and pulled him along, careful to lead him around patches of mud. The idea of slipping in over one's head in a mudhole still made her laugh and still made him cringe. It wasn't long before she found what she was looking for.

The trees opened into a clearing, a foreign sight in the dense woods. Meg led Gregry to the center to reveal a wide, rocky hole at their toes. He looked at the dark opening, at her, then down again.

"That's a big hole." He leaned forward a little to get a better view of the darkness below.

"Yes."

Gregry picked up a rock and lifted it over his head.

"No!" Meg shouted, grabbing him by the arm.

He froze.

"Don't throw it! You'll crush them."

He leaned over again. "Crush who?"

"Lean a little further. You'll see."

He lowered his rock and, finding his footing solid, leaned further forward.

"See them?"

A smile spread across his face.

She yanked his hand again. "Come on. This way."

She led him over to a smaller hole hidden by a pile of rocks. She slipped in and waited for her companions to follow. Not far below the entrance was a natural path that ran along the wall of the cavern, more treacherous in some places than others. Trickles of water weaved their way down the wall and gathered in a warm little pool at the base. Carefully they made their way down to the floor of the expansive cavern, the hole in the center of the clearing a skylight four men above their heads. A patch of delicate pink flowers swaddled in green rested directly below it, where the sunlight could reach. Everywhere else was barren rock and dirt.

"This is the only place in my forest they grow," Meg said proudly.

Gregry circled the defiant little garden. "Do you come here often?"

"Only when I am nearby." She grinned, watching him take in this treasure in her forest. "I like to put my feet in that water there. And think. And it is a safe place to sleep."

"It looks like a good place to eat." He sat down on a rock and slung his pack around. He pulled out a cloth and unwrapped a couple rolls. "I saved these just in case I found you. And I have some of Ida's hard cheese."

Meg took a seat next to him and readily accepted the gifted roll. It was a little flat and very dry, but she didn't mind. After giving the cave a thorough sniff, Riff plopped himself at their feet to beg a piece of dried mutton.

Gregry looked up at the sunlit circle overhead. "My father would have liked this place."

Meg's interest was piqued. He hadn't talked about his father since their first meeting in the forest. "What was he like?" she ventured to ask.

Gregry smiled and crossed his ankles. "He was tall and strong. Handsomest fellow you'd ever seen. And he was adventurous—deep down. I know he was. But he never went far from our home."

"What happened to him?"

He didn't look away from the skylight. "I don't really know. I think he was killed, but some say he's still alive."

She fought the urge to take his hand again. "I am sorry, Gregry. I think that is a hard thing to not know. You never have told me how you came to the Snofams."

"No, I haven't." He sucked in a deep breath. "My father's name was MarKus. MarKus Townen Roshton the Third. King of Roshton."

Meg's eyes widened. King?

"When the attacks began on Roshton, people were confused. Then they became afraid. They looked to my father to protect them, of course. And he did his best. At least *I* think he did. But I was only 10 at the time. Just a boy. Anyway, I told you some of this. The attacks continued and then children began to disappear—nine in all. The fear turned to anger quickly after that. King Herrick—the third—wrote to my father claiming his great-fathers had successfully defended his land from the Rathern's kind.

"My father agreed to let his men help hunt it. Or them—however many there were. In places where his men camped, no attacks occurred. But they continued elsewhere. People noticed. Finally, King Herrick himself came claiming my father was not doing his duty. That he did not deserve to be king of Roshton. But that *he* could protect them."

"How?"

He shrugged. "I don't know. I don't think he really could. But the villages that had borne the brunt of the attacks were ready for a new king. Not everyone was, those in the city mostly, so my father refused to step down. News of a secret bounty for me reached him—a pretty good price for my head."

"A turny?"

Gregry smiled, but his eyebrows pinched together. "A little more than a turny, Meg. My head is worth a cart full of them."

Meg nodded. She could see why. It was a nice head. Even as she observed that, the reality of what he meant dawned on her. "But they were trying to kill you."

"Yes. They wanted me dead. And any others in line who wouldn't concede—give in to King Herrick. To protect me, my father secretly sent me away. To Queen Iril. My family has always been on good terms with the kings and queens of Turron. She sent me as far from

Roshton as she could. To the Snofam's cottage, way out on the edge of Turron at the base of the mountains. And there I have been. Just Gregry instead of MarKus Idvard Greagry Roshton the Second, crown prince of Roshton."

"And your father?"

Gregry cleared his throat. "He went into the forest with some of his best men to hunt the Rathern himself. But he never came out. A small sort of war broke out, more of a single battle, I guess, that lasted only a few days. King Herrick offered to stand in my father's stead as steward. Took possession of everything my family had." He laid back on the rock with his eyes closed. "If I ever get the chance, I will take back Roshton as rightful king. And make it what it should be."

Meg felt his sadness gather and wrap around her like a cold mist. She tucked her knees up under her chin and rocked back and forth a few times. They sat in silence for a great while before an idea entered into her head.

"I'm going to make you supper."

Gregry opened his eyes. "Make me supper, will you?"

"Yes. Fish and leaves. Mickelby's favorite."

"Fish? From where? Meg, I can't eat anything in this forest."

"Don't be frightened, good prince," she said, using a stolen line from his storybook. "I've eaten in my forest my whole life, which I happen to think has been rather long." He squinted one eye. Evidently he still didn't believe she was the little Megnolia in her book. "And also, Mickelby eats it. And he's human."

Gregry laughed. "And you aren't?"

Meg's cheeks burned. "I mean he's a man. I just mixed up my words. A man, the same as you. You will be fine. Wait right here."

"Not a chance. I want to see this."

They clambered toward the entrance, racing to be the first one out. Riff yipped a few times, and while they took turns holding each other back, the dog darted up and out. It was agreed that Riff had won, and a more civilized exit was made.

When they reached the stream, Meg rolled her leggings above her knees, then waded into a section where the water slowed. Within a minute, a curious fish darted about her ankles. She struck, and her quick hands seized the slippery thing with precision. She lifted it from the water, triumphant.

Gregry stared at her for a moment, then softly clapped his hands. "Hm. I was expecting more of a show to make me laugh but am nonetheless impressed. I'm still not going eat it."

"You are being hen witted. You will see."

They returned to the cave, Meg gathering her favorite plant stems and leaves on the way and Gregry bits of dried wood. The sun was beginning to fade, so a fire was built to serve more than one purpose. Meg skillfully cleaned the fish and tucked sprigs underneath the scaly skin. While it roasted, Gregry whittled a thick stick he had picked up and continued to tell stories from his childhood.

"I guess that's why I like to hear Jem play so much. My father tried to get me lessons with the best musicians in the city, but I didn't have any patience for it. I was always off running through the gardens or getting throwing lessons from the blacksmith's son. One time I had been forbidden to step outside, but I wanted to practice, and the only ax I could find was—well, my father had this ax. I wish I had it. It had been handed down a couple generations, a gift from somewhere. It was beautiful—small with a handle made of silver molded to look like a branch and three jewels—"

Meg straightened. "I have seen that!"

"No, Meg. This one was—"

"Silver, with three jewels. Two red and one green. Yes, I have seen it. In Davare. On Herrick's belt. I am sure."

The light of old memories in Gregry's face went out. An odd silence filled the cavern.

Meg swallowed. "They took it from your father, didn't they? It should be yours."

Gregry shook his head and went back to work on his piece of wood.

So Meg began making schemes in her own head.

Herrick was a thief. He had stolen everything that belonged to Gregry's family. Meg knew she couldn't get back a hundredth of what Herrick had stolen from others, but she was determined to get this one thing back for her friend. This was what she could do for him.

In recent months, she had nearly forgotten about the tall, dark tower at the base of a mountain. But now it seemed to be calling to her once more. She would go at night so she could hide in the shadows. She could—

"You look serious about something," Gregry said suddenly. Meg looked up with a start. He grinned at her wide-eyed expression. "Your face was twitching. What are you thinking over there?"

"I was just making a plan to search the castle at Davare."

"You what?" He laughed. "Come, tell me the truth."

"That's it. I have told the truth. King Herrick has your ax. And I am going to get it."

His working hands froze. "Meg, you cannot be serious. It's heavily guarded. You won't even get past the curtain wall."

She smiled, knowing how easily she could pass any wall. "Never mind about it. I shouldn't have told you."

"No, I'm glad you did." He slid off the rock and knelt beside her.

He placed one hand on her shoulder and made her look at him. "Meg, don't be stupid. You can't—"

"I'm *not* stupid," she said with a glare.

He dropped his hand and sighed. "I didn't say you were stupid. I said don't *be* stupid. Tell me you won't go."

"I won't go."

He sat back on his heels. "You're still planning to go. I can see it in your face."

"You told me to tell you, so I did."

"Don't just repeat what I say. Promise me you won't go, then don't."

"I cannot make a promise I won't keep, just as you won't. And I said never mind. I don't want to talk about it anymore." She checked the fish and tried to put on her cheeriest smile. "Your supper is done anyway."

His dark expression didn't lighten. "Meg."

She batted a hand at him. "I'm only *thinking* about going," she lied. She lifted the fish on the hastily made spit and pinched off a piece. "Here. Give it a taste."

"I am telling you, it is poisoned. I can't eat it."

She popped the pinch into her mouth and swallowed. "See? I am not dead."

His mouth twitched into a half-smile. She pinched off another piece and held it out to him, her fingers almost touching his mouth.

"Try it," she coaxed. "Just a bit. Then if you die, I won't make you eat anymore. Come on, open your mouth. Try it!"

She pushed her fingers into his closed lips as he turned his head. The pinch of meat bounced down his chest and fell into his lap.

She snorted. "You're such a mule."

She popped a few larger chunks in her mouth and sucked the juice off her fingers. She could feel him watching her eat and tried to make it look as delicious as possible.

Determined to try once more, she held out a pinch. A smidgen. "Just like fire-breathing deer and the hungry mudholes." He stared at her fingers for a moment, exhaled a deep breath, and opened his mouth. Delighted, she flicked the flake in and watched him swallow without chewing.

They stared at each other for only a moment before breaking into laughter.

"See? Just stories your people make up."

"Yeah, stories. Pity you've eaten most of it."

"I can catch you another!"

"That's all right. Somehow I really don't want any more."

She grinned at him, knowing he was still leery. He moved back to his rock and picked up his whittling.

"I hear you talk of Mickelby often but don't know much about the man. Where does he come from?"

"He's from Davare, I found out. He doesn't speak with his mouth. I don't know why. He—" She watched Gregry set down his whittling and take a deep breath, the color flushed from his face. "Are you all right?"

"I'm fine. I just feel a bit warm." He scooted back, away from the fire.

Meg compared her distance from the fire to his. He was a good deal further away, and she didn't feel too warm. She didn't think his face could pale anymore, but then it did. "Gregry, you look terrible."

"So kind, you are." He tried to laugh but instead lurched forward onto his hands and knees and began to heave.

Everything was out with only a few squeezes of his stomach, but he didn't stop. His gags were so relentless Meg didn't hear him even draw in a breath. When she got over the shock of this sudden change, she crawled over to him and placed her hand on his back.

"Gregry, are you all right?"

He didn't look up.

"Gregry?" She placed a trembling hand on his forehead to lift his face but pulled away from the heat radiating from his skin.

He finally gasped for a breath, heaved a few more times, and collapsed onto his side. Not minding the mess he had just made, she knelt close to him and took his unnaturally warm face in her hands.

"What's the matter?" His breathing turned ragged. "Open your eyes and look at me." She blew in his face a few times. No response. She gently patted his cheeks, then slapped his face harder. After pinching his chest, she opened one eye with her fingers. Nothing. As a last effort to get a response, she bit his shoulder. Hard. But still his eyes remained closed, his mouth silent.

Riff seemed to sense trouble and timidly approached, sniffing at Gregry's face and chest. The dog whimpered a few times and dropped to his belly with his head between his paws.

Meg swallowed hard. She glanced around hoping someone would appear to help her—to help *him*—but there was no one. She could shift and rush him to Mickelby or the Snofams, but what would happen if he woke in the clutches of the Rathern? Or worse, if Mother saw him? Surely neither situation would go well. She placed her hand across his damp forehead and felt the burning. She watched his chest rise and fall in quick drops.

"Gregry?"

Aside from his ribs expanding, his body was still and lifeless.

He was too warm. He needed to be cooled. She removed his travel tunic, boots, and stockings, then ripped a strip of cloth from the bottom of the worn shirt under her own tunic and rushed to dunk it in the pool. She hurried back to the sickbed with the damp cloth and dabbed it across his forehead and cheeks, then his arms and feet. Scurrying back and forth to soak the cloth, she dabbed his face and feet over and over, careful not to let a drop near his mouth.

When no change occurred and his hair and the hems of his trousers were soaked with water and sweat, she crumpled onto her knees next to his head. She put her face low to his, less than a hand-breadth away. His breathing was slowing, and she wished she knew if that was a good sign or a bad one.

"Please...don't sleep anymore. Wake up. Wake up!"

His eyes remained shut. His lips still. She ran a gentle hand through her friend's hair, letting pieces curl around her fingers. With a sudden force that took all the air from her own lungs, she realized he might be dying. Really dying. She had poisoned him. It was her fault.

"Gregry? Gregry, I'm sorry I didn't listen. You were right, you were right." She shook him softly, then with a little more force. "Please wake up."

She touched her forehead to his. His face was still unbearably hot. His breathing shifted into ragged gasps again.

Gently, she lifted his head and slid her legs underneath. She continued to stroke his hair and speak to him in hushed tones. She told him that maybe she wanted to look at his face like Serah looked at Jem. That she didn't want to hide from him and that she liked when he talked to her and touched her hand. That she was grateful he taught her to read.

She told him how much she didn't want him to die.

His breathing drifted back and forth between the coarse, quick breaths and shallow, calm breaths that were barely discernible. She placed her left hand on his chest to feel reassurance from his beating heart. Hours passed with no change. The fire was nearly out, but Meg didn't move to put more wood on. His fever burned on anyway, a different kind of fire burning from within.

Meg's watchful eyes gave out with the last of the coals, and a deadly silence filled the cavern.

Chapter Sixteen

A stirring on her lap pulled Meg from deep sleep. When she felt light fingers take up her left hand, she woke the rest of the way and blinked against the bright sunlight streaming into the cavern from the skylight above. Meg's heart beat with relief when she looked down to see blue-green eyes looking up at her.

"I was so afraid," Meg whispered, her throat dry and sharp from the long night. "I was so afraid I'd wake to find you dead. But you are not dead!"

Gregry smiled faintly and closed his eyes again.

Riff's head perked up from sleep, and he vigorously licked Gregry's face when he found it showing life. Gregry grinned wider and pushed the furry muzzle away. Obediently, Riff backed off and dropped to his belly again, his head on his paws. Meg thought he was smiling.

She looked down at her hand taken up in Gregry's again and resting on his chest. Suddenly, she couldn't bring herself to look at his face. She had almost killed him. A sting in her eyes flared, and she burst into tears.

Startled, Gregry gingerly pulled himself up and turned to face her, supporting himself with one hand on the other side of her legs.

"I'm all right. See?"

His voice was gravelly and barely audible, but oh how sweet it was to her ears.

"I'd rather you hadn't poisoned me but—"

She couldn't stop the new wave of sobs.

"I'm fine, Meg." His arm wobbled and almost gave out. He pulled it to himself and leaned his back against a nearby rock. His face was still washed of color aside from dark shadows under his eyes. "Just need a little more rest."

When his eyes closed, Meg immediately leaned forward onto her knees and placed a hand over his beating heart. His breath caught, and his eyes flew open to look at her face. For a moment she worried he was struggling to breathe, but he closed his eyes again and relaxed under her hand. She checked her tears and settled into a cross-legged position next to him, wiping her wet cheeks with her free hand.

"I really thought I had killed you. I didn't know. Truly, I didn't know."

He grunted what she assumed was a laugh. "I'm not at all suspicious you're trying to kill me. I'd be long dead if that were your intent."

She smiled for the first time in hours. That was true.

"You should have left me alone when I didn't want a bite."

Her shoulders sagged. That was very true. "Was it awful? Did you hurt?"

He pinched his lips together and shrugged. "Burning. Inside and out."

"And now?"

"Empty."

She nodded. Then with a flush of her cheeks, she remembered all the things she had said. "C-could you hear me? At all?"

He shook his head and cracked one eye open. "What did you say?"

She folded her arms across her stomach and carefully selected one thing out of many. "Please don't die."

"Is that all? Hm."

It wasn't very long before he needed to sleep again. She removed her tunic, insisting he use it as a pillow, and started another fire to ward off the morning chill in the cave. As he slept, Meg tried to read some of her favorite pages in her book. She continually found her mind wandering, unable to focus on any of the words before her. It wandered some to Mother and her decline or to the Rathern attacks in Turron. But mostly it wandered to her friend.

She analyzed his face—and even the rest of him a little bit. She had always found him pleasant to look at, but now his figure was very different to her eyes. The events of the night had burst open a seed in her heart that had been trying to sprout for some time. And no matter how hard she tried just now, she couldn't get the sweet, frightening new blossom to stuff back into its shell.

It was a foreign feeling. One that made her feel like singing and cursing and flying and curling up into a ball all at the same time. She didn't want to look at him anymore, and she didn't want to ever look away. Was this what Serah felt? She made it look so pretty. So fresh and rosy-cheeked. Meg feared her love looked like a patch of briar with a few half-dead wildflowers on it.

His father was a king—dethroned and dead or not. Gregry was a prince. She didn't know what exactly that entailed, but it felt like that detail complicated things. In the storybook, the prince always had to have a princess. And Mother? What would she say? What would she do? She felt nothing close to tolerance for humans.

Meg put her hands over her face. Oh, it would never do. None of it. If only he had just stayed away! She never would have known. Humans steal, Mother warned her. Over and over. But she never said anything about the possibility of one stealing her heart.

"You goose, Gregry. Gone and made a mess of everything," she whispered. "You won't like me. I know it."

He slept solidly until the sun was past overhead. It would soon be time for her to return home. When he showed signs of waking, she decided to help him along and gave him a shake. He complained of thirst, so she dug through his pack for his water pouch and something for him to eat.

"What is this?" she asked, pulling out a heavy contraption. Gregry peeked at it and mumbled it was a new type of bow—a weapon devised by a Turron inventor. He was still hunting.

She wanted him to show her how it worked in case she ever encountered one in her forest, but he shook his head saying only that it shoots small arrows with a lot of force. She set the heinous-looking thing down and found his water pouch.

It was nearly empty, and his food supply the same. Feeling like he could keep something in his stomach, he finished what he had. When Meg saw how weakly he stood, she knew she'd have to walk him out. He was in no shape to be wandering her forest.

"My shoulder is sure sore. Like it's…" He pulled back his shirt to reveal a deep purple, circular bruise.

Meg winced. "I bit you."

"You…bit me?"

"To wake you up. It didn't work."

He raised an eyebrow and covered the bruise again.

They both agreed the sooner they moved, the better. Meg hefted his pack onto her back, and with one arm draped over her shoulders, she helped him up and out of the cave, then through the trees, Riff trotting happily about them. Feeling Gregry's physical weight leaning on her added a few weights to her guilt. How long before his strength returned? What if it never did?

Neither seemed inclined to talk. Meg assumed he was too weak to think beyond moving his legs, which was just as well as she was busy attempting to beautify the briar patch in her head.

She had nearly killed him. Her stubbornness had nearly killed him. There was no way to prune that.

And what about being really old? The concepts of years and age were beginning to take root in her head. She couldn't remember all the years of her life exactly, but thinking of the number of times she had seen snow covering the kingdoms and knowing how old Serah was, it didn't seem like there could be more than eighteen of them. But Mother's book proved otherwise. Then again, if Gregry never believed she was the Megnolia in her book, then he would never know she was really an old woman. Thank the heart of the Great Mountains, that bramble was easy to shape up.

But her Raparean blood. What of that? And what she could become at will—a dreaded beast. She could not decide if it was the best part of herself or the worst. If she just never shifted again. Yes, she could just pretend to be human for the rest of her life (how many more hundreds of years did she have?). She could give up soaring over the trees, feeling the wind in her feathers and the rush of blood as she dove, and…no, it would not be easy to give up. And he would never love that vital piece of her.

They stopped for a rest after passing four of his ribbons. The sun was midway to its bed, and Meg bit her lip calculating how much further they had to go.

"Maybe we should have stayed in the cave one more day," she whispered.

"Hm?" Gregry popped his head up off his woolen pillow. He glanced at the sky peeping through the trees and dropped onto the pillow again. "Is it getting late in the day?"

Meg pointed. "The sun is over there." It was so strange she could get direction from the sun, but he could not. She could eat and he could not. It must be her Raparean blood. But Mickelby was fine.

"I feel like I need to get more water in me soon. Moving was a good choice. And I'm not quite so foggy."

While he snoozed, Meg continued to think up thorns. Lezah liked Gregry. How could Meg tell her? She would not be pleased and would no longer be her friend. Then maybe Serah wouldn't either. And what about her castle? Would she leave it for a house like the Snofams? Gregry couldn't live here in her forest, but she could live outside it. She concluded that she could leave her castle, though it wouldn't be her first choice. It wasn't the size or anything. Just that it was home.

She rubbed her aching head. She had never thought so hard about anything in her life. Well, maybe her book, but this was trickier. And what about the Imperald? She needed to find it. She certainly couldn't leave Mother before she did. And maybe she couldn't even after.

She woke Gregry, and they began to silently move again, this time using Meg's direction instead of the ribbons' twisting course. She would strip the trees of the markers later. He no longer needed to lean on her, but they stepped over roots and walked around fallen trees side by side. He didn't reach out to hold her hand like she wanted him to.

Maybe he won't want to hold it ever again, she thought. *I wish he'd just get out of my sight and never come back!*

"I have a friend not far from the border," Gregry was saying. "I think once we reach the edge of the forest, I'll be able to continue on my own."

So! He wants to get away from me. He doesn't want to be near me any longer than he has to! She nodded but didn't speak. She began to feel annoyed with him. And with her thoughts buzzing around her head like flies that wouldn't shoo.

"Are you all right?" he asked. "You seem…agitated."

"Don't use words I don't understand!" It came out uglier than she intended it to.

"Bothered. Troubled." He sounded impatient.

She added that to the list. She didn't know words. He was probably tired of always needing to explain himself.

"I am fine."

He nodded and looked the other direction.

Obviously she was not fine, and he didn't even ask. What was wrong with him anyway? What was wrong with her? Oh, she had never felt so confused before. She had always been Meg, but now she felt like two Megs fighting over the same body. She wanted to crawl under a rock and hide.

When only a few rays from the sun found their way through the trees, Meg could see The Edge. Good! He would stumble away, and she would go back to being one Meg. She would find the Imperald, save Mother, and live quietly and happily with her and Mickelby once more. For hundreds of years if she chose. No tricky things, nothing the matter.

But then she remembered how she felt when Gregry's breathing seemed to stop. If he left and never came back, he might as well be dead. She chewed her lip, fighting the urge to pick up a log and throw it. Before she could put every feeling in its place, they reached The Edge.

"Well, here we are," he croaked. "I'm sure once I get some water, I'll be fine. Marv's house is just through those trees a bit."

She nodded with her lips pinched together, worried what would come out if she opened it. She handed over his pack.

"Are you sure you're all right?" he asked, slipping his arms through the straps.

She nodded again.

He looked in the direction he was about to head and hesitated.

"Tell everyone hello for me," she said with considerable effort.

"I will," he replied quickly. "I'll let them know you are well."

"I give you my thanks."

He took several steps forward and stopped again, half turning toward her. "Be careful. Doing whatever it is you run off all the time to do."

The dark stone Castle of Davare came to her mind. "You as well."

He smiled weakly and resumed his journey forward. Riff, never one to be discouraged, bounded around and sniffed every sniffable surface until he was called back. Thirty paces away Gregry looked over his shoulder to see her still standing there watching him go. She forced a smile before he turned away again.

He hadn't even said he received her thanks.

Chapter Seventeen

WHEN Meg climbed through her bedroom window, it was late into the night. After parting with Gregry and burying his ribbons, she had flown north toward the mountains to get as far away from him as she could. But the time alone had only served to make her more unsettled. And now she feared she had worried Mother and Mickelby. She crept down the stairs into the main chamber and found Mother hunched before the fire.

"Megnolia! Here you are. You are late."

"I was covering a large area and wanted to finish before losing my place." It was the unimaginative lie she had thought out on her flight home. *Lies for everyone!*

Mickelby came hobbling down his tower steps and stopped just at the last. His eyes searched over Meg anxiously.

"Mickelby, why are you standing there stupidly?" Mother said impatiently. "Get Megnolia her plate."

He bowed and disappeared through the kitchen door.

Mother gestured for Meg to sit. "Were there more humans?"

Tired of complete lies Meg replied, "No, I did not find any new hunters." *Only a very familiar one, she thought. I almost did away with him. You'd be pleased,* she added bitterly.

Mickelby returned from the kitchen carrying a plate of cold stewed squash and a freshly cut pear. He handed her the plate and briefly touched her head. Meg smiled up at him and Mother dismissed him to stand at the back of the room. In silence, Meg ate slowly, forcing each bite into her mouth, and gleaned the thoughts she would share with Mother. When she finished, Mother asked directly for the report. Meg told Mother where she had searched. Then, with some hesitation and careful not to use names, asked Mother if the Imperald could be outside of their forest.

"No. Impossible." She glanced at Mickelby. Meg saw him duck lower out of the corner of her eye. "What gave you the idea?"

"Nothing. Or just…we have searched our forest well. I just think it could be outside."

Mother shook her head. "I searched among the humans long ago. I searched well. It never called to me. It would have called to me amongst so many unworthy creatures. *Pestilence.*"

Meg bit her tongue only a few seconds before it willed its way loose. "Mother, what if not all humans are bad?"

Mother's hand jerked Meg's hair forcing her to look up. *"Not all bad."* Mother released her and crushed a handful of her skirt in her fist. "Humans are deceitful, dirty creatures, Megnolia. They lie. They steal. They want us dead Megnolia. All of them want us dead." She sank back in her chair and clutched her hand to her chest. "Not one…"

"But what if you are wrong?"

"I am not!"

Meg glanced at Mickelby but couldn't see his face. She laid her head on Mother's lap. "I am sorry," she whispered penitently. "I will not speak of it again."

Mother would never accept Gregry or the Snofams in the condition she was in. Meg needed to find the Imperald to have any chance.

"Say it."

Meg stared into the fire. "The Imperald is my heart."

Three days later, Meg packed her satchel with her knife, cloak, and food from the garden. She debated whether to take her book or leave it and decided to leave it. It would be safer tucked deep under her mattress. Before turning in for the night, she had told Mother and Mickelby she wouldn't be joining them for breakfast. If she saw either of their faces, she might lose her nerve. Gregry had made it clear this wasn't a good idea. But it had to be done.

She moved for the window and hesitated. Mickelby had watched her closely yesterday, his eyes concerned though she had not been able to tell him of her plan. After a moment's thought, she pulled the book from its hiding place. Gently, she tore a blank page from the binding. With a bit of charred wood, she drew the lines of the castle in Davare, shading it black, and two curved lines above it—what she thought looked like a large bird. She laid the paper on her mattress, hoping Mickelby would find it and know where she had gone. Should she not return.

"What if I am caught?" she whispered. What would happen to Mother if she failed to return? Or Mickelby? And what of the Snofams and Gregry. She would never see them again or gain Gregry's forgiveness. She shook her head. She shouldn't think that way.

The sun winked at her as she climbed onto her tower, filling the sky with the colors of its warmth. She hesitated on the roof longer than she normally did, feeling the rough shingles under her feet. With eyes closed, she leaped and shifted, instantly feeling the comfort of her alternate form. Though covered only in feathers, it felt like armor. Her fleshy human form was vulnerable, but as a falcon, she felt invincible.

When she arrived near The Edge and changed feathers for skin, she hesitated again. Spending time with the Snofams had prepared her for moving among people, she reminded herself. She would be able to blend in better than she did before. She wrapped her cloak around her shoulders and fastened the clasp.

With a breath that filled her lungs almost to bursting followed by a quick release, she crossed the forbidden line into the dwarf trees and moving air. This time she knew her direction and moved easily through villages and forest until she came to the city that lay at the castle's feet. Her plan was to use the daylight to scout the outside of the palace, then move in after dark.

As the morning was cool and others on the crowded streets wore hoods over their heads, she kept hers on as well. But she had a hard time avoiding the impulse to look at the faces she passed. There was a hunger in the eyes that met hers. The smell of cooking foods wafted out of doorways, and the vegetable stands were stocked, though the produce was neither fresh nor from healthy fields. If the people were physically hungry, at least they were not starving.

Even with sprouts of smiles and laughter, the whole city felt dirty and heavy. Like an invisible river of darkness rolled in the streets. It was so different from Turron. A powerful feeling of sympathy rooted in her heart.

A troop of filthy children scurried past her. The little girl at the tail end stopped. With her grubby hands held out, she looked up with pleading eyes that reminded Meg of Riff waiting for a treat. Meg produced a perfect, yellow apple from her satchel, and the round eyes widened further. Just before it touched the tiny hands, an image of Gregry's lifeless body flashed through Meg's mind. Poison.

She jerked the apple back and dropped it safely into her bag. She would not risk harming another human with something that grew in her forest.

"You cannot have it," she whispered. "I'm sorry." She quickly turned away from the confused and hungry face and felt her stomach lurch. If only she had barrels of kingdom-grown apples instead of a poisoned satchel full. "Never mind. You can't think of that just now," she told herself.

She turned a corner and entered a cleaner block than she had seen. The buildings were not extravagant but were neat and trim. The street was not as crowded, and she noticed more eyes following her as she passed, especially those of the armored men who stood with spears in hand. These faces were clean and full. The castle was near.

Meg ducked into an empty alley between two stone buildings and, fitting her fingers and toes into the grooves of the stone, climbed to the rooftop. She stayed low and glanced around. The opposite building had no windows along the alley, and she couldn't see any part of the street. Unless someone climbed after her, this perch would be as secure a place as any to scout out the castle.

She peeked over the roof ridge at the massive structure with less wonder than she had before and with a more practical eye. A tall wall of large, black brick separated the expansive castle grounds from the city. Outbuildings lined the far side and tucked around back, and a garden of sorts spanned the front of the castle. A pristine, circular pool rested in the middle.

The castle itself was at the base of one of the mountains in the range that surrounded the Three Kingdoms and her forest. The steep mountain of pale gray was jagged and rocky, and the contrast of the black stone structure commanded the eye. The darkest section was built just the same as her castle, a square of walls with four towers on each side, only the front tower stretched higher than the other three. Armed men peeked out between battlements on the six-story tower.

"Wretched pointy sticks," she said.

As she studied the castle from her new vantage point, she noticed other differences. Five vertical slits about half a man long strung up the center of the tallest tower. An additional rectangular section, built of stone a shade or two lighter, swallowed up half of one of the short towers where it attached to the square. It, too, was lined with men on the rooftop, though the roof sloped behind them. Balconies and recessed cuts sporadically appeared across the castle and windows—both clear and colored glass—heavily garnished the walls.

As a whole, the castle was magnificent. And she suddenly wanted nothing more than to get inside.

When she had studied all she could from her lookout, Meg slid off the roof and silently dropped to the alley. A few people passed but none looked her direction. She crept to the corner and peeked at the two nearest armed men. Finding neither looking her direction, she slipped out into the street. She was anxious to get back to the crowded part of the city where she felt more comfortable.

Meg hurried the way she had come and rounded the corner that served as a divider between the two worlds within one city. The sun was midway down, the day still hours from dark. Unsure what to do, she found a stretch of blank wall and sat down, pressing the back of her head against the cool brick.

She closed her eyes.

"This will be easy," she whispered. *This will be easy.* The moon would be a sliver and the night dark. She could move her falcon form stealthily, but she was a large bird. Her gut told her it would be difficult not to be noticed.

"Are you all right miss?" a man's voice broke through her thoughts.

Her eyes popped open to see a thin face hovering above hers. He pulled back.

"I didn' mean to disturb you, miss," he said almost apologetically. "I just...see this here is my wall. Most everyone knows that. But if you need a good spot to rest then it's all right with me."

Meg cleared her dry throat and stood, taking him in as she did. He was a small man, with dark, wavy hair streaked with silver. His face was whiskery, and his nose was crooked along the bridge. The clothes he wore were worn and patched but had a neatness to them that surprised her. He also smelled strongly of many things, all of them unpleasant.

"I'm sorry. I did not know walls had claim. You may have yours."

He looked up at her and smiled pleasantly. "I'd rather share it, if you don't mind the company." He moved around her, dropped his rolled pack, and lowered himself to the ground.

Meg looked up and down the street. She shouldn't be making friends. But the man patted the space next to him, so she took the offered seat.

"Monte's my name," he said, obviously pleased she had chosen to sit with him.

"Meg," she replied.

He took a flask from his chest pocket and took a sip, then held it out to her. An odor wafted to her nose and made it wrinkle. It wasn't water. She shook her head.

He took another swig and put the flask back in his pocket. "I seen you once before—months ago. You're not the sort one forgets. I'd remember the likes of you even if I hadn' seen you stand between royalty and common. But that just clamps a memory. You don't live here?"

"No. Just arrived today. And I'm not staying long."

"Ah, going back out to the country. That's probably best. I'm sure you've noticed," he leaned over and lowered his voice to a whisper, "this city is beatin' a failing rhythm." He let out a dry laugh and his warm breath battered Meg's nose. Then he leaned back and clucked his tongue, erasing his smile. "It won't be long 'til the rest of Davare stops with it. Not long at all, if it hasn't already. I guess I don't know for sure, haven't been out for some time." He gestured toward one of his lower limbs. "This leg here don't let me go too far."

"What happened to it?"

He looked at her and smiled. "Just a regular ol' battle wound. Hurt in Roshton, when it was taken."

A quiver of anger rose in Meg's chest. This man had been a part of the ruin of Gregry's kingdom.

Her face must have moved with the jolt, as the man hastily continued, "I was in King Herrick's army, it's true. Who wouldn' be if he had the chance? You get all the meat and drink you could ask for. And if you've a family, which I haven't, they're taken care of, too. Mostly." He pointed in the direction of the nicer streets. "But sometimes things ain't what they seem."

"What do you mean?"

"I mean you're never as important as you think. Didn' take more than a popped stitch for Our Highness, may his bones be in peace, to throw me to the dogs."

Meg thought of Riff sniffing her out. "He keeps dogs?"

He laughed. "Sure, in the kennels. But I didn' mean that literally. I meant Old King Herrick threw me out of his keeping."

"So you do not serve the king anymore?"

"That's what I'm sayin'. Not by choice, of course." He looked up at the people passing by, then dropped his gaze to his feet and scratched his neck. "But now given the chance, I think I'd take the dogs over the cushions."

Meg studied his profile, his tongue continually rolling against his cheek. He seemed honest in his words and looks. It became apparent he wasn't going to say more without prompting.

"Why?"

He looked up quickly, then back down at his feet. "You're a nosy thing, ain't you. Well, I suppose I've seen the world from the dogs' point of view, so to say. When you're the one sitting on the cushion…it's hard to see any problems with it." He looked at her puzzled face and let out another husky laugh and shook his head. "That is, I didn' see any trouble with the way things was run around here. I wasn' getting any harm, so I saw no harm. But now I can see how things is going a bad way. Folks is hungry. Hurting. Getting desperate."

"What has happened?"

He looked at her impatiently but smacked his dry lips and continued in a low voice, "Well, there's difference of opinion, but you know I think it started clear back with King Herrick the Second. Poorly managing his farm tenants. Using up resources without putting anything back. Raising taxes. The Third only did worse. Cut back the private-owned mines to keep it all. And you was probably just a little one when he took on Roshton and all those folks.

"But I don't think he took any thought as to how he'd manage another flock when he couldn't manage his own. There's difference of opinion, but that's what I say. And now this Fourth. He's the worst of them all. Just like his father but worse. Most'll agree with me on this. Even old Phil down at The Tipper agrees with me. Only group this one knows how to take care of is them men in fancy armor. And even them he just lies to. I'd testify to that." He lifted his leg. "A whimpering little piglet."

Meg fiddled with her toes a moment. "Why do people listen to him? Why don't they get a new king?"

He let out a crack of laughter. "For one so nosy you sure ain't got much figured. How are these people supposed to take on a man with an army? They've nothing but pitchforks and sticks."

"They hunt, don't they? What do they use?"

He licked his lips again. "Your head in a hole? How do you live without…King Herrick burned or stole most of the weaponry. Didn' leave regular folks with much. Did the same in Roshton. It's forbidden to make any form of weaponry outside the King's smithies."

"What about Turron?"

"Well, I'm sure they've gotten some things from Turron, but trade ain't what it used to be you know. Stuff like that has to be done in secret. That's another problem the Third created. Queen Iril is no young cluck—she's the noble sort that has more in her head than our last three kings combined. Most people in Turron don't associate much with anyone from either of Piglet's kingdoms."

Meg chewed on this information for a bit. She could feel the bitterness in her new friend's words. He was not on King Herrick's side. At all. He seemed to like having someone to chat with and to educate. It suddenly occurred to her how much this man might be able to educate her.

"What happened to Roshton's king?"

"Don't know."

His tone had flattened, and his eyes cast down. Meg narrowed her own eyes. "That's a lie, isn't it? You know what happened to him."

He looked at her sharply, then raised his eyes to the sky.

"Monte," she whispered. "I can help these people. I'm not really from Davare. Turron is being attacked just like Roshton. They think it's the Rathern, but I know it is not. It's something else. I have friends there, and I do not want them to live like this. Anything you could tell me...I would be very grateful. Please don't lie anymore. It does not suit a man like you."

He straightened his back and thought for a moment. "So that's his game, huh? I wondered what they've been preparing for." After another pause, he scooted himself closer, near enough their shoulders pressed against one another. "I could be hanged for this Miss Meg. Hanged." He looked at her for a moment with shrewd eyes, wiped his hand over his jaw, then went on. "I was regular infantryman. But my cousin was higher up. He was one of them hunters that went in looking for the Rathern." He shifted his eyes up and down the street. "You never speak where you got this information. Hanged, Miss Meg. Understood?"

She nodded solidly.

"Those attacks in Turron. I don't think they're what they appear to be either. I...I thought we was saving Roshton when we went in. But the years since have given me time to think. And I think it was a set up."

"A set up? What do you mean?"

"Rigged. Put together. Planned. It was a set up. I think—" he lowered his voice again. "I think Piglet Senior set it all up. I can't say how 'cause I don't rightly know. But it seems mighty suspicious to me that one kingdom had attacks and the other two none. And now the last is having attacks but the other two none. There's a mouse in the pudding, if you get what I mean. A mouse in the pudding."

Meg shuddered. She didn't know about mice and pudding, but the rest was what she had believed all along.

Then she recalled her unanswered question. "And King MarKus?"

Monte turned his head the other way and muttered a few words under his breath before turning back to her. "Hanged, Miss Meg. Hanged. I must be off my thinker to…you've…King MarKus is alive. Or he was. My cousin and his men found him in the Death Woods, his own men all dead, him barely hanging on. They brought him to the king in secret and was told to keep it quiet until it was sorted out. My cousin, he told me what he'd found late that night when he got back. But Herrick didn' never say a word. And the next morning my cousin and his men were sent back in. But none of them ever came back out." He slid his thumb across his neck. "Knew too much."

"But is he yet alive?"

"My cousin? No, this," he ran his thumb across his neck again, "Means he's dead. Killed."

"No, I mean is King Markus alive?"

"Oh. Don't know. Made it easier for Piglet to take what he wanted with King MarKus out of the way. But if he is still alive, which I'd bet my tongue he isn't, he'd be in the dungeon of that castle. I don't know what you're going to do with that bit but know he'd be guarded like the roasting pig at Holiday." He licked his lips nervously and looked around again.

Meg chewed her lip a moment and watched the people of Davare's Heart pass. Many of them gave Monte a friendly look or a wave. "If the people were armed, would they fight?"

A cart rolled by, the wheels a hand-breadth from Monte's feet. "I think so. Well, I don't rightly know, I guess. Scared. Many of them scared. Half his army serves now because they're scared. I'd bet my tongue on that, too. But you get them angry, and mix that with being afraid, you might get a stir." He looked at her again and shifted his back against the wall. "You sure got me talking. I suppose I've always been a talker, but this stuff. The hanged thing and all. But I like you, Miss Meg. There's something about you that's different from the rest of us poor sucks."

Meg nodded and leaned back to let the information she had just been given simmer in her mind. Things that appeared one-sided now needed to be looked at from all directions. If King Herrick was behind it all, then it could be stopped.

"Would that he would come in and take back his throne," Monte said suddenly. "That would lighten things."

Meg grabbed his arm. "Who?"

Monte looked almost startled by her reaction. "Well, that young Prince MarKus who disappeared. Some say he was killed for bounty, others say he's hiding out. If Roshton was under its own king...Or, you know, even better if she—our own princess—returned. But that's just legend."

"Legend?"

"Yeah. You never heard the Sleeping Princess?"

Meg shook her head.

"Well, sit back sister, and I'll tell it to you. Long ago there was a great king of Davare. King Jonef was his name."

"Jonef?" Meg couldn't keep the surprise from her voice.

"Yes, King Jonef. Don't interrupt the story, now," he chided. He cleared his throat. "King Jonef was a great man. Beloved by all. He took a queen from the forest—all forest women are enchanted, you know. He took a queen from the forest as fair as any woman ever seen. Under their reign, land and happiness flourished. Eventually, they was blessed with a baby girl. The last princess of Davare. Then—how exactly no one knows—but King Jonef betrayed the Great Forest— the Death Woods as you probably know it by. One terrible day, King Jonef was found dead in his castle, first victim of the Rathern.

"But Queen Masabeth was nowhere to be found. Some say she had something to do with the king's death, but I say the forest took her back, swallowed her up. That's how the Herricks came to be kings. Anyway, a curse was cast over the trees. I say by the ghost of the elf king, but there's difference of opinion here. But that's how it came to be called the Death Woods, if you didn't know. Now the baby. How's that child's rhyme go again?

> In the Death Woods, thick and deep,
> Lies a baby, fast asleep.
> Left to 'wait the curse to lift,
> For to bear us all a gift.
> Daughter of King Jonef, sure an' true,
> His departed crown will shine anew.

"Now let's see. This is my favorite part...er...

> Adorned in feathers she will come,
> Restoring peace to our king'dom.

"Adorned in feathers. Ain't that a pretty thought—a princess all decorated in feathers." He looked around. "Near as I can tell, that baby ain't awake and the curse still goin' strong."

Meg stared at the man. "Tell it to me again."

Monte squinted one eye at her, shifted in his seat, and repeated the whole bit.

"King Jonef," she whispered to herself. Mother's husband—Meg's father—was *King* Jonef. A human. Deciding not to announce she was the Sleeping Princess, she went the other route. "I know where Prince MarKus is." Monte looked at her wide-eyed. "I do. And he should— will—help his people. This King Herrick is a wicked man and must be punished. I'm not afraid of him."

Monte shifted again, scooting away from her a bit. "Nicked in the nob," he said under his breath. "Well, Miss Meg, I wish you luck in your quest. When you next see the Lost Prince, tell him to get a move on things if he's to do anything. The king's men will be marching for Turron soon, mark my word. They've been camped in the woods just to the south for a couple weeks now. I myself have received a golden invitation from the Turron queen and am going to pay my respects. Of course, I'll travel on one of my flying pigs and donate it for the feast, along with ten kegs of the finest whiskey. Bet she's a fine dancer, the queen, when she's loosened up."

He laughed merrily, but Meg did not join him.

"I give you my thanks, Monte," she said getting to her feet. "I hope we shall meet again. Keep to your wall and watch."

She strode away, his laughter following on her heels.

Chapter Eighteen

THAT night Meg found out when darkness falls, the guards come out like bats. Every ten paces, a shiny guard stood against the wall, spear centerline and handy. She wouldn't be able to go in on foot. It was also unfortunate to find most people went in as soon as the sun went out. Aside from a handful of stragglers wandering home and clusters of people tucked against the walls asleep, the streets were empty. Meg was far less inconspicuous as she moved through the city than she had been during daylight.

After a filthy man grabbed her around the waist, breathing hot air into her face and forcing her to bite his greasy nose, she gave up her discreet pace and ran for the forest with only a short, staggering pursuit. She didn't stop until the trees surrounded her like her own personal guards. The air outside the city was instantly cooler, and she breathed in deep to calm her lungs, taking in traces of the forest's heavy mood but also allowing the peace of night into her bones.

"I can do this. It will be easy," she repeated.

She jumped and shifted in one sweeping motion and shot straight up. The higher she flew the smaller she would appear, attracting little attention as she neared the castle. Surely the jagged cliffs gave Herrick the feeling of security from behind. She would start there. As she made her way, her eyes found flickers of light to the south. A good number of fires dotted a concentrated area. The camp Monte had spoken of.

Suddenly the castle was below her. She circled a few times, reassuring herself of the plan. There was no wall behind the castle. No wall meant no line of guards. She'd only need to be mindful of the few on top. She swooped in low, keeping to the mountain as she descended, and silently coasted right up to the base of the castle and shifted. She pressed her back against the wall. A tiny, astonished laugh escaped her throat.

Now what? She waited a few minutes for her pulse to slow and her mind to clear. What would Mother say if she knew Meg was standing against the Castle of Davare right now? Meg shook her head. It was better not to think about that.

With no low windows on the tower, she began making her way across the wall of lighter stone. She slunk along, stopping to listen under windows and occasionally peeking in. Most rooms were dark or nearly empty, revealing nothing. Then she came to something that held her interest longer than a second. A large, well-lit room with windows rising three quarters of the way up the wall. An intricately designed rug stretched across the floor and chairs unlike any Meg had ever seen sat empty. Opposite the window, a fireplace three times the size of hers at home stood proudly ablaze. A painting of a man she immediately recognized as Herrick hung over the finely carved mantel. But the mantel was not as beautiful as the one Gregry had made at the Snofam's, she thought smugly.

She moved on and made it to the opposite corner. Moving around to the front of the castle did not seem wise, so she decided to move up. With her bare feet easily finding footing, she climbed to the second set of windows. She pressed her ear to the windows of the dark rooms, careful not to scrape against them and make noise. When she came to the high windows of the large lit room, she found herself stuck. The window panes were narrow and her fingers were beginning to cramp from pinching the thin ledges of the stone. Also, she imagined alarm would be raised if anyone entered the room and discovered a girl sprawled out against the glass. She leaned away and looked up to see if she could go above the glass. A balcony was over-head and back to the right a ways.

Chewing her lip for a moment and feeling her legs beginning to shake, she lifted her foot to a ledge above and pushed higher, making her way to the balcony. She gave her thanks to the person who had designed the newer portion of castle with places to rest from scaling. When the balcony was an arm's reach away she stopped to listen again. She shuddered at the silence of the massive building. It seemed unnatural to be so hushed. It should be full of people, a living building. Hearing nothing for several minutes, she grabbed ahold of the carved stone railing and pulled herself up. Like a mouse, she scurried to the recess between the door frame and the railing and tucked her knees under her chin with her back solidly pressed against the wall.

Suddenly she heard voices. Low and gruff. Meg pushed even tighter against the wall. It was several moments before she realized she was hearing a conversation between a couple guards atop the castle, still one story away.

"I think...I would rather be eating rolls with Serah just now," she mused in a whisper, feeling her heart in her throat. It seemed such a little idea. Sneak up to a castle and creep around it until she found what she was looking for. But it was not the same as creeping around her forest. She should have practiced on something a little smaller and a little less likely to get her killed.

She took a deep breath and leaned forward onto her knees, curving her body around to peer into the room on the other side of the glass-paned balcony doors. She slid back to her place in the shadows. Her legs felt rubbery. Scaling all around the outside was going to take all night. And she didn't much feel like coming back. The sooner she went in, the more likely she'd find success. There were plenty of windows. If discovered, she could bolt out the nearest one, shift, and be gone before anyone saw her nose.

Meg moved onto her toes, keeping her crouched position, and crept toward the doors. Slowly she reached her hand up to the latch and gave it a tug. A quiet click whispered success, and the door opened with a little pop. She slipped through and pulled the door closed again before passing through heavy drapes. The darkness she found on the other side created phantom figures all around her. She stepped back until she found the wall and pressed into it, waiting only seconds more for her eyes to find enough light to see. A large bed first came into focus. She could see the tall posts and puffy bedding. It appeared empty. She made out a few chairs, a little table, and a tall solid something in the corner.

Summoning the courage to cross the room, she glided noiselessly to the crack of light that signaled a door. Opening it ajar, she could see a long, empty hallway. Candles on sconces provided dim light all along the space.

She sucked in a deep breath and slipped out. The rug that spanned the corridor was soft under her feet, and she wiggled her toes a moment as she debated which way to go. The castle was as silent inside as it was outside, and she wished someone somewhere would scream or smash something or do anything to signal where in this massive place they were. As she padded down the hall she began to worry she had entered the wrong part of the castle. Where would King Herrick keep the ax? And his dungeon?

She continued to tiptoe, stopping to listen for something—anything. At the end of the corridor, she found a spiral staircase and decided to go down.

Before opening to the next floor, the polished stone steps flattened into a landing. A large door with metal hinges and an interesting latch stood guard. Meg twitched to continue on but stopped before taking another step. The door, rustic and unadorned, looked out of place considering the rest of the castle.

She placed a hand on the latch. Despite the large keyhole, the latch lifted and with a firm push, the door moved several inches. She pulled it closed, unsure she really wanted to go through. The shuffle of shoes coming down the winding staircase entered her ears. Meg's heart tucked into a tighter ball. The footsteps were drawing nearer. She could hear the voice of a woman, muttering under her breath.

Meg lifted the latch again and found herself on the other side of the closed door before she really had time to think. A stone wall was before her with a corridor to the right, and a little off to the left another stairwell. Just as she exhaled a breath of relief, the door behind her pushed open and bumped into her back. With light feet she scurried to the stairwell and ducked around the bend.

"Hello?" a woman's voice echoed.

"Yes?" a distant voice responded.

"Is that you Crag? Did you just come through the door here?"

The tread of boots moving down the corridor sounded dangerously close.

"Lirpa, what is it you're jawing about? I can't hear you from around the corner, mumbling like you do."

"This door," she replied in a clipped tone. "Did you just come through?"

Meg sucked in a breath and held it.

"I've been at my post this last hour. Haven't moved."

"I'm sure I heard it close as I came down the stairs. You haven't seen anyone then?"

"Not a soul."

"You might have a look about. I'm sure I heard someone, and none of my girls are out."

A grunt came from the man that indicated he would do so. Meg squeezed her eyes shut and let her lungs release a little of the air that struggled in her tight chest. Where were all the windows?

As soon as the door scraped closed, his boots clodded back down the hall. Meg exhaled the rest of the way. Footsteps and voices quiet once more, she stood on the steps frozen, pressed against the cold stone. *This was a terrible, terrible idea,* she thought. *Trapped. Trapped. Trapped.* Windows were supposed to make for a quick exit, and here she had wandered into solid corridors she couldn't predict. *Think, think, think,* she commanded herself. The towers. She glanced around at the stone. It was dark, almost black. Like the older section of castle on the outside.

The question was whether to continue down the stairs or not. Afraid to go back through the door and certain she couldn't go in the direction the man had gone, it seemed down would be best.

Light was scarce, only a little glow from the torch at the head. Keeping close to the wall, she made her way. With each step, the feeling of being trapped drew up. There were no windows, no doors. No place of escape. A cool draft snaked its way past her body. It wasn't long before another faint glow came from somewhere below, and with relief she found another torch at the foot of the twisting steps.

A cough bounced off the stone, and she jumped back around the turn. A second cough followed, then faded into snores. *Frelick?* She nearly laughed at herself for thinking Frelick would be here at the bottom of the castle of Davare. No, not Frelick, but someone snoring. Someone asleep. She peeked around the corner. She could see no one.

She crept forward, each step ready to turn and run. A pair of boots came into view. Then legs. Then the rest of a man, seated in a recess in the wall. His hands were clasped over the armor on his belly and his head was slumped forward. He sucked in a loud, gurgled breath that made Meg gag.

Slowly, she tiptoed past the man, staying pressed against the far wall. Ten paces away from him she turned a sharp corner and continued down a long, low-ceilinged corridor. Doors were sporadically placed along both walls. By the scant number of guards inside compared to outside, it was clear Herrick didn't expect anyone to get into his castle. The place she found herself in was empty of persons and almost empty of light. Another draft shivered down the stone. Far at the end of the silent passageway, a torch burned.

She swallowed hard and pressed on. She passed one door, then another, wondering what was on the other side. By the third door she had gathered enough courage to lift the latch. Slowly, she pushed it open and put her head through the crack. And found...darkness.

"Meg, of course there's no light," she chided herself under her breath.

She pulled back from the door and, leaving it open, moved for the torch at the end of the hall. Her head bumped something. An unlit torch. She didn't know what awaited down the long hallway, but she knew what was behind her, so with torch in hand, she retraced her steps back to the sleeping man. She lit the thing without the slightest disturbance to his snores and after granting him a taunting face, ran back to the open door. She stepped inside and pushed it closed.

The room was full of furnishings. Dusty paintings. Shabby chairs. Vases. Nothing worth discovering. She searched behind the first two doors she had passed and then a fourth, finding much the same. Stacks of old armor. Piles of moth-eaten tunics. An entire room of buckets, tools, and dusty old things. Meg could not understand why all of it would be placed in these rooms rather than given to people to be used.

She reached the end of the hall and turned a corner. More doors. She continued forward and discovered another descending staircase. She took it and weaved through more passageways and checked a few doors. Behind the final door before another corner, something made her pause. Long sticks spread over the floor and piled to the side next to a crumbled heap of cloth. Large papers covered in drawings and writings were nailed to the far wall.

In the center of the room was a splintered contraption consisting of slender pieces of wood and torn fabric. Meg circled the thing, noting the wood pieces tied together in a triangular shape. A long, curved piece extended from one side. She sat on her heels to run her hand over the fine fabric that stretched over the structure. Something about the shape was familiar.

A wracking cough echoed down the corridor making Meg jump. She moved to the door and listened. In the silence, she thought she could hear voices. Meg slipped out the door and crept toward another corner. Then down the corridor until the voices grew loud enough for her to make them out. Two men. Neither asleep.

She leaned against the wall and listened. One man was telling of his son—his ability to get a hold of any sweet in the house. The other man seemed to be enjoying the story, chuckling at the description of the little boy climbing shelves like a squirrel.

"He's just a little pup, you know. No bigger around than this. But he has another sense, my boy does."

"Just like his father." The second voice sounded further away. In another room?

The man laughed. "I suppose that's true. I've a sweet tooth of my own. You've seen that."

"Yes, I have. I should like to meet him someday, Kam. I wonder if he is much like my MarKus."

Meg straightened and leaned her ear nearer to the corner.

"Was—I mean is he a strapping lad with neatly kept hair and clean hands? If so, then my Staven and he are not much alike. I wish I could bring him to meet you, sir."

There was a pause. "I know, Kam. I know it isn't possible. But I like to think of it all the same."

The men went on talking about the man's ill wife and then about horses. There was no mention of the name Gregry, but Meg felt certain she was listening to his father. Though his voice was coarser—older—he sounded much the same. Something in his way of speaking. And he had the voice of one who could command.

She dared a peek around the corner. A young man sat sideways on a chair—his back to her. She leaned out a little further. She couldn't see the other man but made out a large, solid door. A staircase stood coldly about twenty paces from the men. She leaned back and chewed on her lip. The man sitting guard sounded nice enough. He might be friendly. It might not be difficult to convince him to release the imprisoned man to her. But the staircase was a good distance away. And what or who was at the top of the staircase she couldn't guess. She couldn't take risks. Not with another's life. And not before she had the chance to tell Gregry what she thought she had found.

She listened a minute longer, then made her way back the direction she had come. Or the direction she thought she had come. She came to several dead ends and found more unexplored doors. Soon she was quite lost in the maze of stone. She opened one door—larger than the others—to find a dark tunnel instead of a room. It was musty and cold and unwelcoming so she backed out. As she tiptoed past another passageway she had not met, a voice called to her. She paused in the silence and shook her head.

"Now you're imagining things, Meg," she whispered to herself. *I must get out before I go mad.*

Still, it wouldn't hurt to check a few more doors. Glancing around, she entered the passageway. It was not long, and as she silently neared the end, she heard more voices. Real voices. She set her torch down on the ground and crept to the very corner.

Then she heard the first voice again. With a shock, she realized she didn't so much *hear* it as she had *felt* it.

She couldn't understand the words of the whisper, and once she had caught a few sentences from the two men, she wished she couldn't understand their words either. Several of their coarse words were lost on her, but she understood enough of the vile things they said to feel sick inside. She tried to shut her ears to their words and pick up the other voice. It was soft like the call of a songbird, but it wasn't really musical either.

She felt a strange pull in her chest. An urge to find the source. She peeked around the corner. There was no staircase in the distance this time. Just another corner. Two men sat outside a door, one with his back to her and one facing her. She pulled back before he looked up.

The voice called to her again. She wished she could make out its words, that it would give her instructions. She felt helpless knowing it was just right there yet she couldn't get to it. She pushed both hands through her hair trying to decide how to proceed. She couldn't fight off two men like this, not in this form. And the passageway was too narrow for her to fly through. She would have to escape on foot. But she had to get into that room.

Meg jumped low and shifted in the small space, her wings scraping the stone walls before she tucked them to her side. Picturing herself, an immense bird hopping down a narrow hallway, would have made her laugh in any other circumstance. But instead of laughing, she hopped around the corner and screamed.

The two men startled out of their seats, one to his belly and the other to his feet, both with their hands over their ears. She half skipped, half lunged toward them, shrieking and snapping her beak. The one standing had drawn his sword, but as she neared, he turned and ran. She reached the one on the floor and pounced on his back, poking the tips of her talons into his skin. She was hoping he would also run when she hopped off, but he bellowed in agony and tucked into a ball. Dismayed, she hopped back a few more paces and shrieked again. Seeing his chance, the man scrambled to his feet and loped toward the opposite corner.

Meg shifted and pulled at the door. Locked. She looked around for a key but found none. She swiped her fingers through her hair again. There wasn't any way for her elfin form to get the door open.

With an exasperated cry, she shifted again and went to work with her powerful beak, twisting and gnawing at the hinges. The top hinge cracked and popped loose quickly but the bottom gave her trouble.

She went at it from all angles until it finally gave in and allowed her to pry it from the door.

She shifted again, bumping her head hard on the ceiling, and scooped up the thick sword the gutless man had dropped. Wedging it between the door and the frame, she forced the barrier open a crack. No longer on its hinges, the door was offset and difficult to move.

The whispering grew louder. More urgent. The pull in her chest pulsing with her heart. Frantically, she wedged the sword in further and tugged. Surely the men had made it to reinforcements by now. Time was burning low. Finally, the door hung open enough for her to climb through. She snatched a torch off the wall and scrambled into the room.

It was a treasury, with ancient war pieces hanging on the walls and gold and precious gems gleaming at her from all directions. Scattered around the room, fine cloths draped over items, hiding them from view. The pull grew almost unbearable.

The Imperald was in the room somewhere, screaming to be found. Meg yanked cloths away from piles and pedestals. She ransacked small boxes and ran her hands through a few large chests, but nothing had the appearance she was looking for, nothing responded to her touch.

In desperation she dropped to her knees and listened, fearing at any moment the clang of guards returning would be all she heard. Like the breath in her lungs, the whisper moved from inside her chest up to her ears. When she opened her eyes, Meg knew where to look.

Her slender fingers moved over the floor searching for a defect, a crack, a loose stone. Crawling on her knees, she moved forward until she found it. Grabbing a nearby gilded dagger, she pried a stone away from the rest.

Meg stared into the hole. Several items nested in a rotted piece of cloth—a wooden toy horse, a tiny pair of stiff leather shoes, and a book. Small and calf-skin brown. She reached for the leather-bound paper and lifted it from its tomb to tuck it safely into the bottom of her satchel. Then, with a trembling hand, she pulled back the cloth.

And there it was. The Raparean Imperald. An unshaped crystal, rough and jagged, about the size of her fist. Black with a green sheen. Or was it a red sheen? The color wasn't important. She grabbed the relic, but a jolt through her hands made her drop it back into the hole.

She snorted. "You don't have time for this, Meg!"

She snatched it up again and placed it in her satchel, ignoring the vibration that lingered in her hand. She glanced around the room once more. Then she slipped out the door and ran like wildfire.

Shouts came from behind. She thought she could hear voices ahead but it was impossible to tell, the clattering and shouting echoing off the walls. Rounding a corner she slammed into something, feeling fur brush against her skin before she fell backward onto the hard stone. A cloaked man stood over her, a silver ax in his hand and two guards on either side. Her eyes met Herrick's.

"You?" he said in surprise.

In a split second, Meg sprang forward, throwing her shoulder into his stomach and pushing him stumbling back against the men behind him. The ax clattered to the ground. Meg twisted away as one of the guards lifted his sword. There was a flash of silver.

"No!" Herrick shouted. "I want her alive!"

The guard's hesitation gave Meg just enough time to grab the fallen ax and scramble past him.

"Here!" she heard Herrick screaming. "This way!"

Meg could feel his men closing in. She passed the big door she had discovered earlier and skidded to a stop. The tunnel! Just as a group of men rounded the corner behind her, she yanked the door open and bolted into the cold.

"You! Stop! Stop in the name of King Herrick."

"I'll do nothing in the piglet's name!" she shouted back.

She ran through the darkness until torches from behind lit her way. Unhindered by heavy boots or metal plates, she moved swiftly down the damp tunnel. The clamoring of armor forced her heart higher into her throat.

Suddenly the ground disappeared from under her feet, and she dropped awkwardly, splashing into inches of foul water.

A light appeared ahead, a soft cold light. Moonlight!

Allowing herself no more than a couple gags in reaction to the smell, she sprinted toward the light. A metal grate covered the high opening large enough for her body to slip through. On either side of her was another dark tunnel.

Instantly, she decided she was done running through tunnels and muck and pulled at the grate with both hands. It budged slightly. It was not built into the wall, but set on a rusted track. She stepped to the right and pulled the grate with all her might.

The clamoring was growing louder and the orange glow she had left behind growing dangerously near again. The grate slid with a terrible shriek and dropped to the ground, nearly yanking her down with it. With both arms reaching for freedom, Meg jumped to pull herself into the hole. She pushed onto her elbows, but before she could get her upper body through, a hand caught her satchel and yanked her back to the floor of the tunnel, contents from her bag splashing about her. More orange glows were swiftly nearing.

On her belly, she scrambled for the ax and swung at the guard, slicing the blade across the back of his leg. He cried out and dropped into the water beside her clutching his wound. Without losing a second, she took up her satchel and jumped up to the hole again and pulled herself forward through the short tunnel, her hands raking across packed earth and clumps of grass that had found their way into the vent. She gulped in air. Fresh air!

A strong hand grabbed her foot.

One yank and her head bumped hard against the stone. She gave a swift, hard kick with her free foot and connected her heel with the guard's nose. He bellowed, and her other foot, still slick from the muck, slipped out of his grip. Meg squirmed forward, out onto the castle grounds.

Shouts continued to erupt from the hole, but not one of the men could hoist himself through quickly enough. Meg dashed across the lawn as a whiz sounded in her ear. An arrow stuck in the grass just before her on the left. She raced toward the mountainside on foot, afraid to shift in view of the guards. Another arrow. Then another. Before one could strike her in the back, she threw out all caution and jumped into her falcon form.

Like the thief in the night she was, she glided stealthily up the mountainside toward the sky, out of reach and out of sight.

Chapter Nineteen

MEG lay against the cool bracken of her forest, dew seeping through her tunic. The sun was beginning to stretch, the sky fading to dawn. As her heart continued to pound, her mind wrapped around the events of the night. Scaling the wall. Sneaking through the castle. The maze. The guards. The Imperald. The *Imperald*.

A slow laugh started in her stomach and bubbled out her mouth.

"I did it," she breathed. "I did it!"

She sat up and fumbled through her satchel to find the crystal. Seeing it again, she realized it was not a pretty thing like she had expected. And yet it fascinated her. For a moment, she couldn't take her eyes from it. She could see where pieces had been broken off, like the piece in her ear.

She clutched it to her chest and lay back into the earth. As she ran her fingers over the spikes and edges, she imagined the look that would come to Mother's weary face when the crystal was placed in her hands. She would finally be happy. And maybe then she would be willing to tell Meg more about her father.

She sat up suddenly and felt around in her satchel again. Her fingers took hold of the cool silver and pulled out the jeweled ax. With a cringe, she wiped the blood and muck from the blade, then gently set it in the grass next to the Imperald. It was the ax Gregry described. And the imprisoned man the rightful owner. Meg felt it in her bones. A different feeling prickled her skin. What if she had put the king in great danger by entering the castle? Gregry needed to know his father was still alive. And soon. She looked from one item to the other.

"Mother can wait," she said, tucking the items back into her bag, and with a leap, shifted and took flight, excitement fluttering under her feathered breast.

The trees could not pass swiftly enough as she neared the eastern mountains. Nearer to The Edge than she usually dared, she shifted and dashed out of her forest. Instead of taking roundabout paths, she cut through the trees of Turron to save time. She did not slow until she reached the Snofam's home, her throat burning and her mind all astir with her news. Lezah was standing at the edge of the pigsty, shovel in hand.

"Lezah!" Meg called as she jogged to meet her. "Where is Gregry?"

At the sound of her voice, Serah came running out of the barn. "Meg! Where have you been? It's been so long. But you're here now and—oh!" She wrinkled her nose and jingled. "What in—dear friend you are filthy!"

"Yes," Meg said looking herself over. She had hoped the flight would air her out. It hadn't evidently, but there were things more urgent than a wash. "I need to speak with Gregry. Now."

Serah looked to Lezah.

The girl grunted and drove her shovel into the mud. "I do not keep his time." She paused, then said, "But it is past midmorning. He was supposed to return today from Rrr—his friend's and meet up with Papa near Grosbek. He should be here soon."

"My thanks!" Meg exclaimed as she turned to search them out. She stopped suddenly and ran back to take Lezah's hand. "I should tell you…I—I've changed my mind. I do *like* Gregry. Like enough to…" She pressed her lips together and let them open with a pop.

Lezah rolled her eyes. "I *know*. I knew that well before you evidently." She pulled her hand away and bent over to pick up her bucket. "It's fine, Meg." She looked up and smiled weakly. "Really. It's fine."

Meg swallowed. She didn't know what else to say. So, with an apologetic glance at Serah, she turned and took off down the trail. Just after passing Jem's sheep pasture, she saw Frelick's wagon coming up the trail with Gregry walking beside it. When he looked up to see her coming, he jogged ahead to meet her. The shadows were gone from under his eyes, Meg noted with relief.

"Have you come again for a visit?" he asked.

"Yes! I mean no. No, I've come to tell you something. I went into the Castle of Davare and—"

"You what?!" It was an exclamation of surprise rather than doubt. He looked her over with a troubled expression. "I asked you not to— do you realize what could have happened?"

She grimaced, feeling the cold hand around her ankle again. "Never mind that," she swung her pack around and pulled out the ax. "Look!"

His eyes widened. Slowly he took it from her hands. "My father's ax. Where…how did you get this?"

"I took it. And I…I think I heard your father. I think he's alive."

He looked up sharply.

"I can't be certain," Meg continued quickly. "I didn't see him so I can't tell you what he looked like—but I heard him speak. He spoke like you. And he talked about a MarKus."

Gregry looked the ax up and down. "Meg, I…" He trailed off and they stood there in silence until Frelick rolled up beside them.

"Hello, Meg, my girl! Haven't seen you in a good bit. How have you—" He stopped and let out a whistle. "Where in Three Kingdoms did you get that?"

"From Davare," Gregry said without looking up. "It's my father's ax."

Meg placed a hand on Gregry's arm. "I spoke to a man who used to be a soldier in Herrick's army. He said they found your father in the forest. Wounded but alive. And Herrick has kept him ever since. He didn't know if your father was still alive, but I went into the castle to get your ax and found where they keep him. I didn't escape without notice and now I worry he is in danger. Because I was down where they keep him. And! My new friend has reason to think Herrick is behind the attacks. Not the Rathern. It makes sense. His father used fear of the Rathern to work his way into Roshton. And now he's trying for Turron."

Gregry studied her face, and she could see thoughts turning in his eyes.

"There could be truth to that," Frelick said. "We've thought something was going on, and if you could convince the Noble Queen…"

"I think she already suspects something. Marv said she has been organizing her troops. His man reported so last week."

Meg heard this with relief. "If the people of Roshton were armed, too, you could stop Herrick. The people in Roshton and in Davare are tired of suffering."

"I know," Gregry said quietly, gripping the ax.

"And Herrick's guards are on the southern side of the city, moving from there. If you went in from the north—through my forest—you could get to the castle without meeting them."

"If the Noble Queen is organizing as you say," Frelick put in, "we could be ready within days, if not already. I think it's time, boy. Time for you to fight."

Gregry looked up from the ax and stared into Meg's eyes. She watched uncertainty harden into resolve. He nodded, inhaled a sharp breath then looked at Frelick.

"My thanks to you Frelick. Keep your family safe. Come with me Meg." He grabbed her by the hand and together they ran to Jem's.

After a quick exchange with Jem, they hurried into the barn.

"This might be a fool's scheme. What if…" He placed a saddle on Jem's strongest horse. "Do you really think we can move through the forest undetected? What about the Rathern?"

Meg bit her lip. The truth had almost slipped out. "Leave that to me. I promise you and anyone who enters will be safe. Just stay close to the edge and don't eat anything."

He nodded and didn't speak as he fastened the saddle. Then he grabbed a bridle and slid it over the horse's muzzle.

"And you stay here with the Snofams." He briefly turned to her with a wry smile. "I don't trust you to stay out of danger."

"No, I'm coming with you."

His fingers stopped working the buckle. "This is not your fight, Meg." He jerked back into motion. "I won't risk you coming to harm."

"But if I stay here, how will I protect you from the Rathern?"

His mouth twitched into a half smile, and he smoothly mounted the horse. "All right then, go into your forest. But stay there. Don't come out until I come to find you."

Meg grinned. "*You* find me?"

"I always do."

The horse shifted under the weight upon its back. Without warning, Gregry dismounted and in three strides was before her, his hand enveloping hers. He kissed her cheek, creating a flow of warmth that consumed her from head to toe, and pressed his forehead to hers, nose brushing nose.

"I give you my thanks, Meg."

Before she could think of anything coherent to say, he pulled away. Without a word he mounted the horse again, and the animal turned and left in a gallop.

Meg watched him disappear into the trees from the stable door, her fingers to her kissed cheek. Her heart thumped loudly in her chest long after he was out of sight.

"Stay in my forest," she mused. She bolted out of the barn in the direction of the Snofams. When she arrived, the family was gathered inside the cottage, Frelick in the middle of relating the news.

"Has he gone?" Frelick asked as soon as Meg walked through the door.

"Yes, on one of Jem's horses." Meg took Serah's offered hand and let herself be pulled into their huddle.

"Good." Frelick finished telling the rest.

"So what do we do now?" Lezah asked.

"Gregry has slowly been gathering men in Roshton into a resistance, but I don't know how many. I'm sure Herrick has numbers and experience on his side."

"He has numbers now," Meg interjected. "But I don't think he can hold onto them. The people are ready to be rid of him. My friend said so. They just need reason enough to move."

Judging by the shocked look on Serah and Lezah's faces, Meg guessed they had no notion of this. But Ida didn't look surprised.

Frelick nodded. "I knew things have been bad for Roshton for a while, but I didn't know Davare, too."

"So really then," said Lezah. "What do we do now?"

Frelick ran a hand over his bearded chin. "I'm not sure. But I can't sit here..." he moved for the door. "I'm going after Gregry. You four stay here."

"I'll come with you," Meg nearly shouted.

Frelick stopped. After one shake of his head, Meg continued.

"I—I forgot to tell Gregry some things."

Frelick sucked on his cheek for a few seconds before he nodded. "Come on then, girl. The rest of you stay here."

"Wait, Papa." Serah grabbed Meg by the hand and led her upstairs. "You can't go to the city like that." She lifted the lid of a chest and pulled out a bundle. "Put these on. My travel clothes. They might be snug but..."

Meg dropped her satchel and quickly made the switch. Serah's leggings stopped mid shin, but the rose-colored shirt and dark gray tunic were long enough to fit. After replacing her own belt, she wiped her face, hands, and feet with a damp cloth. Serah dabbed her neck and hair with a flowery scented oil.

"There. Now they won't throw you out the city gates."

The friends embraced and hurried back down the stairs. Serah hugged her father, begging him to be safe. Ida handed her husband a filled pack, kissed his cheek, and sent him out the door.

She turned to Meg. "Watch over him, please. And if we aren't here when you get back, tell him not to worry. The girls and I can't just sit here, either. We're going to find some way to help."

Meg nodded and hugged the woman tightly.

"Be safe," she said as she slipped out the door and ran after Frelick.

They jogged to Jem's and borrowed two more horses. While Jem helped Frelick ready the horses, Meg peeked into her satchel at the Imperald. She should get it to Mother soon, but she had waited years for it. She could wait another day or two.

Within minutes Meg found herself seated on a horse, gripping the saddle with damp palms and tight legs.

"You know how to ride, don't you?" Jem asked.

"I rode on the back of one once."

Jem pinched his eyebrows together. "That's not exactly the same thing. Move up on the saddle a little, there you go. Now tighten down on the reins." She gave him a blank look. "The strap there in your hand. Wope, wope. Steady. Move your hands up—yeah like that—point your thumbs there. Hold on, don't pull too hard. There just like that. Now, when you want her to turn this way, give a little tug with this hand and lean. Same with the other side. When you want her to stop pull back evenly with both hands. You sure you'll be all right?"

"Uh...yes."

He nodded, his eyes full of doubt. "Good because I don't think Serah would forgive me if you broke your neck."

Meg put her shoulder to her ear and rolled her head around. "Right, I don't want to break that."

He slapped the horse on the rump and the mare trotted out of the barn after Frelick.

"Get comfortable. It'll take us a bit to get to the city."

Meg nodded and wiggled again in the saddle. At first, they rode at a walk. When Meg felt more comfortable sitting astride the horse and Frelick had given her more instructions, they increased to a trot. But still it did not feel fast enough. With the speed Gregry had taken off,

Meg was certain he would arrive hours before them.

Why must horses be so slow? Birds flit and bounced overhead and glided to unseen destinations. It was hard for her not to feel pricks of jealousy. Why could she not be a tiny bird when she shifted? If she could use her wings, she'd be there in half the time. To distract herself from the length of road ahead and her waning patience, Meg worked her mind around what she had not yet taken time to process.

She was the daughter of a king.

A human king. One who lived long, long ago but was not forgotten. Memories smeared together in her mind as she tried to remember her years. Tried to remember her father. It didn't seem possible, and yet she was sure the Jonef Mother had written about in her book and the King Jonef in Monte's story were one and the same. And it became clear to Meg why Mother would refuse to speak of him. Why Mother would hide the truth. A part of Meg was everything Mother hated. A part of her was human.

"Not long now," Frelick broke in.

She inhaled a deep, calming breath. The now familiar whisper tickled the inside of her chest. She reached into the satchel hanging at her hip and felt the Imperald. She fingered the edges and listened, trying to understand. How could such a thing contain the sort of power needed to save Mother? She reached up to feel the piece in her ear. Mother had sacrificed the only piece she had for her. Mother loved her.

When they topped a particularly stiff hill, the City of Turron came into view. Green farms and forest surrounded the settlement. Buildings in a neat, distinct order, spiraled from the edge to the center, surrounding a cream-colored castle with three slender towers and walls that dipped gracefully in the center. It was a beautiful city from afar, which was the only view Meg had ever had of it. She itched to see it up close.

Just outside the gate, Frelick dismounted and instructed her to do the same. "It's rude to ride in the city streets."

Meg obeyed and dropped out of the saddle. Her legs ached from the long ride, and she suddenly felt the weariness of being awake for so many hours.

As they guided their horses through the streets, Meg could not help notice the contrast between this city and Davare's Heart. The streets were cobbled with small, smooth stones of blue, gray, and white, and swept clean. The buildings were in good repair with colorful flowers adorning every few.

Just like in the Snofam's village, the people here were a stark contrast to their counterparts in the west. Most of their faces shone with a brightness, even if lacking a smile. There were disturbances but none that compared to Herrick's brutal acts. The thought entered her mind, if she ever ruled a kingdom, she would want her people to be like these. Another street gone by and she determined even if she never ruled anything, she wanted the people in Roshton and Davare to be like these.

Using zig-zagging cross streets, they reached the castle's high curtain wall, made of peach-colored brick and washed with thinned mortar. They followed the wall until they came to a black iron gate guarded by four armored men, each with a long sword and shield.

"We're looking for a friend who's come to see the Noble Queen," Frelick announced. "I believe he might already be inside."

"Sorry, you'll not be going in to find out," one of the guards replied. "The queen is not taking visitors at this time."

"But our friend has surely been through?" Frelick persisted. "A young man about her height. Light brown hair. In…what was he wearing Meg?"

"A dark green shirt—with the sleeves rolled up and one button missing—under a buckskin vest that has a pocket on one side and a dirty spot above it, and dark brown trousers thin on the knees."

Frelick briefly squinted one eye at her, an amused expression on his face. "Right, that. Has he been here?"

"Sorry, sir. Not at this gate. You might check the other two. I assure you, though, we've not let anyone in."

Frelick bobbed his head and informed him they'd check just the same. They moved to the next gate and then the last without any luck. None of the guards admitted to having seen Gregry.

"Will you give the Noble Queen a message then?" he asked one of the last guards, who responded with a patronizing nod. "Tell her Frelick Snofam is here. Frelick Snofam."

As they walked away defeated, Meg heard Frelick mutter a string of curses under his breath. He had as much faith in the young man relaying the message as she did, apparently.

"Come, my girl. I know of a good place to stay if you feel you can walk a little more."

Meg's eyes burned and her legs felt as if they might give out any moment, but she nodded, summoning her last bit of energy to keep moving. The light of day was beginning its fade by the time they reached the quaint, pink-bricked inn on the far end of the city near what Frelick told her was the market. He purchased two meals and rented a room for the night. He apologized for not having enough coin for two rooms. Meg assured him she didn't mind. She didn't say as much, but his snores had become a comfort to her sleepy ears.

They ate their supper of mutton stew and red potato pastries in silence. As she chewed, Meg felt her anxiety increasing. Where was Gregry? Was he safe? She hadn't seen any bodies on the side of the road. No saddled but riderless horse. But if he had made it to the city, how would he get in to see the queen if she wasn't allowing visitors? Surely Herrick would move soon. She needed to be warned.

When the dining room clock chimed, both companions were ready to turn in for the night. Just as they reached the first landing of the staircase, a familiar jingle came from the receiving room below.

"You were right, Mama! We have come to the right place."

Meg turned on her heels and skipped down the stairs two at a time. "Serah! Ida. Lezah."

Each of the women grinned in triumph and Frelick joined them with a bewildered face.

"We knew you'd be here," Serah said taking Meg's arm. "Come, show us to our room, and we will explain."

When Frelick closed the door behind them, he turned to face his family with his arms across his chest. Their room was small, but it felt strangely comfortable with the five of them filling it.

"Now, what in the Three Kingdoms are you doing here?"

Ida made a dismissive sound. "Don't start swearing at me. You and Gregry both scurried here without this." She held out a leather strip with an embossed wreath. Meg instantly recognized it as the one from Gregry's book.

Frelick's shoulders relaxed and a sheepish expression washed over his face. "Praise you, woman." He reached out to her and pulled her in for a peck on the forehead.

Serah must have seen Meg's confusion and spoke in a low tone. "Mama says it's Gregry's token to see the Noble Queen. She gave it to him when he came to us and said he may use it any time."

"Along with his own pass phrase," Frelick added. "Do you remember it, Ida?"

She nodded. Frelick exhaled heavily. It wasn't a given the token would allow them through, but he said it improved their chances. The time was getting late but with renewed hope came renewed energy. Frelick determined they should try the castle again and received no push-back. He left word with the innkeeper they would return late and ushered his family out the door.

Lamp lights were lit, and the streets still bustled here and there with evening activity. Meg walked arm in arm with Serah as she searched each head of hair, each face, for the one she knew. Where was Gregry in all of this? As if reading her mind, Serah gave her arm a squeeze.

"He's fine. He is here somewhere. I wouldn't be surprised if he is sitting with the Noble Queen right now."

Meg smiled at the reassurance. "Where is Jem? Why did he not come with you?"

Serah cocked her head with a sly grin. "We've stolen all his horses. And I refused to share mine. I wasn't about to have a sore bottom from being shoved to the back of a saddle! Besides, someone had to stay behind and feed poor little Riff and the other animals."

Meg laughed. Poor Jem. She could picture his expression after finding himself left behind with no horse. The group moved on and on through the streets letting Serah tell Meg about her first and only other visit to the city. The shops. The street music. The friendly folks at the inn. Meg was happy for the distraction and allowed herself to be carried away in Serah's words until they reached the castle gate.

A new set of guards stood at attention, and Frelick asked again if they had seen Gregry. They had not. Frelick looked back at Ida, who stepped forward pulling the leather piece from her pocket.

"We need to see the Noble Queen. Will you take this and a message to her?"

One of the guards standing on the other side of the gate nodded and reached through the bars to take the token.

Ida stepped closer and lowered her voice. "Tell her, 'The sword of Brando defeats the troll.' "

He nodded again and disappeared behind a hedge not far beyond the wall. The family stepped to the side where another guard indicated to wait.

"The sword of Brando defeats the troll?" Lezah scoffed in a whisper. "Of all things."

Ida grinned. "He was only a boy, Lezah. He was told to come up with something he could always remember."

A smile touched Meg's lips picturing a small Gregry carrying his book and showing pictures to the queen.

A short while later the guard returned. "Queen Iril will admit the owner of this token."

"We are all going in?" Frelick asked more than he told.

"No, sir. She will admit only *the* owner. Just one of you. Who was given the token?"

A noise squeaked from Frelick's throat but before it became a word, Ida spoke up.

"We will wait for you here, dear Meg," she said quickly, stepping forward to give her a squeeze. She stood on her toes and whispered, "You have the most information to give. Go in his place. Warn the Noble Queen." Ida stepped away with a reassuring nod.

"Leave your pack," the man instructed.

Hesitantly, Meg slid her satchel off her shoulder and handed it to Serah. "Do not let anyone take this."

Serah nodded solemnly, and Meg drew in a deep breath as the gate was unlocked and she was allowed to pass through.

Chapter Twenty

MEG followed the guard as he weaved through a maze of tall hedges and rose bushes with sure steps. Meg recognized the scent like the yellow wild roses Serah picked by the creek, but these roses were different. Even in the dim light of the guard's lantern, Meg could see the bright pink and creamy white petals that grew layer upon layer. A few times her tunic caught on stray branches reaching into the path, and she had to tug it free from the thorns.

The maze ended and a short, lush lawn began. With her view no longer obstructed, Meg took in the castle she was about to enter. Faint imprints of vines and roses in vertical rectangles broke up the smooth building material, and several lit windows gleamed gold against the milky background of the castle. It was lovely. Meg wondered if the woman inside matched her castle and grounds.

The guard led her through an arched door guarded by four men dressed the same as those at the city wall. After a wide entryway, they entered a great room with polished stone floor and columns, and two large, carved seats at the head shrouded in green and purple strips of cloth from floor to ceiling. More guards dotted the room.

Meg felt anxious to see the woman they called Noble Queen but found herself oddly comfortable following the guard through the room. Being allowed into a castle was a very different experience than sneaking into one.

The man led her into a hallway and past several doors before he turned and entered a room. Meg gasped. In the center of the far wall was a large fireplace flanked by two windows, filled with colored glass plated in a garden design. But the real beauty of the room was the shelves and shelves of books. Of all colors. How could anyone ever read so many?

Blinking away her amazement, Meg searched over the room for a person. Two guards stood opposite each other on the side walls, and in a corner by a clear, circular window stood a small, gray-haired woman. Her dress was fine but simple, no jewelry but a single ring and a thin gold crown. Meg liked the way her green gown folded into two loops at her hips.

The woman turned from the window and a look of surprise passed over her shrewd face before she expertly masked it.

"Leave us," she said to the guards without taking her eyes from Meg. "But stay outside the door."

The guard who had accompanied Meg nodded and preceded the other two men out. When the latch clicked, Meg instantly looked toward one of the colored windows. It would be a shame to make it an exit.

"I always knew you would grow tall, but your hair has surprised me and grown quite dark since I last saw you as a child, Prince MarKus."

Meg looked around and behind herself, confused. "I am not Prince MarKus."

The hint of a smile pulled at the stern face. "I know. Who are you and where is the owner of the token you gave?"

"He has not been here then?"

233

"No." The queen tucked her chin and looked at Meg expectantly. Though small in frame she seemed to grow taller the more she spoke, her every look and word threaded with the control she was used to possessing.

Meg swallowed. She did not like the pressure of the queen's gaze on her. But she was Raparean and royalty herself. She squared her shoulders. *I am the daughter of King Jonef and Queen Masabeth* were the words that first came to mind. Instead, she said, "I am Meg."

An eyebrow arched. "Are you? And tell me, Meg. Why do you have the young prince of Roshton's token?"

"He has gone. I do not know where. I thought he was coming to you. But I came with the Snofams—Frelick and Ida. Serah and Lezah. They gave it to me. And I have just come from Davare this morning." Had it really been just this morning? This would last in her memory as the longest day of her life. "I bring you warning. Herrick has guards set to move. They are coming this way."

One of Queen Iril's gray eyes narrowed briefly. "How do you know?"

"I saw them gathered and camped. And a friend of mine in Davare's Heart said they would move soon. He said they would be coming for your castle. Just like Herrick the Third did for Roshton."

"And who is your friend?"

"Monte."

The same little smile returned to her lips. "And who is this Monte? An adviser to King Herrick? A captain of his guards? A nobleman?"

"He...he isn't any of those I don't think. He lives by a wall."

"A wall?"

This was not going well. The queen was full of doubt. She needed to say something different. "King MarKus is alive!" she blurted out.

Meg didn't think it was possible, but the woman stiffened further. "What do you mean?"

"I mean what I say. King MarKus is alive and inside the castle of Davare. I heard him. And I found his ax. And Gregry—MarKus—has…" Suddenly she knew where Gregry was. "He has gone to rescue him," she said quietly. She licked her lips. She was sure of it. "He has gone after his father. The Rathern is not to blame for the attacks. Herrick is. I do not know how, but he is behind it all. To make your people afraid and take your castle, just like he did to King MarKus."

The queen's lips tightened, and she turned back to the window. "I knew it," she said to herself through clenched teeth.

Moments passed, and Meg was made very aware of the ticking clock above the crackling fireplace. She wiggled her toes against the soft carpet beneath her feet. She had to go after Gregry. He needed her. Finally, the queen turned to face her again.

"Four days ago we apprehended a man in possession of a flying device of sorts and kerosene. We assume he is from Davare, but he refuses to speak. Do you know anything of that?"

Meg shook her head.

"I have no doubt now, regardless. Herrick has not corresponded with me since I refused his help months ago, and attacks have only increased. He is not as patient as his father. So he is coming for me?" Queen Iril crossed the room to a desk littered with papers and began sifting through them. "Well, he shall find I am not one to tremble in my slippers. I feel I can trust you, Meg. And I trust Frelick. He would not bring you to me if he doubted you. Thank you for your warning. Where might I find you and the Snofams?"

"At the pink inn by the market."

She nodded. "I know the one. Any—what is that in your ear?"

Meg reached up and combed her hair forward.

"Where did you get that?" the queen asked.

After a pause, Meg replied, "My mother." She hoped that would satisfy. She didn't want more questions. She needed to go.

The queen swished toward her and held out her hand, not for Meg to take but to see. A green gem with a black sheen gleamed on her middle finger. "It is the same is it not? The only others I have seen...do you know what it is?"

Meg set her jaw.

The woman dropped her hand. "This ring has been in the line of Turron for over a century. It was a gift from the queen of Davare long ago. She was from the forest, they say." Silence prodded her to continue. "When it was passed to me, I was told if I took care of my people, the ring would take care of the land. Silly notion, of course—ancient enchantments. But my people are happy and our land is strong. Did your piece come with a promise?"

"No."

The woman tipped her head back and clasped one hand over the other. "I see. Any more you can give me?"

Meg shook her head. Her feet needed to move.

"Jon!"

The door instantly opened. "Yes, Noble Queen?"

"Take Meg back to the gate. Send a message to Captain Rossed and Crown Princess Marrie. I need them immediately."

"Yes, my queen."

Meg was relieved the guard felt a sense of urgency and kept their pace near a run all the way back to the gate. Once through the bars, Meg continued her pace.

"Meg! Wait for us!"

Serah's call pulled her out of her determination. She had forgotten about the family waiting for her, and she hurried back to where they stood against the wall.

"I know where Gregry is," she whispered. "He didn't come here. He went to Marv's. I'm certain of it."

"Marv? Of course." Frelick pounded a fist against the wall. "Bumbling idiot, coming here. Girls, you go back to the inn. Meg and I are going after him."

Meg looked at him in his rumpled shirt and disheveled hair. The man was exhausted. She could reach Marv's home much faster if she went alone.

"You should stay here, Frelick. The queen might need you."

"I can't let you go scampering into the dark alone. What if—"

"Don't worry for me. I'm used to being in the dark alone. It will be better if we part. We will...accomplish more."

"What if you're wrong?" Lezah asked. "Do you even know where to find this friend of his?"

Deep in her bones, Meg knew Gregry was heading toward Davare, but she didn't want to completely disregard her friend. "I'll find it. And if you do find him here, tell him I've gone to my forest." She held out her hand for her satchel. She had almost left without it!

Serah's eyes widened as she handed it over. "*Your* forest? What forest?

"He'll know. Be safe," Meg said as she turned and broke into a jog.

"Meg! Meg! Surely you don't mean..."

Serah's calls trailed off as the distance between them quickly grew. She was sorry to leave her friend without a thorough explanation, but she didn't want to get into those depths at that moment. Time was too precious to waste. And Serah would want to know every detail she had hidden about her forest, her castle, her life. Everything.

In the time she had been in the castle, the streets had grown quiet but not still. On almost every corner a soldier stood alert. Moving the same path she and Frelick had first used to reach the castle, Meg stayed close to the buildings and easily passed each guard until she reached the city wall and the gate. To her dismay, she found it locked and heavily guarded. Firelight flickered on the other side of the gate, and her eyes made out the shapes of wagons and animals camping for the night, waiting entry.

She left the gate and found an unguarded section of the wall. She ran her hands over the barrier. Smooth. There were no crevices to wedge into and climb. No trellis or vine.

Annoyed, she stepped back into the shadows. The heavy feeling of exhaustion came back into her body, and she slumped against a wall to think. Why had Gregry insisted on going without her? He needed her. And she needed to get out of this city. She could shift and in one quick motion be out. It wouldn't be hard, and it was unlikely she'd be seen. She rested her elbow on her knee and placed her cheek in her hand. She couldn't stop the memory of Gregry's kiss, his face so near hers. She closed her eyes to visualize her escape.

Yes…it would be…easy.

Meg startled awake. She was still sitting against the brick building facing the inside of the city wall. She looked up at the sky. Night was just starting to wane. How long had she slept? A loud clanking came from somewhere just out of sight. The gate. It was opening.

She returned to the point of entry in time to see the first carts roll in. She received a strange look from one of the guards as she moved against the flow, but he said nothing.

When the people were out of sight behind her, she turned off the road and entered the forest. After treading under the protection of the trees for some distance, she shifted and took flight, pushing herself high into the sky, hoping not to be seen ascending in the dawning daylight. When she transitioned into her horizontal plane of flight, she consciously felt the wind gliding around her body and sighed. Freedom.

As she silently moved over the forests of Turron, she arranged the coming events in her head. First, she would find Gregry and make him tell her his plan. Frelick had said he had men from Roshton. That was good. She would guide them through her forest. Then, before they broke away from her trees, she would go to Mother and give her the Imperald. Then it would be safe, and Mother would be healed. Then Meg would rejoin Gregry and together they would sneak into the castle, and she would guide him to his father.

It all unraveled naturally before her, a clear path marked. What else would she need to plan for? If the same friendly-sounding guard was on duty, it wouldn't be difficult to get the king free. Then King Mar-Kus and Gregry would have their kingdom back.

A feeling of dread snaked its way under each thought. Deep down, she knew it would not be as simple as her mind made it. There were swords and arrows, angry men and tall castle walls. Everything would be less frightening if she could go in as a falcon.

Through the trees, she glimpsed pieces of a trail and followed it until she was near the edge of her forest. She didn't know where Turron ended and Roshton began, but she did know she was just south of her favorite cave. She flew back and forth, scanning for a little cottage that might belong to Marv. When she spotted one, she cut into a stoop, shifted, and jogged to the little home.

When she knocked and the door opened, she was greeted by a little gray-haired man with mismatched ears and jelly on his shirt.

"I am looking for Marv."

The man shook his head and pointed. "You got a little more to go. Take that road. It will lead you straight to him."

She thanked him, and just as he said, a good ways up the road, she came to another cottage. It was dark with every shutter closed up tight. Five horses stood tied outside the house, and the nickers of several more could be heard from within the barn.

She walked up the porch steps and knocked. There was a shuffling on the other side of the door before it cracked open. A middle-aged woman in a frilly nightcap peeked out.

"What is it?" she asked gruffly.

"I'm Meg. I am looking for someone."

The door opened a little more for the woman to give Meg a good look up and down.

"Yes, he said you'd come looking. He isn't here. They've gone already."

"Where?"

"To Davare. Through…the forest."

A small girl appeared and tugged at the woman's apron.

"Who's she, Mama?" she whispered.

"Never mind, child. Back to bed with you." She gave the girl a gentle push and turned back to Meg. "They left before dusk. A gathering here, and Marv said there were more being sent for." She inhaled a deep breath and swiped a rough hand across her face. "Been praying all the night they're safe. I think it's foolishness to try for it. Numbers low as they are. But maybe some of the Roshton men will surprise me and get a spine. So you saw King MarKus then? He's alive?"

"Yes," Meg said, feeling a sting of guilt for stirring up so much hope on a little scrap of certainty. "I, er...I didn't really see him. I only heard him. I think it was him anyway."

The woman nodded, her face doubtful. "And the Rathern? Gregry promised my Marv it would be safe to move through—" She nodded toward the forest not far off. "Said you knew the habits of the beast. You better know what you're about girl. Or I'll have your skin."

Meg felt a sudden need to get away and backed down the stairs as she replied, "They will be safe. I promise you."

With that oath she turned and ran. When she glanced back and could no longer see the little home, she shifted and took flight. If they stayed near The Edge as she told Gregry to, they would not be lost and should not be difficult to find. She glided and weaved back and forth over the border, disregarding another one of Mother's rules.

She glanced south and spotted the castle of Roshton. The men should be near. She kept her sharp eyes constantly scanning the spaces between trees. She spotted movement below and turned to find a safe place to shift.

On foot, she sprinted in the direction she thought she had seen the man. She zig-zagged past trees and over bumps in the earth. When she could see The Edge, she stopped to listen. Nothing. The forest was as still as always. Where was this group of men?

She began to run along The Edge heading west and bounded up over a rocky ledge.

Whiz.

A hatchet whirled past her ear and struck into the tree behind her with an awful *schunk*. She dropped to her stomach and covered her head.

She looked up when she heard footsteps. Three men cautiously neared, one of them she knew.

"Why are you throwing things at me?" she shouted, her words muffled by the soft earth. Surely he recognized her—that would explain the miss. She had seen him throw. If he had wanted to strike her, he would have.

"Up, Meg."

Her name sounded more like a warning than a happy-to-see-you. She got to her feet and immediately noticed another hatchet ready in Gregry's hand. The two men with him held crossbows, both still raised and ready.

"Why did you lie to me?"

Meg looked him in the eye. Unable to determine which lie he meant, she stood silent, hoping he would give her a clue. The fury in his eyes sharpened.

"Why did you lie to me, Meg? Is this a trap? I trusted you."

"A trap? No. I don't know what you mean."

"The Rathern. We were attacked. Before light. You said it was gone. That it wouldn't be near us."

"Attacked?" She looked from one unknown man to the other, both clearly on edge, clutching their weapons tightly. "Gregry please, put that down. The Rathern wasn't—"

"We were ambushed. We lost five men. Five! The rest scattered and fled from the forest. We're scattered once again. Who put you up to this?"

Heat flared in her chest. How could he think she had purposely arranged an attack on him?

"I made this plan alone." When she saw him flex his grip on the handle, she shook her head. "I mean the plan to move through the forest. I don't have a plan against you. I'm not working with anyone. Except you. You weren't attacked by the Rathern. It must have been something else."

"Enough! Enough lies. I saw it, Meg. You can't lie to me about it anymore."

"It wasn't what you think, Gregry."

"What else swoops in and carries a man five stories in the air and drops him? Or slashes throats with its talons? I trusted you. Those times you went to Davare. Are you working with Herrick? Luring me in so his seat in Roshton is safe?"

"No! Believe me, no! It wasn't the Rathern."

"How do you know?"

"I just know!"

"How?"

"Because I didn't kill anybody!" The strangled words shot from her lips like a bolt from the sky.

The other two men stepped back, and the hatchet lowered several inches.

She looked down at the ground, not wanting to see their faces. She wanted to turn and run and hide under a rock. But there was no hiding now. Still unable to look up, Meg took a deep, burning breath and surrendered. "I am the Rathern, as you call it. And I didn't kill anybody. I wasn't here. You were attacked by something else."

"What's this about, Your Highness?" one man stammered.

Through her lashes, Meg saw Gregry's arm drop to his side. "Meg, just tell me the truth."

"I am!" she snapped, raising her eyes to meet his. She lifted both hands out to the side. "Raparean. I am not a Rathern. I am Raparean. I...change form. And I've protected my forest for years. But I have never killed anybody. It wasn't me. I wasn't even—" She froze, her throat tightening. Meg hadn't been near the men. But she wasn't the only Raparean in the forest. Her voice barely pushed past her lips. "Mother."

The three men stared at her, but she no longer saw any of them. Meg had never seen Mother shift. She had always been too weak. But if she had a reason…

Meg took several steps back. "Gregry, I'm so sorry. Gather your men. You may move through *my* forest. You will be safe. I will see to it this time."

"I don't understand. I—"

"You will be safe!" she stated again. "Gather your men and go. Your father is in danger. I… I am so sorry for the men lost."

With that she ran toward the nearest fallen log, leaped, and without hesitation, shifted. She did not look back at the men's faces as they watched the beast take to the sky.

Chapter Twenty-One

WHEN her castle came into view, Meg felt her stomach twist. She had never confronted Mother before. Had never truly been angry with her. Up until a few months ago, she had done everything Mother had asked her to do. She had hunted and searched and protected. And now Mother had descended upon her friend.

She landed on Mother's tower, shifted, and slipped swiftly through the window. She did not care if Mother was asleep.

"Mother!" The bed was empty. "Mother!" She screamed, as she bounded down the steps.

"I am here, Megnolia. Stop shouting."

Meg followed her frail voice and found Mother slumped in her chair before an empty fireplace.

"What have you done?"

Mother barely turned her gray-streaked head toward her. "What do you mean?"

"The men. In our forest. You attacked them."

Mother lifted a defiant shoulder. "So I did. They should not be here, and *you* were nowhere to be found. How did you not notice so many humans in our trees? I could feel them from here."

"You hurt them. Killed some even!"

"They have no right to enter! Unworthy creatures. But where were you? Why was I forced to cleanse the forest?"

"I…" Meg's voice faltered. She felt her courage fleeing like a traitor before battle. "I was in Turron."

Mother's golden eyes bore into Meg's, and she attempted to prop herself up. "I forbade you go there." She clutched at Meg's wrist. "I forbade you."

Meg knelt down. "I know, Mother. But people—the humans—they aren't as wicked as you say. Most of them are good."

Mother roughly released Meg's wrist. "No. Deceivers! Thieves."

A new thought made Meg go cold. "Have you been to the kingdoms? The field fires and stolen children. Was that you, Mother?"

Mother hesitated. "Stolen children? Do not be a fool. What would I want with small humans?" She wiped the sweat from her brow with the back of her hand. "They have taken so much from me, Megnolia. I could not let them remain in my forest."

Meg suddenly felt the weight of her satchel and remembered. She whipped it around from her back and reached in. Feeling through the folds, Meg startled and looked into the bag. "My book," she whispered. It was not in the bag.

"What?"

"Nothing." Somewhere she had lost her new book. Brushing aside the stab of regret, she pulled her hand out of the bag and produced the gleaming crystal. "I found it, Mother."

The woman's eyes widened as she reached for it. "Give it to me."

Instinctively, Meg pulled the crystal back. "Mother?" She paused. "Mother, what will happen now that we have it?"

Mother eyed Meg for a moment. "Everything will be made as it should be. We shall have the strength of our forest. We will live in peace. Now give it to me, my eyas."

Slowly, Meg placed it in Mother's outstretched hands. She moved her fingers over the rough surface, her face full of wonder. "Where, Meg? Where was it?"

"It was in the castle of Davare."

Mother looked at her sharply. "You went there as well? I forbade you ever to go to the humans." She tucked the gem to her chest. "I forbade it, Megnolia."

"Yes, I know, Mother." Meg remembered the story Monte had told her. Of King Jonef of Davare and the Lost Princess. She summoned some of her fleeting courage. "Who is my father?"

"Your father? How do you know of…never mind. I do not want to speak of him, Megnolia. Do not ask me. Going to the human king-dom has put the thoughts in your head I have kept out. Do not ask. Do you understand?"

"Yes," she replied softly, though inwardly she felt confused. She could not understand why Mother would keep thoughts from her.

Mother's pursed lips slowly relaxed, and she held out a frail hand. "Never mind. Never mind all of it. Come."

Meg accepted Mother's hand and helped her to her feet. "Are you going to sleep?" Now that she had given Mother the Imperald, Meg was burning to return to Gregry.

"Yes." She sighed. "Yes, I must. Going out took almost all. So very tired. Oh, my eyas." She gave Meg's hand a squeeze. "I cannot believe you have found it. Everything will be made right now."

Everything will be made right. The attack. "Mother, how could you kill those men? I had given them permission to move through our forest."

Mother stopped. "You should not have done so."

"I didn't think you would know," she answered honestly. "And the king in Davare. He is the type of human you speak of. A wicked man. He has tricked the others. He has starved the people and taken much of what they had. He is the one who had the Imperald, Mother. He must be stopped. And those men you attacked were…how could you kill them? What of their families—?"

Mother stumbled on a step, Meg catching her under the arm. Slowly, she lowered herself to sit, the Imperald clutched tightly to her chest. She began whispering to the Imperald, words Meg didn't understand. Meg watched Mother, her eyes closed. Meg felt a thump in her own chest, an energy flashing through her body.

Mother stood and began climbing the stairs again. When they reached the bedchamber, Mother instructed Meg to retrieve the silver scepter above the main hall mantelpiece. She did as she was told and watched Mother carefully place the silver rod on the ground, the cage in the center preventing one tip from touching the floor.

Mother held the Imperald over the twisted silver and whispered a few words. Meg felt the pull in her chest again as a bright light flashed. When the light was gone, the Imperald was safely wrapped in its cage, its dull spikes protruding from the silver bars. Mother picked up the scepter and laid herself on the bed.

"You have saved us, Megnolia." Her eyes closed and the lines of her forehead smoothed. "You have saved the forest. Everything will be as it should now. Everything will be as it should. I will help you."

"Mother," Meg said. Mother's eyes didn't open, but it was just as well. It was easier to continue without having to look into her eyes. "I am going to Davare. I must help my friend."

Mother's face tensed. "I forbid it," she said groggily. "You will stay here."

"You misunderstand, Mother. I am not asking permission to go." She had begun firmly, but the last few words came out so softly, Meg barely heard them herself.

Mother's eyes opened. "So they are suffering in the kingdoms. There is a stirring of war?" She nearly sat up. "They do not deserve our help. Let them destroy themselves!" She dropped back to her mattress, her chest falling and rising rapidly. "You are not one of them. You will stay."

Meg placed a hand over Mother's, willing her to understand. "We should help them. When all is right, it will be better for us, too. We can live here peacefully."

Mother looked at her skeptically.

"Please. Please understand why I must go. I love them, Mother."

Something flickered in Mother's eyes, and she squeezed them shut. "Place your hand on the Imperald." Meg did as she was told. "Do you feel it?"

Meg felt the energy pulse through her body. "Yes."

"Say it."

"The Imperald is my heart."

"And do you give it to me?"

"Yes." A strange sensation stirred in Meg's chest. "But Mother, I cannot stay."

Minutes passed. Finally, Mother inhaled a deep breath. "Go then. But do not return to me when it is finished."

Meg was still. "Mother?"

"You have already left me, Megnolia. Do not return."

Meg moved to take Mother's hand, but she pulled it away, gripping the scepter tighter. Silence lingered between them until Meg stood and turned for the door. She hesitated.

"And you will stay here, Mother?"

"Yes, my eyas," Mother said quietly.

Meg watched for signs of sleep to overtake the woman, took one final look, then dashed back down the steps.

"Mickelby!" Meg's call echoed through the great hall. "Mickelby!"

All was silent. She ran up his tower steps but found no sign of the old man. She hurried out to the orchard but did not find him there, either. After minutes of searching, she determined not to lose any more time and took to the air.

By the time Meg found Gregry again, the regathering was well under-way. Men were strung along The Edge in clusters moving toward a makeshift camp. Most of them must not have gone far after the attack—perhaps lingering near the border waiting to see if their prince would emerge from the forest.

The entire flight to him, Meg had tried to work out what she would say. How she would explain. She was relieved no one apprehended her when she walked into the camp. Gregry and the other two men must not have mentioned they had seen a girl morph into a beast.

She spotted Gregry deep in conversation with four other men near a poorly constructed tent, his back to her. One of the men saw her approaching and stepped back with eyes wide. Gregry must have no-ticed the change in his friend's face. He turned his head to see what had raised alarm.

His face hardened. She waited a safe distance away while he cut off the discussion and came to meet her.

For a moment neither spoke. She tried to read the lines of his face and the thoughts in his eyes, but she couldn't.

"I can explain."

He grabbed her firmly by the arm and pulled her out of the camp and into the trees. With the other men still in sight, he stopped and took a seat on a large rock.

"Go ahead then. *Explain.*"

Meg shifted her shoulders. She didn't like feeling as she had as a small child before Mother, giving reports and accounts of all her time and doings. But she stifled her pride and opened her mouth.

"I am neither a beast nor human. I am Raparean. The elves of your stories." She held her hands out to the sides. "I never meant to deceive you. Not in a wicked way anyway. But Mother told me humans were dangerous and could not be trusted. So I didn't tell you. And then I didn't tell you because I didn't want you to know. Because I was afraid of what you would think of me."

His face remained impassive, his posture stiff. Her simple words had not been enough.

Meg tried again. "I didn't come to you to trap you or trick you or cause any harm. I only wanted to read my book. But then I wanted to keep feeling what I felt with the Snofams. I hadn't realized how lonely I was or how much I wanted to learn. And then I wanted to be…" She felt a burning in her throat and tried to swallow it down. "And then I wanted to be near you. Because I felt more myself with you than I ever have anywhere else. I am not who Mother thinks I am but I hope to be who you think I am. Or thought I was. Or…" She saw a flicker in his eyes but it went out as quickly as it lit.

"What about the attacks?"

"It wasn't me. I promise you. It was Mother. Only this attack though, not the attacks in Roshton or Turron. She isn't well. I haven't ever even seen her shift. She's been too weak for years. I didn't think she would know you were in the forest, so I thought you'd be safe. But she found out somehow. And when she could not find me, she went on her own. I've never killed anyone, Gregry. Please believe me. I've scratched and frightened but never killed." She placed a hand on her forehead, nearly covering her eyes. "I'm so sorry," she whispered.

They sat in silence for a few moments. Then Gregry stood and drew so near she thought she could feel his breath on her face.

"Go home, Meg," he said in chilling calm. "We will leave your forest tonight. You and your mother can rest assure we will not enter it again."

She dropped her head. He would not forgive her. He would not see her as anything more than the beast he hunted. He backed away several steps before he turned and strode back to his camp. She could not raise her eyes to see him go but listened to his steps grow further and further away from her. She felt her heart crack in her chest with each twig he snapped under his boots. When she could bear it no more she turned and ran.

Meg ran until her legs felt no stronger than a sapling and her chest felt burned to ashes. She stumbled up to the base of a giant, flung her arms around the trunk and broke into choking sobs.

Never had words been so painful to her heart. The finality of Gregry's instructions. *Go home, Meg.* She was glad she had not looked at his face. There might be nothing left of her if she had. Tears scalded her eyes and the rough bark scratched at her cheek, but she went on clutching the tree, feeling a small amount of solace in its firm stance.

When her eyes could produce no more and her shudders had subsided, she slumped to the ground. She could not face Mother yet. She could not confess that she had been rejected. She wanted to stay in this spot until the moss covered her body, and she felt pain no more.

Eventually, the night robbed the forest of the sun's rays, and she curled into a ball for sleep. She felt relief as her body relaxed and her breaths deepened. She listened to the stillness of the forest. The night hoots and the scritch-scratching of small critters rooting for their first meal. She hugged Serah's tunic tighter around her body and let the lullaby of the forest soothe her aching heart.

Meg woke before the earliest rays of the sun. Wanting moss to grow over her no more, she sat up and a wave of memory from the day before washed over her. It still stung.

She ruffled her fingers through her hair, pulling a few leaves from the straight strands. Her stomach reminded her how empty it was with a loud rumble, and she scrounged around in the dark until she had a raw meal of mushrooms, wild onions, and a couple eggs she stole from a nest.

When her stomach felt satisfied, she returned to sit by her tree and tucked her legs up under her chin. Gregry had said they planned to leave the forest during the night. She wondered if he and his men had already made their exit. She hadn't even had a chance to tell him the set up of the city or guards or where to find his father. A panicky feeling of helplessness rose up in her chest.

'Let them destroy themselves,' Mother had said. 'You are not one of them.' Mother's words were true. She wasn't one of them. And she never would be.

'Go home, Meg,' Gregry's words repeated in her mind. Meg covered her ears. 'This isn't your battle,' they seemed to say. 'You're not wanted. You have no place here.'

She straightened. "But I have," she said aloud.

Gregry was the son of King MarKus, the rightful prince of Roshton. And he was now on a path to take his kingdom back.

But *she* was the daughter of King Jonef. She was the sleeping princess of Davare. That meant Davare was *her* kingdom. King Herrick sat on *her* throne. He wore *her* crown upon his head. And the people were waiting for her to return.

Chapter Twenty-Two

IN the grayness of fog, Meg made out the castle, tall and proud. As she neared, she could hear the shouts of men. Small blazes burned about the grounds. Her heart hitched in her chest. Mother's words echoed again in her mind. 'Let them destroy themselves.'

Beyond the far side of the city, the field where she had seen the glowing fires of Herrick's army was blank. She hoped the troop had already marched for Turron and left the castle to only a handful of guards.

Instead of going directly to the castle, she glided into the city and shifted in the street, just before reaching Monte's wall.

"Monte!" she called out. She ran a few buildings down, toward the castle. "Monte!"

"Here, girl," a voice came further down the way. She ran toward it and found Monte, huddled with several other men, the battle in view down the street.

"Monte. You said the people would fight if they had reason. That reason has come."

He looked at her blankly.

"Prince MarKus of Roshton is here. They've come to get his father and take back their kingdom. And I am here to take back mine."

"Yours?!"

"Yes, mine. But we aren't very many in number. We need more."

He laughed mirthlessly. "And you want me to get a troop gathered up right now? That ain't done like gathering chickens in a coop, sis. But what do you mean by—"

She squatted down to look him in the face. "You have experience in battle. We need your help. Any you can summon."

The man didn't move for a moment. Then he looked down the way at the source of shouts.

"Please, Monte. You know what kind of man Herrick is—think of your cousin. And all the people suffering."

"Most of the troops have moved out, Monte," one of the other men piped up. "We wouldn't have to go up against the entire army. Some might even change sides."

Monte rolled his tongue around in his mouth. "All right. I can't promise they'll listen to an old drunk like me, but I'll run it like a horse."

She took up his hand. "I give you my thanks. You are a good man, Monte. You probably don't need horses, though." She glanced down the road again. "I must go. Send them as you gather. Hurry!"

Before she finished speaking, she was running down the street, away from the battle. She jumped and shifted into her falcon form and shot up through the air.

She circled widely above, unable to pick Gregry out of the crowd. They all looked the same, like ants fighting over a hill. The castle roof was lined with archers, and more arrows shot out from the slits in the walls of the main tower. The men of Roshton had just broken through the curtain wall and a hand-to-hand battle was taking place on the grounds as they moved toward the doors. It appeared some men had tried approaching from the side but had been unsuccessful, their bodies strung along the curtain wall.

The archers on the roof were dropping men on the ground quickly. She would begin there.

She pushed to a higher height, then turned sharply and tucked into her stoop. The wind in her face brought comfort as her heart raced into the unknown.

None of the men looked up to see the missile shooting toward them. She pulled into a horizontal strike at the last moment and sped across the front of the line of archers, her talons flicking up bows and helmets as she went and knocking several men to the ground. When she reached the end of the line, she had disarmed twenty men.

Shouts of alarm reached her ears as she pushed back into the sky. She rounded and darted down for her second strike from a lower height. She needed the men to have little time to anticipate her.

This time she let out a fierce scream, causing some to drop their weapons to cover their ears. Others, undaunted, turned their aim for her, and several arrows whizzed past her head before her claws raked over the second string of men. She screamed again for good measure. She pulled up a second time and circled the castle. Herrick's archers were fleeing the roof, only a few stubborn soldiers held their ground, firing arrows futilely in her direction.

She shot down in another stoop, this time toward the men on the ground closest to the castle, their glinting armor helping her sort them from Gregry's men. She swooped over, shrieking and flicking up weapons and pushing guards to the ground.

Once again overhead, she could see the men of Roshton gaining ground. Now that the roof archers were nearly snuffed out, the men were not dropping so quickly. There wasn't anything she could do about the archers shooting from the crenels, so she went for another strike at the men on the ground. This time her sharp eye caught Gregry, wielding his ax on the center right, nearing the main entrance to the castle. Her heart skipped. He had not fallen.

A ruckus came from the gates and a wave of men and women rushed in from the streets of the city, armed with shovels, hoes, and clubs. Monte had come through. As she pulled back up, Meg felt her heart jerk. It was hard to feel victory in such an ugly scene, humans fighting over the top of one another. But she only had seconds to lament when she spotted Gregry and a group of men rushing to the large door. She dropped and shifted paces away from them.

The men startled and stumbled away from her. But Gregry only nodded.

"This way," she breathed, leading him down the slope around to the side of the castle. "We can enter through the side."

They reached the escape hole she had used only days ago. She dug away the dirt and sod to enlarge the hole, then leaned through to the grate. It didn't budge. She pulled out and one of the men crawled in to try.

"Will it move, Marv?"

"Not a bit, Your Highness."

Meg glanced around. The battle continued to rage. All of Herrick's men were occupied. No one had noticed them. They had time.

"Wait for me," Meg said as her fingers found holds in the stone.

She scaled the wall to a window high above the grate. It was locked. Gripping the ledge with one hand and her feet securely between bricks, she pulled back and punched her fist through the glass. Sharp edges sliced across her skin. Surprised but undaunted, she pulled the front of her tunic free from her belt and wrapped her hand. The glass fell away in large shards as she cleared the remaining fragments with her covered hand. Then, she pulled herself up and slid through the window.

As she had hoped the small room was empty of persons. She hurried out the door and down a short flight of steps. She froze on the last step when she discovered a small huddle of women staring at her.

The eldest woman met her eyes and after only a second, flicked her head to the side in a nod.

Meg darted around the curved wall to the steps that led down, only looking back once to see the women still standing where she had found them. After two more flights of stairs, she sprinted down the corridor until she came to the large door that led to the tunnel. In minutes she reached the grate and exhaled when she found Gregry and the men still waiting for her.

A shiny latch blocked the grate from sliding, a mark Herrick realized his castle was not invincible. She undid it and pulled the grate aside.

The others swiftly joined her in the tunnel, and wordlessly, she led them back toward the door. Once in the hallway, Meg had to regain her bearings. The maze of halls and doors blurred in her mind.

"This way," she whispered, taking them away from the stairs. They turned several corners before she had to stop again to determine which way to go.

She suppressed the feeling the next turn would bring them face to face with guards. Surely Herrick knew what the men were after. Or maybe he had not connected it. They reached a staircase that signaled she had led them astray. She retraced their steps and moved down a different passageway.

"Meg, hurry," Gregry whispered, frustration lacing his words.

She led them around another corner and stopped, the men in the back bumping into her. A guard shot to his feet from his chair and drew his sword.

Gregry raised his ax. Meg lifted her hand to his chest to stop his charge.

"We are here for King MarKus. Give him to us," she commanded the man.

He studied her face and tightened his grip on his sword. Maybe this was not the same guard. She wished she had seen his face.

He glanced toward the stairs, then back at them. He sheathed his sword.

"Kam, who is it? Who is there?" came a voice on the other side of the door.

Gregry lowered his ax and ran to the cell, the guard stepping out of his way.

"Father?"

"MarKus? My son, MarKus?"

From a narrow opening cut into the door, thin hands stretched out and clasped Gregry's.

"It's me, Father. We've come to get you out." He gave the frail hands a squeeze and stood to address the guard. "Unlock it."

The man shook his head. "I can't. The king only trusts a few men to hold keys." He glanced down at the cut in the door. "I would open the door if I could."

"Help me!" Gregry called to his men and together they drove their shoulders into the old door. The first blow yielded nothing and after several tries it was clear it would not budge.

Gregry laid several chops into the door, each time his ax blade being swallowed by the thick, solid wood. It would take longer than they had to create an opening wide enough.

Meg fingered the hinges of the door. They were the same kind as the others she had cracked to get the Imperald.

"Stand back."

Without hesitation, the men did as they were told. She shifted in the narrow space, and the guard stumbled and fell on his backside with a startled cry. Ignoring the gasps, Meg set to work on the hinges, cracking the metal with her beak as she had done before. After some effort, both were broken into pieces.

In the time she had worked, the circle of men around her had tightened, and she had to hobble back and forth a couple times and shrug her wings to create enough space to shift again. The door was wiggled and jerked and pulled from its frame. As soon as the gap was wide enough, Gregry pushed into the cell to embrace his ragged father.

"Your eyes," Gregry whispered, touching the old man's scarred face, his one open eye clouded with white. Before the king could speak a shout came from the stairwell down the hall.

"They are from Roshton! I want him moved now!"

The clattering noise of armor and boots echoed down the corridor.

"Hurry, this way," Kam instructed.

Gregry pressed his father to his side and looped his arm around him for support. The small group moved as quickly as the king would allow down the hall. In a harrowing replay from her previous visit, another shout came from the end of the hall before they reached the first turn.

"Stop!" The clamoring grew louder as Herrick's men began to run.

Meg turned and was surprised at the number of heads. They were out manned three to one at least. Before she turned the corner, she glimpsed King Herrick still standing on the steps.

They weren't moving fast enough. One of the men turned to face the slew of armored men alone. It was Marv. Meg gave him a push to turn around and keep going.

"Stay with your king." She would not break her promise to the woman he left at home.

Without hesitation he turned. She whipped herself around and shifted just as the guards rounded the corner. She let out a war shriek unlike any she had before.

The men skidded to a stop and a few swords hit the stone floor.

"Trap her!" their king shouted.

At once they rushed her. Unable to move freely in the tight space, she bounced forward as much as she could and collided with the first string of men. Her talons sliced through the air as the swords jabbed seeking a soft spot. She swung her head a few times, knocking men into the stone walls and snapped her beak, catching a sword blade.

She shrieked again when she felt a blade slice across her leg and hot pain jolted through her body. Most of the men turned to run but several kept coming. Then from behind she was pushed aside and a hatchet flew through the air striking one of the men. Gregry scooped a sword from the ground and with the jeweled ax in his other hand, clashed with the remaining men. He wielded the sword as easily as he did an ax, his expert swings finding openings and his blocks stopping blows. The last man turned to run as his companions slumped to the ground, exhausted or too wounded to continue.

Gregry turned to face her.

"You..." he breathed, "are a very large bird." A faint smile came to his lips.

She shifted her form and stepped toward him, but the searing pain shot through her body again, and she instinctively clutched her leg.

"You're hurt!" He dropped the sword and pressed her to his side. "Move. Before another string comes."

They hurried down the hall, this time as quickly as Meg's pace would allow. They rounded the corner leading to the hallway with the tunnel door. She stopped him. Sounds from the approaching second string echoed at the opposite end of the hall.

"They're coming. We won't make it."

"Back this way then."

They turned back the way they had come just as the din from the soldiers became certain. Presently, they were stepping over downed men and tufts of feathers and hurrying past the prison cell to the stairs.

"Keep going up. If we get to a window, I can get us out."

They limped up the steps and rounded the corner to the tower staircase. The first two doors they encountered on the climb were locked, but they continued up, afraid to turn back. The burning in Meg's leg worsened with each light step.

They reached a third door at the top of the stairs, left ajar by a care-less soldier. It opened into a sitting room of sorts, with playing cards and half-empty plates strewn about several tables. Shouts of triumph flowed through the three small windows.

Gregry released her and stepped up to one of the windows. "I can't see the courtyard, only roof."

They were in the tower between the new and old sections of the castle.

"Out the door," Meg said. "Try from out there."

The door pushed open easily, and they found themselves on the long rooftop of the old keep. The sky was purple with early dawn on the other side of the east mountains and a thin fog from the forest still rolled low over the earth. The roof was empty of soldiers, and they crossed the space, stepping over fallen helmets and bows, to look over the edge between battlements.

Gregry leaned out. "We've taken the courtyard! A heavy cost, but we've taken it." He moved over a few spaces. "I can't see my father."

The battle had ceased, all Herrick's men having either fallen or surrendered. It appeared the doors and windows had been barred from inside.

Gregry jumped onto the battlement. Cheers with renewed vigor erupted when his figure was spotted from below. A rhythmic pounding of tool handles and fists against stone began.

"I still can't see him," Gregry breathed.

Meg leaned out further. She couldn't see King MarKus or any of the men he had been left with either.

"Maybe they've taken him into the city. Let's go down to see what we can—"

"Don't move," a cold, confident voice came from behind.

Meg closed her eyes and felt a chill move up her spine. Her instincts knew what she would turn to see.

Chapter Twenty-Three

GREGRY cautiously jumped down from the battlement, and Meg forced herself to turn toward Herrick, his arm wrapped around King MarKus, a knife to his throat. Five armored men stood behind him.

"MarKus," the frail king choked out.

"Not exactly as I had planned but still, it has been worth it to keep the old man alive. Prince MarKus. I knew one day we would meet." The jewel in Herrick's silver crown caught an early ray of sunlight and gleamed like the eye of a monster. "Do you know how many nights I have laid awake wondering if you were on your way to slit my throat? I had to have a bargaining chip. Now here we are, a knife to his throat, you soon to be on your knees."

"Put the knife down, Herrick." Gregry's hand moved to his ax.

"Ah-ah-ah." Herrick tucked his face further behind the king's head. "My blade will be across his neck before your ax is out of your belt."

Gregry looked from his father's face to the man holding him captive. Slowly his hand dropped. "What do you want?"

"I want my playthings back of course. Your victory here means nothing. My army will return after it has taken Turron. The peasants running the streets will be beaten into submission. And you and your father will permanently and publicly renounce your family's claim and once again be lost. Or dead if you choose."

"What makes you certain your army will return?"

The man laughed under his breath. "You cannot make me feel concern on that point."

Gregry said nothing but reached for Meg's hand.

"Ah yes, the girl. My Lady Meg, isn't it? I thought there was something about you the moment I laid eyes on you. Yes, my mother read me stories of the forest elves. Tall, striking creatures." His head tilted, considering her. "But they left out one very important detail. So all this time, the dreaded Rathern was simply a Raparean girl. Beast and legend. The last of your kind, are you?" He sucked on his bottom lip a moment. "I'll give you this one if you give me her."

Gregry pulled Meg back, tucking her behind him.

Herrick's lips curved into a wicked grin. "Come now, little prince. Are you sure you want to protect her? Do you want to know in what condition your father was found in the forest? Do you not see his scars? I'm surprised you would form an alliance with such a monster." Herrick tightened his hold.

Meg knew she wouldn't have time to shift before the knife cut skin, but there had to be another way out. The men standing behind Herrick didn't look as sure as their king. Meg could see it in their eyes. Fear. All of them watched *her*.

She stepped around Gregry, his hand catching her wrist. "This is my kingdom, and I've come to claim it."

Herrick's face flickered before he regained his indifferent expression. "*Your* kingdom?"

"I am the daughter of King Jonef. The last worthy and rightful king of Davare. This kingdom is mine."

"Meg," Gregry whispered. His grip on her wrist loosened.

A strange quiet settled over the rooftop. The banging below seemed to fade, Meg's pulse pounding over the sound of fists.

"Well, this is a turn of events. Have you really been asleep all this time, little princess? 'Adorned in feathers she will come.' I wonder if the poet knew how accurate his little rhyme was. Yes, you look just like the portrait of your mother my father had burned." He smiled with delight. "So, the Lost Prince *and* the Sleeping Princess. On my roof. I think I will take them all. Be still or the old man gets it."

The men moved around him and rushed Gregry and Meg.

"I'd really watch my step around this one, Prince MarKus. I take it her forest born mother was also Raparean. Do you know her father's fate? Like mother, like daughter."

Meg shook her head and felt a wave of helplessness. She didn't want to hear anymore. If she had already been in falcon form, it would be over. She stood still as the men looped a rope around her wrists. When their hands were tied behind their backs, Herrick pushed his prisoner into the hands of one of his guards.

King MarKus was out from under the blade. Meg smiled to herself knowing the rope binding her hands would not hold her shift. She jerked her shoulders free from the guard's grip and ran toward Herrick, preparing to jump. A whisper in her chest stopped her mid-stride, and a guard barreled into her back. Her hands still tied, Meg tumbled forward, feeling a shock of pain when her face hit stone. But she could still hear it. She raised her head and glanced around for the whisper's source.

Her eyes fell on Herrick just as a giant owl swooped in and took him down with one solid blow, crushing him to the ground. In a burst of confusion, the guards scrambled for the door without even a glance at their fallen king.

"What is happening?" King MarKus whispered, groping the air around him.

The owl looked at each of the faces still before it, the round, yellow eyes known to Meg. Slowly, Gregry moved in front of his father. As Meg continued to stare she realized she should not be startled to see a massive bird, but Mother was magnificent, her white and black feathers gilded with gold. The talons at the end of her yellow, feathered feet were twice the length of her own. Mother chattered her beak.

King MarKus gripped his son's arm. "That sound. I know it!"

"Stay, Father. Be still," Gregry whispered.

With a swoosh, the feathers melted away and Mother stood before them. Her long, dark dress had been replaced with a purple tunic that reached her shins and was belted around the middle with a silver band. Two loose straps of leather crossed her chest and wrapped around to her back. The tip of the Imperald scepter peeked over her shoulder.

"Mother," Meg choked out in a dry whisper.

"Your line has done well, young king," Mother said calmly, looking down at the lifeless body under her feet. "Just as I wanted." She stepped toward Meg and stooped down to pick up the silver crown that had clattered to the ground. "At last. The time when all shall be made right has come."

Meg rolled onto her side. "You've come to free the humans from their king? To help them?"

Mother laughed, a deep, bold laugh. "Help them? No, my eyas. Look around you. Do you not see their destruction? They are so close. It won't take much. We will soon be free of the plague of their kind!"

"No."

"Listen to me! Stay with me and we'll rule this land as we rightfully should, as our kind did for centuries before they came!" She held out the crown. "This crown. It was meant for you!"

"And my father's kingdom. I know my father was King Jonef."

Mother's eyes flashed. "Do not speak his name!"

"Please…" Meg begged.

Mother's voice turned venomous. "Your father was one of them, but you do not have to succumb to his blood. Do not make the same mistake my sister did. Do not trust them."

"I don't understand."

"Listen to me, my eyas. From the time we could shift, I cared for my sister. Protected her. Did all she needed." Mother began to move, circling Meg. "When she and I alone remained, we kept the forests. But she, too, could not resist pitying these creatures. And then that man. He discovered us, and she foolishly loved him. Loved him more than me!"

Meg closed her eyes and shook her head, trying to shake the pieces tighter together.

"It was all because of *him*!" Mother continued. "I had no other choice. He turned Masabeth against me! Said I was a danger to you. To her. Me?!"

"Masabeth? My…my mother?"

The old elf's hands clutched at her chest. "I am your mother! As one who has every right to be called so."

Meg flinched as she neared. The diary. Her mother's diary. It was not from this woman. "Torah."

"What did you say?"

Meg looked up, realizing she had spoken the name aloud. "Torah," she repeated.

A smile spread across the woman's face. "Yes. That was my name."

Torah turned her head to the side. "Where did you—?"

"My book." Meg shook her head again. "Masabeth's book."

Torah's eyes flicked to Gregry. "Book? So you have been mixing with these creatures for some time. Megnolia, I beg you. See them as they are. Liars! Thieves!"

Meg pulled herself to her knees, shaking her head. "No."

Torah's words came quick. "I will tell you all. You must understand. You will see I did right. Masabeth was splitting the Imperald. Dividing its power among humans. Because he refused immortality, she did, too! She wanted to grow old. She gave up the life it gave to her. To us! She said nothing of this to me—betrayed me with her secrets! But I found out. I tried to save it. It was my duty. But she was too powerful with the Imperald bound to her heart, and I failed. She hid it from me and would not let me near after that, but I watched her. I was her protector! She was safe because of me. It was his own family that threatened you."

Meg remembered the diary entry. Masabeth had said they were in danger.

Torah took several steps forward. "I heard them. Greedy, black hearts. I knew they would bring ruin. They would have the crown! So I gave it to them! Their descendant deserved his fate."

"What happened? Tell me!"

"He left her in the forest. He abandoned her. I told her. I knew he would not be faithful."

"But she went after him," Meg whispered.

"Yes. She cast the Protector's spell over the forest and put you to sleep. Even then, she did not seek me out. She left you in the care of a human. A human! A weakling. Nothing more than a mouse. She left—but I never meant for..."

Meg squeezed her eyes shut.

"She was not careful when she left the forest, you see? And only your father's cousin knew her. His men were prepared to take her from the sky." She quieted. "She only meant for you to sleep until you were safe from your father's kin. They wanted you dead! But you looked so like her. I knew if I woke you, you would age too quickly, and I would soon be alone. I had to find the Imperald. I searched. For so many seasons. And I grew weak without it. But you. She left you strength she did not give to me. I had to wake you. You were so small, my eyas. But I have protected you and taught you and loved you as my own. See? I alone love you. More than any human has or ever could."

Meg shook her head. "No, that's not true."

Torah's eyes narrowed. A finger pointed at Gregry and his father. "This one? Them? You would choose them over me?"

Images snapped before Meg's eyes. She thought of Mickelby in the orchard. The Snofams in the cottage around the fire. Villagers gathered for united celebration. She thought of Monte sleeping on the cold street. The grubby little beggar girl. Slowly, Meg struggled to her feet, bracing against the pain in her leg and in her heart. "If it must be a choice, Mother, yes. I choose them. I'll let no one in this kingdom come to harm."

A strange look overtook Torah, filling Meg with dread. Shouts of "Hoorah!" came from the castle grounds below. The celebration continued, unaware of the clash just beginning above.

"And you will not change your mind," Torah said darkly.

It wasn't a question, but Meg responded with a shake of her head just the same.

Torah placed the crown on her head. "Then you are every bit a fool as your mother." She lifted a shaky finger at Gregry again. "He has taken you from me. Just as that man took your mother. I will have him first!"

With a war-like scream, she leaped at Gregry in a swirl of feathers.

At the same moment Meg jumped into her falcon form, and the two collided, talons slicing through the air like fistfuls of daggers. Meg tumbled onto her back, and Torah's powerful, feathered feet pinned her to the ground. The strength of the old elf was astonishing. If only she had known the whole before handing over the Imperald!

Meg squirmed and writhed against the stone. She kicked her legs, forcing her body to turn under the weight pressing against her. She was smaller than Torah, but her body was also sleeker, quicker. Now on her side, she arched her middle to loosen the cage of claws, tucked her wing, and rolled out from under the owl. She shrieked and took to the sky glancing back several times to be sure she was being pursued. If she could pull Torah away, Gregry would have time to run.

Careful not to fly too fast, she climbed higher into the sky. Then in a quick motion, she tucked back down and dove. Torah turned to the side, and Meg missed the strike. But she caught site of the blank sheet of stone. The rooftop was empty.

A feeling of control took over—the two she most sought to protect were safe—and Meg swooped up and turned into another stoop. With both her wings tucked, her speed increased. At the last moment, she opened her wings and threw her legs forward, her talons finding their target. She ripped sideways and pitched Torah into a faltered flight. With her feathered back stained red, the old elf regained her composure sooner than Meg hoped and clicked her beak in warning.

Meg dived again despite the short distance and, inside a brief struggle, was brutally made aware she was no equal to the owl in matched combat, ground or air. She tore herself away in a mad flight of escape, relief filling her hollow bones as the threatening sound of wings lessened behind her. She pushed higher and higher toward the clouds, one wing trying to lag in force. But she would not let it.

Ignoring the pain throbbing under her feathers, she dove.

The air parted for her sleek form, stepping aside for her royal blood and whipping only at her tail. Her heart quickened as the owl and the earth hurtled toward her. Torah was almost above the castle.

Nearer and nearer she came, until the blades at the tips of her toes touched feather. She gripped Torah's beak with one foot and her neck with the other, and in one swift jerk, flipped her head upward. The great owl shrieked, and Meg watched the feathered body careen toward the ground.

With everything she had left, Meg forced her burning, wounded wing to carry her to the rooftop. She stretched out her feet to land as Gregry ran out from the tower.

"Meg! Watch out!"

Suddenly a force launched into her body, raking talons across her back and the side of her head. She hit the hard stone and rolled feeling a new burning and a strange wind all at once. She lay face down for a moment, the wind sweeping wildly over her body, the cool stone under her skin. *Skin.* The wind ceased.

She looked at her wings and found only arms. Warmth oozed down the side of her face, and she reached up to feel her ear, a shredded bit of flesh. Paces away from where she lay, a gleaming green crystal shone against the gray. With an agonized cry, she raised herself on one arm to find herself alone.

"Gregry!"

She looked frantically in all directions and found him slumped against a battlement. The owl landed next to his still form and shifted. With slow sure steps, Torah came toward Meg, her shoulders heaving.

"I have tried to wash away your tainted blood, to overthrow your human nature, but Raparean is too weak in you. Your mother saw it and wept over it. And now the enchantment she gifted you is broken. You are nothing. Neither human nor Raparean." She stood over Meg, her golden eyes cold. "I should have killed you when I killed your father."

Torah shifted again, and in two bounds was upon Meg, the weight on her chest and throat crushing. Meg gasped but her lungs would not expand. A gleam caught the corner of her eye. The jeweled ax. Gregry had dropped it.

Slowly she inched her arm up until her fingers touched the handle. A jolt moved through her body as she worked it into her grip. With as much force as her arm would allow, she swiped the blade over her head, connecting with Torah's leg.

The beast hissed and stumbled off. Meg rolled and pushed herself to her feet, the ax firmly in her hand. Through her palm she felt energy course into her body. She couldn't shift, she knew that power was gone. But strength was returning. As the earliest rays from the sun stretched across the heart of Davare, Meg glanced down at the ax. Buried in the handle was a green jewel, no greater than the length of her little finger, with a faint black sheen. Imperald.

Meg looked up as the owl morphed into elfin form. Torah, with her weight leaning on one leg, drew the scepter out from behind her back. A gentle whisper moved inside of Meg. The Imperald called to the worthy, Torah had said.

"I am sorry it has come to this, my eyas, but I must. For my forest. And for my people."

Meg felt what was happening before she understood. A sharp jolt thumped in her chest. Her knees all at once felt weak. Torah was drawing strength from her. Before the next jolt, she darted for where she had fallen before, slid onto her side and snatched up the piece that had once been in her ear and rose again to her knees, an Imperald piece in each hand.

She closed her eyes. *The Imperald is my heart.* She searched over her body with mental fingers, pushing down the pain, pushing out the chaos. Deep in her chest she *felt* her heart beat. Another thump and she felt her grip on the ax lessen.

"My heart." She was among her giants again, their still strength settling over her like the rays from the morning sun. And then a lost, vague memory was before her. Her mother's face. Masabeth. Her heart began to beat anew. She felt the push and pull, the force of the Imperald pieces in her hands against the scepter, but no more than that. Slowly she rose to her feet. Meg felt a gathering inside herself. The whisper in her chest grew.

She opened her eyes to see the frantic look in Torah's face. A rush of wind broke over Meg, as Torah fell to her knees, the scepter clattering to the ground.

"The Imperald is *my* heart," Meg whispered, her chest heaving in gulping breaths. She stepped toward the woman and tightened her grip on the ax.

"No! No, please. Harm me no more. Please."

Meg hesitated. Here was the woman she had known. Feeble and afraid. The fierceness in her eyes was gone, replaced with a dismal desperation that was painfully familiar. She was Mother. She was *Mother.* The ax dropped to Meg's side. She would not—could not— do any more to her. She took the crown from Torah's bowed head and picked up the scepter.

"Go. Take what strength you have and go."

"Give me some," Torah begged. "It is all gone from me."

Meg tossed the ear piece to the ground. The woman scooped it up and placed it in her mouth. Without looking at Meg again, she uttered, "You fool," and shifted and fled.

Meg watched Mother Torah's fleeing form for a moment before a moan drew her attention.

Gregry.

Still clutching the ax, she ran the width of the roof to his side. He was unconscious but breathing steadily and seemed to be coming around.

"Gregry—"

The next moment she was on her back, pinned beneath the great owl, like a recurring nightmare. The ax slipped from her grasp as the weight of the bird pushed heavily into her throat. She felt her strength recede and all the pain flood back into her body. *Breathe. Breathe!* she commanded her lungs but with no response.

A loud thump with a simultaneous *crack* sounded in her ears. Torah jerked one foot off of Meg, a strange noise rolling from her throat. Another thump, and the weight completely lifted from Meg. Gasping, she rolled to her side, staring at the feathered lump. She lifted her head as a crossbow clattered to the ground.

Mickelby came to her side.

Chapter Twenty-Four

"THE third room has been emptied, Your Highness."

Meg turned from the window of the small library and winced. She had done too much that morning—the muscle and bone aches worsening already. "I give you my thanks, Janie. And the sorting?"

"We have distributed two cartloads from the first room. But I'm afraid it is more of a mess than originally thought."

Meg smiled at the nervous woman. "Then we will continue to work."

Four days had passed since the death of King Herrick the Fourth. The Nobles of Davare had gathered one day after to determine their new ruler. Mickelby had brought with him a deteriorating scroll—official papers of the royal birth of Crown Princess Megnolia Masabeth Miricam Davare, which made a considerable stir.

There had been some doubt of the legitimacy of Meg's bloodline, but with a written testament from King MarKus and verbal witness from many others of her significant, feathered role in the rescue of Davare, enough of the nobles were convinced that she was indeed the daughter of Jonef the True King. The news was widely welcomed and accepted by the people across the kingdom. And the few who still questioned did not dare cause another uprising.

She was not officially queen yet, but she did not intend to sit idly until her coronation—still fourteen days away. All morning she and Mickelby had assisted in the cleanup of the old keep's dungeon rooms. The burden of distributing years of confiscated tools, goods, and equipment was heavy, and she was anxious to get it off her back. The people—her people—needed the wrongs made right as soon as possible.

When the door closed behind Janie, Meg resumed her gaze out the window. The library was on the third story and overlooked the city. In the courtyard below, people were busy moving to and fro. Everywhere she went there were people.

Slowly her focus left courtyard and settled on the faint reflection in the glass. She gently pulled back her raven hair. Dark scabs ran along her jaw from her chin to her hair. She couldn't see her mangled ear in the reflection, but she knew what it looked like. The physician told her when the scabs fell, the deep marks left by Torah's talons would always remain. She wondered if she would be scabbed or scarred on her coronation day.

Soft footsteps shuffled behind her. She knew those footsteps like she knew the beats of her heart.

"Mickelby?" she said without turning around. "Do you think all those people out there really want me for a queen?"

When he didn't join her at the window, she turned. Her old friend stood with a rolled canvas under his arm, his face beaming. He nodded.

She returned his smile halfheartedly. "But I don't look like one. You should see Queen Iril. She—what is that you have?"

He stepped closer and unrolled the canvas to reveal a cracked and discolored portrait of a man standing behind a woman, a dark-haired baby in her arms. Wrapped around the baby was a cloak made of white feathers. Meg stared at the man for a moment and then the woman. It was almost like looking at her own reflection.

"It's me. And my parents," she whispered.

Mickelby nodded again. She limped toward him, and he held the portrait out to her. She took it and together they sat down on the settee. Meg traced a finger over their eyes, then their noses, careful to not disturb the fragile paint. Although she was seeing their faces for the first time, she knew them. In her heart, she knew them.

"Where did you find this?"

Mickelby pointed down.

"In one of the dungeon rooms. Did you find anything else belonging to them?"

He shook his head.

She stared at the portrait, afraid if she looked away it would turn to dust. She had asked Mickelby a question the evening after the battle, but he had refused to answer it, insisting she needed to rest. "You knew both my parents, didn't you, Mickelby?"

She could see him wrestling with an answer, his eyes unfocused and full of thought. Finally, he nodded his head.

Meg released a deep breath she had not realized she had been holding. He had known them. She gently wrapped her fingers around his hand. He squeezed it and nodded. He pointed to her father. Then slipped off the settee to his knees and pretended to remove something from Meg's bare foot.

"You...took his shoes?"

He squinted at her, a shade of annoyance in his face. He shrugged out of his jacket, placed it on her shoulders, and picked up a tray, holding it out to her.

"I don't understand."

He sighed, walked out to the hall, and returned with the guard who had been standing outside the door.

"Yes, good idea," Meg said. "Monte, will you please help my stupid self figure out what my poor friend is saying."

"Certainly, My Feathered Princess."

Mickelby repeated his charade with a little more finesse.

"An esquire attendant?" Monte suggested.

Mickelby pointed to Monte and nodded. Meg was utterly confused, and Monte explained an esquire attendant is a special kind of servant. Similar to her lady's maid, one who is dedicated to the service of a certain man.

"So you were my father's esquire attendant."

Mickelby nodded and returned to his seat. Monte bowed to leave, but Meg quickly requested he stay in case his services were needed again.

"Please, Mickelby, tell me how you came to be with me."

His shoulders slumped and looked at his feet. He shook his head. Meg could see the memories were painful to him. Badly as she wanted the last piece, she would not ask him to walk through them against his will. But after a long pause, with the aid of Monte, Mickelby recounted his past.

He had returned to Davare's Heart with Jonef, who was hoping to resolve the conflict with his cousin, Herrick. Mickelby had been in Jonef's bedroom when the great owl had attacked. Terrified, he had fled, leaving his king to his fate. Guilt drove him into the forest to tell Masabeth what he had seen. Alone, she left sleeping Meg in his charge. But then...with trembling hands, Mickelby opened his shirt to reveal old scars across his chest. Torah. He pointed to his throat.

"She attacked you. And took your voice."

He nodded. And Masabeth never returned.

Meg took up his worn hand and kissed it. He had been terrified of Torah, but he had stayed. All those years. For Meg. What would she have done without Mickelby? Without her companion, her mentor, and her protector?

"You needn't be afraid anymore." She squeezed his hand again.

The following morning Meg awakened with the earliest rays from the sun streaming through her window. For a moment she was unsure where she was, the four-post bed and beautifully furnished room not yet familiar. She wished she knew what had been brought in by the previous four kings and what had belonged to her family. She would rather have an empty room than one full of things that didn't mean anything to her.

She pulled the bell rope and within minutes her lady's maid entered to help her dress. It was such a silly thing, to have someone help you dress. She almost let the girl go, but Monte assured her it was a good situation for the maid. She would be able to send the money she earned home to her family. And that seemed right.

And it still hurt to bend and twist dressing alone.

As the buttons were fastened down the back of her dress, Meg stared at the black urn on her mantel. The ashes of the great owl were locked inside. She looked away when the girl's fingers dropped from her back.

"I give you my thanks, Linn. You may go."

"Your breakfast, My Princess?"

"Not yet. But soon."

Linn curtsied and left the room. Meg sighed. What a strange new life she had suddenly found herself in. For years she had only known two other faces doing the same things every day. And now she was surrounded by countless people doing different things all the time. She didn't know if she would ever get used to it. A small voice in her mind begged to return to *her* castle, and she reminded herself once more that this *was* her castle now.

She tucked herself in the window seat nook and stared out the glass. It would be easier to get used to these things if everything wasn't quite so new. Or rather, if every*one* wasn't so new. Arrangements had been made last night for a messenger to be sent to the Snofams. She hoped they would come to her coronation. It felt like years since she had seen Serah, not days.

She placed her chin on her knee when she thought of the other invitation she had sent. The one to the castle in Roshton.

Gregry had left Davare mere hours after the dust of battle had settled. His father had instructed all those from Roshton who had been wounded or slain to be returned to their kingdom immediately. Meg had watched anxiously as injured men were loaded into wagons, Marv among them. The physician assured her he would live.

It was also discovered that a handful of servants in the castle were from Roshton. The missing children of the "Rathern" attacks had been found. Lirpa, the head housekeeper, identified them all. Though Herrick the Third had robbed them of the childhood they should have known, at least he had spared their lives. They were all returned to King MarKus.

With a stab, Meg recalled her last conversation with Gregry.

"Have you had word of the whereabouts of Davare's army?" he had asked.

"Not yet," she'd replied, "but Lord Hapwood has issued the recall. It should reach them by nightfall."

"Then they will return in the next day or two. We will take an upper road to avoid passing. You will be all right?"

She shrugged.

"MarKus," his father called from inside the borrowed carriage.

"I must go. I give you my thanks, Meg. For everything."

She had gripped his hand tightly hoping it would keep him, but he had simply shaken it off and climbed into the carriage, eager to get away. She had caught a glimpse of him looking straight ahead as the carriage rolled past. He hadn't waved or smiled or even taken one last look at her.

Meg leaned back and thunked her head against the wall. It was no matter. She had Mickelby. And all her people. Thousands of them probably. She had lived a hundred years without Gregry. She could live some more. Never mind she had been asleep for most of those years.

Feeling suddenly restless, she pushed away from the window seat and crossed the room. After pausing for a moment, she knelt before the chest at the foot of her bed. Slowly, she lifted the lid and felt the whisper enter her chest. When she had asked Gregry how a piece of Imperald had come to be inlaid in the ax handle, he didn't know. And he wouldn't bother his father with the question. "There are far too many things on his mind right now," he had said. Gently, she lifted the Imperald Scepter from the folds of velvet. She listened to the ancient language of the trees and whispered it to herself.

She waited to feel the same power she had felt on the rooftop but nothing except a whisper came. As the people in Davare and Roshton healed, she knew the trees surrounding the kingdoms would heal as well. But that would take time. And maybe gifts that she didn't have. Holding the scepter, it was difficult to forget Torah's words. She was neither elf nor human.

She went down to breakfast to find herself alone at the table. *Mickelby must still be asleep,* she thought as she poked at her bowl of mush and fruit. An hour later she still had not seen him. When no answer came to the knocks on his door, she pushed it open.

"Mickelby?"

A weak hand raised from the bed. She stepped inside. "Are you all right?"

He waved her to him. His breathing was irregular, and his face sickly and pale.

"You are not. I will get the physician."

The physician came and assessed the old man. Meg sat at his bedside as the woman poked and prodded her friend with various devices. The physician had given her a tonic the first day to ease her pain. And it had helped. Surely the magic-worker could heal Mickelby.

"His heart is failing. Days probably. That is all that is left for him."

The words robbed the warmth from Meg's body. Days? No, she needed him for years. She followed the physician out and asked for more information. The physician prattled on with many words Meg did not understand, but she listened intently. She begged for a fix, but there was nothing to be done.

For two days Meg kept to Mickelby's sickbed, speaking to him and dabbing his mouth as he slept, feeding him broth and reading him books when he awakened. She never left the room, requesting all parchments and various counsels be handled there. No one argued, no one balked.

In many respects, she had everything just the way she liked.

But what she wanted most was to take Mickelby home. To walk with him around the forest castle wall and sit with him in the orchard.

"I want the seventh room emptied today," Meg said to the man named Balter. "And also, another cart of fruit to be sent out for the children."

"Yes, Your Highness. Right away. I will send the list of items when the room has been cleared." He bowed and quit the room. She liked him. He was old, though not so old as Mickelby. And he had kind eyes, anxious to undo all the suffering.

Monte stepped in. "A bundle and letter for you, My Feathered Princess."

Meg sat up. A letter! He handed her a small item wrapped in linen and tied neatly with string, along with a folded piece of thick paper. Meg traced her fingers over the strong, slanted markings. Gregry.

She burst the seal, tearing a layer of parchment, and took in the words written in his hand.

Dear Meg,

I hope this letter finds you well. I will be attending your coronation, but I am anxious to put this in your hands. Serah found it when her family returned home and sent it to me with my other belongings. While a man should never read a lady's book, if he does, he should confess it. Forgive me for my intrusion and forgive me for doubting you.

Gregry

Meg dropped the letter and pulled the package string loose. Beneath the layers of linen, she found the little book she had discovered hidden with the Imperald.

In the light of day she could now see the seal, lightly embossed in the stiffened leather. She traced a finger over it.

"Mickelby, another book. Another one of Masabeth's books!" She settled herself on the bed and, with a deep breath, read aloud the faded words.

To my dear Megnolia on your second birthday,

My Eyas. This book has been especially bound for you, to one day keep your thoughts and dreams safe. Your father says it is too early a gift for one so small, but I could not wait. Now, a wish for you. I wish for the life you live to be one of peace, unlike the one known by those who have come before you. I hope it will be one filled with all the good things of our world.

Your father has passed to you noble blood, but do not forget Raparean royalty flows in your veins as well. You have a Raparean heart you cannot surrender. I can feel it in your tiny chest. As such, the Imperald is bound to you. I hope I will be able to pass it on to you myself, but if that is not my fate, know it's strength will seek you. Once in your hands, you must learn from the Imperald itself. Do your father and me honor, Meg. Live loyally to the life we dream for you. Show love, have compassion, and be strong. Mortality is uncertain, and I cannot pretend to know what your life will be. But if you allow the heart I know you have to guide you, all will be as it should.

Your father loves you, Meg. As do I. With all my heart.

Meg read the message once more, letting each word sink into her mind, then set the book on her lap. Like a gentle breeze through the forest, an idea weaved through her mind. Noble blood and Raparean royalty flowed in her veins. *Together.* All at once. There was no separation and never could be. She was made from two parts that were one within her. She didn't have to choose to be Raparean or choose to be human.

She only had to choose to be Meg.

Though the peace she had known living in the forest was no more, she understood the worries of the world had always been. She was just no longer asleep to them. And she would wade through the doubt and unknown to find ways to put things right.

Mickelby's hand suddenly covered hers. She looked at his face and returned the faint smile on his lips that had been absent for days.

"I am one, aren't I, Mickelby?"

He nodded.

"And I am where I am supposed to be."

He nodded again.

There was a faint squeeze of her hand, then his grip loosened. A gentle peace overtook the room, and Meg knew he had gone to sleep for the last time.

Early the next morning, Meg prepared to enter her forest. Not on an excursion of pleasure but one of pain. She dressed herself in a long, emerald green tunic with a black shirt and leggings. At the last moment before leaving her room, she grabbed the urn on her mantel. She had two things to do today.

She rode into the Great Forest with a caravan of visibly nervous mounted guards, Monte bravely at the head. A wagon rolled slowly behind her conveying the mortal remains of Mickelby.

The road was overgrown and rutted, but the narrow, one horse wagon she had chosen, with frequent dismounts of the guards to clear the way, was able to slowly wind its way through. When they reached the gate of the castle it was late evening, the last of the sunlight filtering through the giants.

While a grave was dug in the resting place she had chosen, Meg climbed the steps to the top of Mother Torah's tower, a black urn tucked tightly under her arm. She had been uncertain what to do with the ashes when she had asked them to be collected, but as she ascended toward the sky, the way became clear. So, when the window shutters were unlatched and the roof shingles were beneath her feet, the lid of the urn was removed. In one smooth motion, the ashes were released and immediately caught up in the new wind that moved through the great trees.

Her eyes closed and her heart searched for peace. When she found it, she climbed back through the window. Lingering only a few minutes inside her home, she left the keep for the orchard. There, under the pear tree closest to the wall, she watched the simple casket lower into the ground. With trembling hands, she pushed the first cover of earth onto the casket. Then from her knees, watched the men cover it completely. Monte placed a small, glittering stone carved with a tree at the head of the grave. Meg placed her hand over the stone.

"I give you my thanks, Mickelby. Over and over, I give you my thanks."

And she knew he received her thanks—his wordless presence changed but with her just the same. Here in his orchard where he was happiest.

Chapter Twenty-Five

T HAT will never do!"

Meg sat at the writing table in her bedchamber, quill in hand. Tomorrow was her coronation. She had to get this right.

She crossed out another line.

At a council last week, Lord Hapwood informed her tradition dictated the new king or queen must announce a decree at the ceremony. Today was the first day she had found time to think about it.

Since Mickelby's passing, she had worked tirelessly to set things right in her kingdom, putting into motion a process to restore what vocational equipment she could and organize citizen apprenticeships with royal smiths and tradesmen. She had held a request day for the public (the line was so long she grew sore sitting on her cushioned throne), distributed food from the royal storehouse, and worked to rid her castle of all signs of any Herrick, including the daunting task of sifting through soldiers, guards, and courtiers for weeds.

Meg brushed the feathered quill across her chin. She breathed in the faint scent of the bird it had come from and felt a stir in her chest.

She used to smell like that, too.

She leaned back in the delicate chair. Daily, she was made aware of more laws or unwritten principles. She laughed mirthlessly at herself for thinking Mother Torah had a lot of rules. She was catching on to the traditions and ways of Davare quickly, but there were gaping holes in her knowledge. When she became overly anxious, she read the letter from Mother Masabeth. Her parents had ruled rightly and had faith she could as well. The energy and excitement she felt in those all around her added to her motivation.

Her only complaint was doing it alone. Surrounded by people but alone. No Mickelby in her orchard. No Serah to do chores with. No Frelick or Ida or Lezah around her fire. And no Gregry to talk to in the dark hours of the night.

"Monte?"

The man's head poked into the room.

"Come in, please. I need a counselor."

He straightened his back and adjusted his tunic as he strode toward her. "Yes, My Feathered Princess?"

She smiled at the name he refused to give up using. "I am trying to find a decree. It will be my first official one, and I want it to be perfect. I've already crossed out sugared plum cakes for all every Sunday—I didn't think Cook would like that one. Sweep the streets daily—too boring. And no taxes. I like the last one, but Lord Hapwood says there must be taxes. What do you think?"

"I'm afraid I agree with Hapwood. You need moneys for keeping your kingdom. A lesser one would be a fine idea, though. People could keep more in their purses."

She scratched down a note about taxes, then held up the cream-colored parchment. Her letters were not pretty or straight, but she was pleased they were still legible. "Have I spelled everything correctly?"

Monte looked over her shoulder. "I wish I could tell you, My Princess. But I can't read."

She turned to look up at him. "You can't?"

"No. Too low. Only highest of nobles and royalty. Draw me some pictures, and I'll get it. Them letters, though…"

Meg remembered Gregry telling her it wasn't right for Serah or Lezah to read. "All three kingdoms are that way?"

"Yes, it's been the rule for…well, I don' know how long, but long."

Meg brushed the feather across her chin again. She glanced at the bookshelves she had ordered moved to her room. The colors on the bindings were faded but still gave life to the shelves.

The sound of carriage wheels crunching the gravel outside made her heart skip. Tonight there was to be a supper party in her honor. The noble men and women of her kingdom were expected to attend, and she hoped with every breath the faraway visitors she was expecting would arrive in time as well.

She scrambled to the window. A large man was handing a honey-haired young lady out of Meg's own carriage that she had sent to the border on a special mission.

"My thanks, Monte!" Meg squealed as she darted past her guard. When she reached the landing, she shouted, "Open the doors!"

The sentinels hastily obeyed, and Meg fairly threw herself out the door and into Serah's arms on the steps.

"You have come, you have come, you've come!" Meg squeezed her friend and bounced on her toes.

"Well of course we have, you chirp," Serah said jingling in her throat. "We were ready to leave before your messenger was back on his horse. You don't ignore an invitation from the princess of Davare."

"You don't ignore one from a friend, either," Ida chimed in, taking her turn in an embrace. "We would have been here sooner, only we had to detour to the city for a few things."

"A fine place you have here, my girl. If we'd have known…" He cleared his throat and lowered his voice. "We'd never have made you sleep on the floor."

Meg grinned. "I would rather sleep on your floor than any bed in the Three Kingdoms. Come in, come in." Meg took Lezah's hand. "I have so much to tell you all."

She led her family to the smaller sitting room and when everyone was comfortable and fed, she related all that had happened. The Sno-fams laughed and gasped, questioned and cried as the story unfolded. With them in her sitting room, everything felt right. Almost.

When the clock chimed the supper hour, Meg stood at the head of the table, Serah and Frelick on one side and Lezah, Ida, and Monte on the other. At the foot of the table stood Queen Iril. The rest of the long table seated thirty dignitaries and guests from her own kingdom. Remembering the instruction from Lord Hapwood, Meg bowed and announced all may be seated.

As she adjusted her skirts her eyes settled on the two empty seats next to Frelick. She should have found occupants for them. Then the absence wouldn't be so glaring.

The stew was dished and roll baskets were placed on the table. Meg smiled at the food in her bowl. She had added her own favorite leaves to Cook's pot. The woman had wanted to make the supper a finer affair, but Meg insisted it be simple. She could not eat and eat while so many were still hungry. This meal felt just as it should.

As she lifted a bite to her mouth the side door opened.

"King MarKus of Roshton and Crown Prince MarKus," the foot-man announced.

Meg's spoon nearly dropped into her lap. She fumbled to place it back on the table and stood with stew dripping down her skirt. There was Gregry, a tri-pointed crown on his head and his finely dressed father on his arm, a silver band tied round his eyes. The rest of the table stood and waited for the two latecomers to be seated.

"We give you our thanks, Princess Megnolia," the king said facing her end of the table. "Please accept our apologies for our late arrival."

"I receive your thanks and am so happy you have come," Meg said with every bit of feeling she had inside. She picked up her spoon and eating resumed.

Gregry gave her a quick nod, then turned to embrace Frelick. With her table complete, Meg ate quietly and happily, allowing all the talk and laughter to fill her chest. When the meal finished, the Snofams— worn from travel—turned in for the night while the rest of the party retired to the large sitting room.

Seated alone on a settee, Meg found herself watching Gregry. Though he looked her way frequently, he had hardly said more than a greeting to her all evening and seemed content to stay on the other side of the room. The crown looked natural on his head, and he spoke to the strangers in complete composure. They were listening intently to whatever it was he was saying. She half smiled at how well both being a prince and being a boy from the woods suited him.

"You are great friends with the young prince, I gather," Queen Iril's abrupt voice cut in on her thoughts.

"What?" Meg said, pretending she hadn't been watching anyone in particular. "Oh. Him. Yes, we are friends."

"Good. Your friendship will aid in opening trade and camaraderie again. It is wonderful he has returned to his rightful place. Roshton will need a man like him when his father's time ends."

Meg knew that was true. His kingdom needed him. She smoothed her wretched skirts, picking off bits of dried gravy.

"I noticed the piece is gone from your ear."

Meg touched the purple scar tissue on the side of her face. "Yes."

"If it was a gift from your mother, and she truly was Queen Masabeth, then I am sorry for it. It was a pretty piece."

"Yes," Meg conceded. It was more than a pretty piece. "But its removal has made the Great Forest safe for all. And has made me…it was necessary."

The regal queen clasped her hands. "I hope you will still keep the Great Forest. Your ear piece may be gone, but your land can still be made strong."

Meg nodded. She had more than a little piece to strengthen her land.

"You have the crown don't you?"

"The crown?" Meg thought of the glittering piece of metal sitting on a pillow in her room. The goldsmith had made it specially for her.

"Yes, the crown. The one with the red gem. I believe Herrick still wore it the last time I saw him. That crown was a gift to King Jonef from his wife. It holds the same promise. Keep your people and the gem will keep your land."

Herrick's crown was her father's crown? She had hardly looked at it before sending it to the treasury.

"Ah, Lord Hapwood, how good…" The Turron queen whisked herself away.

"Monte," Meg signaled to the man who was never far. "Have the crown with the red jewel moved to my room. I want to look at it."

He nodded and left the room. Meg returned to watching the faces around her, absently pulling at the edge of her sash.

"I think the young queen will be a beneficial change," she caught a man in the corner behind her saying.

"Do you? I'm rather doubtful myself," his companion said, obviously thinking them out of her hearing. "Some of Herrick's doings might have caused the failure of Davare—we'll never really know—but he knew how to be a king. A ruler must have a certain air to be successful. Look at the Noble Queen. No one crosses her. This young one, who I still have my doubts is the daughter of King Jonef—"

"But they say she returned in feathers. And what of her features and the papers?"

"Yes, yes. Regardless, she has a weak spirit about her. A naivety. I have my doubts the people will maintain their respect for her."

Music struck up and the men's words became lost to her ears. But she didn't need to hear more. A snake of doubt had curled in her stomach. Suddenly the room was crowded and hot and noisy. Seeing no one looking her way, she slipped out the door and hurried to the far staircase, passing into the old keep. Up more flights of stairs she went and into the highest tower's guard room. The men stood and greeted her respectfully. They were not surprised to see her. She had come their way several times before.

She climbed the ladder and passed through the trapdoor. On top of her tower, she inhaled a deep calming breath. Oh, how she wanted to leap from this perch and soar into the night! She looked out over the city and tried to remember all the faces she had seen. The faces that wanted her for a queen.

"You know," said a voice from somewhere behind, "it isn't proper to run away from a party held in your honor." She turned as Gregry flopped a large blanket onto the roof and climbed through the trapdoor. "But I have found you—without Riff's help, mind you."

She was so happy to look at his face again. How she had missed it over the past weeks. *We shall always be good friends,* she thought.

She looked back out at the lights of Davare's Heart. "I wanted to see the people preparing for tomorrow. I hope they are celebrating."

"Why wouldn't they be?" He stepped up beside her and placed the blanket about her shoulders. "Their Sleeping Princess has returned to save them."

Save them. She chewed her lip. "Everything is moving so slowly. And I hardly know what to do with servants in my castle, let alone an entire kingdom of people."

He leaned on the low battlement with both hands. "You will learn. You're a quick study." He cleared his throat. "And you have courage. A lot of it. That will help." He straightened and fidgeted with a ring on his finger a moment, then reached out and grabbed her hand. She let her fingers slide between his. "And you are brave."

"Isn't that the same as having courage?"

He squeezed her hand and grinned. "Yes, I suppose it is. You just have an abundance of it, so...um...it needs two words."

She laughed, and he laughed with her. "I give you my thanks, Gregry. For my two words."

His grin softened, and he moved a fraction nearer. "The truth is, there aren't any words worthy of describing you, Meg." They stared at one another for a moment before he looked down at their hands. "I didn't leave well three weeks ago. And I'm sorry. I was anxious for my father and for Roshton. I was nervous to be Prince MarKus again instead of just Gregry from the forest."

One person turned into two. Meg certainly understood that.

He swung their hands a little. "And I didn't know what it meant for...us...when I realized you were the rightful princess of Davare. Because I knew you would be queen. And someday I know I shall be king of Roshton. But I've been thinking—and if you don't agree, just speak and I'll never say another word about it. I've been thinking that Davare and Roshton were poorly united by the trickery of a false king, but if the two were united under different—happier—circumstances, then they could successfully be one."

Meg leaned a little closer and cocked her head to the side. "What do you mean?" She wanted to be certain she understood him.

He blew out a deep breath and nervously laughed. "I mean maybe one day, if you'll have me, we can marry. And when Roshton becomes mine, our two kingdoms can—"

"Marry? You mean you want to stay? With me? In my castle?"

He laughed again, more easily. "Yes, well, your castle is bigger than mine so really it's a step up for me. And I—"

She could contain it no longer. With both hands, she grabbed his face and kissed him. She could feel his smile under her lips as he pulled her closer. And she knew—even if she lived hundreds of years, she would never love anyone the way she loved him. If her heart had not been trapped in its cage, it surely would have flown into the sky.

Gently, he stroked her scarred jaw. "You've caught my heart, Meg. And I never want it back."

They stayed atop the tower late into the night, wrapped in a blanket and looking at the stars, dreaming of the things they would accomplish and the kingdom they would build together.

The next morning was the brightest that had ever been, the crisp autumn air over the city welcoming the sun's rays. As Linn helped Meg into her velvet gown, Meg smiled. Purple was Mother Masabeth's favorite color. Though she couldn't see her, she would be with Meg today.

"Will you take the crown on my bed down to be cleaned? It will be the one I use today."

"But the other…"

"I know. It is beautiful and fits my head just right. I will send a message to the goldsmith complimenting his craftsmanship and use it another time."

"Just as you say, my Princess…er, Queen." The girl dashed off with the crown in hand.

The red jewel did indeed have a black sheen. What had made it red over green when it was broken from the mother crystal, she didn't know. But someday she would find out.

The courtyard outside was full and the crowd spilled into the streets of the city. The ceremony was to be held in the large hall of the old keep, the tall doors open for her people to see and hear. A knock at her door sounded, and Serah rushed in fluttering her hands.

"Oh, great mountains, I am so excited, Meg. You will be a wonderful queen. I still can't believe it, but I know it's true. Oh! Your gown. It suits you just right, not too foofy like a pin cushion, but very pretty, just like your face. And you're so tall!"

"I wish I could keep you with me always, Serah," Meg said. "You always still my nerves."

Serah hugged her just as another knock came. Lezah entered in her best blue dress and her hair twisted prettily in a low bun.

"I am happy for you, Meg. You will do well."

Meg nodded and took both her friends by the hand. "I am ready."

Together they walked to meet the rest of the party staying at the castle. The excitement of the event was palpable on every floor and in every room. With Gregry's hand in Megs, they made their way to the main hall. Yellow-leafed garlands wrapped each column and tall vases of autumn flowers had been placed in each corner, by the doors, and on either side of the throne. The room hushed as she calmly walked up the dais to her throne.

Lord Hapwood welcomed all to the coronation of Princess Megnolia. Cheers burst forth, and Meg felt her face flush. How suddenly this had come. How quickly her life had changed. She looked at the faces peering up at her from the front row. The Snofams, the men from Roshton, her loyal guard. Her friends. Her family. Then she looked out at the rest of the crowd. Hundreds of faces she did not know. But all of them her friends today.

"The princess's vow," Lord Hapwood announced with a bow.

Meg licked her lips and stood. Her heart was scrambling for escape but her legs held her solidly. With a clear voice, she spoke her carefully prepared words.

"Raparean blood flows in my veins, Davare is my heart. I will honor those who came before me and respect those still to come, by giving all that is truly mine to give—my loyalty, my strength, and my love."

The high chancellor in white removed the Imperald crown from the pillow. Slowly Meg lowered herself to one knee. *Don't fall, don't fall, don't fall.*

She closed her eyes and felt the weight of the cold metal settle on her head. It tilted back—an improper fit—but the force of power entered her body. She was the daughter of Jonef and Masabeth.

She was queen.

A roar erupted from the crowd, and Meg opened her eyes to the hats and flowers tossed into the air. She rose to her feet to accept the celebratory greeting from her people.

The celebration continued the entire day. The city streets vibrated with music and dance, the courtyard moved with rounds of people wishing to congratulate the new queen, and Meg never tired of any of it. When the sun was behind the cliffs, she made her first decree.

"All shall have opportunity to learn to read."

An audible gasp, then murmurs, echoed in the large hall.

"My Queen," Lord Hapwood began. "Consider—"

"I have considered. I give you my thanks for your support."

Meg walked down the steps to Gregry waiting to take her hand. He kissed it and gave it an approving squeeze. Together they walked into the throng hoping to find a sugared plum cake.

Three days later, a small party left the black castle for the Great Forest. The road had been made smooth, and the horses and carriages moved easily along. When they rolled up to the gate of the forest castle, Meg hopped out and ran through, kicking off her slippers as she did. She wiggled her toes in the fine grass and breathed in deeply the forest air.

"So this is where you live," Gregry said from behind.

She turned to face her guests. "This is where I live." No more secret castle. No more secret Meg. Her heart was free.

"If I imagined a castle for you, Meg," said Serah looking around, "this is what it would be."

Riff, who had been enjoying his days in Davare in the royal stables, bounded around snapping at dragonflies and chewing sticks. A quilt was laid out, and Gregry helped his father to it, describing the surroundings as he did. Ida sat with him while the others took a tour.

First a visit to Mickelby's grave to place flowers from Meg and a carved bird from Gregry. Then one turn on the walking path before entering the keep. To the amusement or terror of her friends, Meg climbed out her tower window to the rooftop to explain her favorite perch to fly from. The afternoon was spent with stories from Meg and the evening stories from Frelick and King MarKus. The pantry and a stream were tapped for dinner, prepared by the newly crowned queen. Monte willingly tested the fish to ensure it was not poisoned.

No one fell ill.

The following afternoon, Meg sat in her carriage with Gregry's hand in hers. The new wind swayed the trees, and she closed her eyes to listen. The trees were happy. They still had a keeper. With the crack of a whip, the carriage rolled forward to take them home.

A new home. Where hope for their kingdoms grew as wild as the Great Forest deep.

Acknowledgments

Special thanks to Jana and Megan for always being ready for a first draft and then a final. Melissa and Tara for loving my characters as much as I do. LeeAnn, Tessa, Tookie, Diana, Lindsay, John, Cheryl, Madie, and Niki, my wonderful family and friends who have read and critiqued and cheered me on.

Additional thanks to Niki for the amazing cover art.

Thank you to my children for being excited about my work and for being nothing but awesome.

Last but not least, a huge thank you to my husband and best friend, Travis. Thanks for sacrificing some sleep to listen to my busy brain every night.

Other Books by the Author

A Pretty Game

Ayra of Darkwater Quarry

www.ingramcontent.com/pod-product-compliance
Lightning Source LLC
Chambersburg PA
CBHW032151190626
46814CB00005BA/1940